THE BLUE DOOR
and More
Accidental Heretics Tales

By E.A. STEWART

ACCIDENTAL HERETICS SERIES
Book 1: *Bone-mend and Salt*
Book 2: *Trebuchets in the Garden*
Book 3: *Crux Lunata*
Book 4: *Song of Valerós*
The Mad Woman of La Catalane: A Novella
The Blue Door… and More Accidental Heretics Tales

LEGENDS OF VALERÓS SERIES
Wheel and Serpent: 1
Traitor: 2
Hero: 3

WRITING AS ANNIE PEARSON
Chaos House
The Grrrl of Limberlost
Artemis in the Desert
Nine Volt Heart
The Pirate King

THE BLUE DOOR
and More
Accidental Heretics Tales

E. A. STEWART

Jūgum Press

First edition: January 2017

Print ISBN 978-1-939423-82-5

Published by Jugum Press
Seattle, Washington U.S.A.
www.jugumpress.net

Acknowledgments: Thank you to my critical readers and
editors: Ajax Bell, Elizabeth Bjorkman, Laurie Cropp, Jacyn
Stewart, and Susan Urban.

For Jacyn, always.

Contents

THE BLUE DOOR

The Blue Door
A Novella

In a later tale, told in Crux Lunata, Book 3 of
the Accidental Heretics adventure series

THE FORMERLY HANDSOME Tomás of Morella y Cyprus studied the caliph's vizier, who claimed to be his cousin. "My own great-grandfather al-Makkzan came from the Rodriguez clan."

"He and his brother came from Morocco. They joined our clan through marriage. They were hired by a widow in Morella, on the Aragón frontier." Rashid ibn Abd al-Aziz spoke Catalan in formal tones, overcoming his Arabic accent. "The brother—my great-grandfather Jamal—married into the clan and returned to serve the caliph in Jaén. Your ancestor, al-Makkzan, married that widow. His grandson Mikhail left for Cairo and Damascus after Morella was joined with Aragón."

"Mikhail of Morella was my father."

"And we are cousins," the vizier Rashid said.

This is al-Makkzan's tale.

1
Silina

THE SUN BROKE OVER the top of the mountain as the men from the local villages lined up, quietly debating who had come first to meet the recruiter for the Veiled Ones. The dawn light burnished the highest peak so it glowed like beaten copper. Shadows fell away from the men, who also shone in the light while painting each other's faces.

The caliph had sent a recruiter to the mountain villages again, seeking Berber men to help bring infidels to the true belief, to expand the glory of Dar al-Islam. Idren's two brothers had come here, one village over from their own, to join. "We need the silver!" Meri said. "We need the adventure!" Juba crowed.

Idren, only there to watch over his younger brothers, let the dawn light wash over him. His two-times great-grandmother claimed that the old fire god lights your flame anew each morning. Whether or not you believe it. He didn't believe, but Idren liked to greet the dawn.

Then dawn burned into midmorning. Idren passed time as if waiting in a hunting blind, sensing what lay around him. The smell of the rocks, the flickering of sunshine and shadow as the sun burned its way across the sky. His nose told him that two men from across the valley had caught a civet cat in a hare trap; his nose told him, but also, the story had already traversed the valley. The homes in this village hung terraced on the hillside, similar to Idren's village, but not as beautiful. It would be unkind to say it aloud, but perhaps this village wasn't as loved by its aunts and mothers as his own home was. And the people here dined on too much goat and cheese, which was why Juba had sternly told Meri that it was ridiculous to think of marrying into the women here.

Then it was midday, and still the men stood in wait for the Veiled Ones' recruiter, the heat now melting the clay painted across their cheeks. Juba's red slashes and Meri's ochre crescents lasted better than most. All these men agreed that they must appear at their best, as if they were preparing for a serious hunt or a manhood ceremony. When Idren agree to only three white dots on his cheeks, his brothers laughed. "Always so serious!" One dot reminded everyone in the valley that Idren had killed a bear on his first hunt, and the second that he'd hunted and killed a leopard that preyed on his aunts' goats. The third dot reminded his two brothers that once he'd had to rescue Meri from trouble that Juba had talked him into, taking too great a risk down where the desert encroached on their mountains. Juba had talked their youngest brother Meri into this new adventure.

While men muttered about the wait, Juba said aloud, "So this caliph does business only after midday. Like the badger sniffing for a late supper where the panther killed a deer for breakfast."

Juba's friends bent over laughing, even if it wasn't that funny. Three were Ali, Umar, and Tariq from this village. True Berbers, those three men were much shorter and paler than Idren and his brothers. Like Juba, they were more eager for this day's adventure than Idren felt the Veiled Ones were worth.

Meri hung close by Idren, smiling but not joining in Juba's jests. When the morning grew too tedious, Meri played on the flute he'd made from a young calf's long leg bone. He'd tied a leather string to the end of his flute and wore it around his neck. That morning, he played festival songs, even though the work of the day was serious.

Idren tried twice again in the course of the morning, but couldn't convince his brothers to heed their aunts' warnings and stay home. As the oldest man in the family, Idren had no choice but to stay home, so the village would have at least one wise hunter. And he didn't want his brothers wandering so far from home.

Just before all the men roasted in the sun, the recruiter appeared, accompanied by four Berber men with spears and swords. They hobbled their horses, then lounged nearby while the recruiter preached a soul-stirring message, encouraging local men to come work for the caliph. Small, lithe, and far paler than Idren or his brothers, the recruiter had an indigo turban and a half-face *tagelmust* veil, a style no one in these mountains had adopted, because it hid everything but a man's eyes. The recruiter held a leather purse over his head, first jingling it, then lowering it to reveal that it was full to its leather ties with silver coins.

"This comes to your families the day you depart to bring infidels into Dar al-Islam. That can be today."

He spoke a Berber dialect in an odd, high voice, so his own people must live in the far eastern mountains, or perhaps the far desert regions where the Veiled Ones first stirred people's passions. Even if he wasn't from this part of the world, the recruiter's speech stirred the local men from the lethargy that overtook them in the midday sun.

The recruiter seated himself on a carpet that one of his spear men unrolled for him under the shade of the village's sole tree. The place he claimed under that tree was where that village's old ones always sat, but perhaps the broken custom didn't matter on this special day. The recruiter asked each man his name, and then wrote it on an animal skin and told the man to make a mark in the place where he pointed.

Then it came Juba's turn. "I'm Juba, the son of the milkmaid and Musa the hunter."

But the man couldn't pronounce that name when he repeated it. "Jamal ibn Musa. Pretty name for a pretty man."

Their little brother Meri laughed at the indignant look on Juba's face. Juba had said his name clearly, as proud as ever that he carried an ancient king's name. Instead, the man wrote another name and called Juba pretty. However, their youngest brother fared no better.

"I'm called Meri, son of Musa the hunter."

The man looked up and down Meri's thin frame. "Truly, Amir ibn Musa? Are you old enough to travel without your father?"

That's when Idren knew in his bones that he couldn't let his brothers go alone.

"My brothers are with me. I'm Idren, son of Musa the hunter."

"Idris ibn Musa," the man said, as if Idren had hissed his name through a mouthful of pebbles. The recruiter wrote on that scraped animal hide. "Good of your father to give you the name of an ancient prophet. From before the Flood, when infidels worshipped fire. A perfect name for a man who will help bring infidels to know the true Laws."

But Idren didn't want anything to do with infidels. His own aunts and uncles had struggled to keep away from the Veiled Ones' righteous soldiers and teachers, hoping these new conquerors wouldn't declare their village to be impious. Idren sought only to keep his brothers safe while they earned enough silver from that leather bag to pay taxes, so the Veiled Ones would leave their village alone.

The recruiter asked all the men to pray, in exactly the way the Veiled Ones demand. When done, he insisted the men prepare to leave that day, though it was long past the sensible early-morning hours best for a long walk in the mountains.

Juba and Meri had brought their travel packs, each wrapped tightly with a *burnus*, tunic, and shirt, plus their spears and bows tied in place. Idren needed to jog home for his hunting pack.

"I'm so happy you're coming. How did we talk you into this?" Meri asked. He and Juba had followed his brother to the trail.

"I lost the sound of our aunts' voices when that man said your names wrong," Idren said.

Juba laughed. "Where we're going, our aunts can't scold."

"That's not what I fear."

"What then?" Juba folded his arms. "We're off on an adventure, yet you have to be so serious."

Idren rubbed at his ear lobe, thinking. Then he pointed to the east. "We've lost too many uncles who walked down that trail to work for the Veiled Ones."

"We're better than our father or uncles. We'll come home." Juba tapped Idren's chest, over his heart, where courage was said to live. "We're stronger. We care for our family more than other men. We shall find our way out and home again."

"Do you agree?" Idren challenged Meri, who'd do anything that Juba dared him to.

"I just hope it's a good time." Meri shrugged. "And that we bring silver home to the village."

"Yes," Idren agreed. "To pay our taxes."

"And for our bride prices," Meri said. "We shall all be able to buy good wives."

Then both brothers looked guilty for a minute. A bride-price wouldn't matter for Idren, since what every father in the valley wanted as a bride-price was for Idren to move to their village. His village needed him too much for Idren to leave. It would take a miracle for Idren to find a wife.

Juba forced a laugh. "Bride prices? All Meri wants is a wife? I want a horse and my own house more than a wife."

"Having a wife sounds good to me, the way our uncle describes it." Meri, the perpetual innocent, once more wandered into a joke for Juba to make.

"Great-uncle," Juba said. "Great-great-uncle, who only remembers his long-gone past. You want a wife so you can leave our village, because you believe what our mama says."

"I never." Meri turned his back to Juba, his eyes pleading with Idren to intercede.

Like Meri, Idren didn't want to believe what their mother repeated, that their father never came home because he'd found another wife, made another family. But no one knew any other story about their father's fate.

"No matter about old tales," Idren said. "Juba is right. We're stronger than our uncles. We're better hunters, better fighters. We know how to do right in the world and come home."

One of the smallest cousins, Tadefi, ducked behind the tall cedar in the village square. Idren snatched her up into his arms, swung her around.

"Where are the aunts and mothers, sweetness?"

"They've gone to their secret place," she said. "We are to hide until the Veiled Ones leave the valley."

"Yet here you are in the middle of the square." Idren set her down, hands on his hips, adopting the stern stance of the old uncles, which he must be now. The little girl pointed up into the tree, where he shouldn't have to glance up to know a nest of small cousins hid there, like he and his brothers did until the magic day when they were old enough to hunt.

The blue door to Idren's house lay ajar. It was never left open unless a woman of the house stood under the crenellated archway, calling gossip across the way to neighbors.

"Why is our door open?" he asked as he boosted tiny Tadefi onto the lowest branch.

"Because Silina insisted," she called back, scrambling up into the safety of the high boughs.

Idren opened the blue door wider and called his sister's name. Then his aunts' names. He stepped inside, his eyes straining in the dark after leaving the bright sun.

No sound but that vague hum he always heard inside the house, as if the stone-and-mud walls breathed, or a creature was caught there, silent while scratching out an existence in a corner of the hard-packed floor. Only in here, in a house his ancestors had built out of mountain's rubble, did life smell different from the mountains that surrounded their tiny village. That day, it smelled of yesterday's tagine, with lamb and lentils. It smelled like a safe place, where a child can always find shelter. However, Idren, full grown, no longer needed that kind of safety, yet it was only here, in this women's world, where he could let down his guard, bask in the dark safety of the world behind the blue door.

"Good morning, Idren." A voice hailed him from the corner. "Is it done?"

"Yes, Grandmother. We have sold our services to the recruiting man. The older men say that you must always send an uncle for our pay each quarter. That way, you won't be cheated."

Everyone in the village called Silina grandmother. His mother called Silina grandmother, but so did her mother's mother, who was old as the mortar between the stones in the walls of their house. Perhaps Silina had always lived in that corner, swathed in indigo cotton, her blue-tattooed lips quivering just before she spoke, her words always the law, her insights never wrong. Perhaps Silina wasn't his grandmother's grandmother but was indeed one of the ancestors, forever living among them.

"And you're going too, Idren?"

"Juba can't look after Meri properly."

"Ah." She lapsed into silence or perhaps fell asleep.

"They gave us new names," Idren said, softly so he wouldn't wake her if she indeed slumbered.

Silina sighed, or the house itself groaned. "Your mother insisted on giving you boys names from the old times. Though we knew that names matter to the Veiled Ones. Bad enough you have to go away. But it's sad they also take away your name." Silina shook her head, white locks tumbling from the comb that held her hair in a knot. "We are from the oldest people, the Amazigh." The free people. "These too-holy men from the other mountains, they speak a tongue almost like ours, but they came here like waves of heat across the desert in a bad season, telling us how we must call on God. Taking away our names, insisting they are the first free people."

"We could abide," Idren said, joining in her resentments, "but the Veiled Ones bleed us with taxes. Otherwise, my brothers and I wouldn't be selling ourselves to the caliph."

"You are wise, Idren. And it's good that you chose to go with your brothers, whatever your aunts said. Please always remember your name from the old times."

"Do you have another name, Grandmother? From before the Veiled Ones came?"

She put her hands on his face, gently, like she used to when telling a story that was important. She whispered, and the sound soothed his ears, but he couldn't understand what she said.

"Say it again, Grandmother."

While she whispered, Silina clasped his hand, her ancient fingers dry, leathery, boney, fragile; they'd break if he gripped her hand the way he'd grasp a man's. But then his palm began to burn, as if she held a coal from the kitchen fire. He pulled away, or tried to, but Silina kept hold of his hand, though it felt as if that coal might burn through his palm. Idren gasped, in too much pain to worry about showing weakness in front of a woman.

When Silina released him, a great wind arose, but no—it was a disturbance created by an enormous bird, frantic and loose inside the house, its sharp flight feathers incising the mud-plastered walls, as if a giant's hand had raked deep grooves. Idren ducked as the creature flew over his head, then he regained his better nature and moved to shield his grandmother. But she held him away, that one burning hand on his chest, holding him back with irresistible force, as if he pushed against a wall.

The bird settled on his shoulder, teetering. Idren reached out to push it off, but the bird dug in its claws and nuzzled its beak in Idren's hair, all while Silina held him motionless with her fragile, leathery hand. Idren couldn't turn his head to look, for fear of agitating the beast on his shoulder.

Not a bird.

The animal craned its neck and peered into Idren's face.

"Animal? Bird? Have I come to a fool?" The creature's voice hummed in Idren's ear, like a woman's or a young man's.

A monster with black wings, an ochre-colored breast, and a face almost human, except for a beak like a booted eagle.

"Almost human? How insulting." Its voice was sultry, alluring, though Idren couldn't see its mouth-beak move. Rather, it spoke with its monster's eyes and heard Idren's thoughts before he spoke them. "Monster is no better, you rude child."

It pecked at Idren's eyes, but the peck felt like a woman's kiss, breathy, full of promise. Yet the way it read his thoughts would unnerve any man.

Silina said, "This most honorable qareen was given to me as my companion the day I became a woman."

"Came. I came to you that day," it said. "I'm never given."

"As you wish." Silina laughed, a deep throaty sound that Idren had never heard from her.

The odd creature grasped his shoulder with its talons, stepping sideways, and gripping again, so that pain shot down Idren's arm.

"Odd creature? She told you what the Lord of Fire made me to be. I'm your qareen." It shouted in his ear like an angry, scolding witch. "Witch? Scold?" It hissed his thoughts back to him while one bird-foot grasped a soft fold of skin at Idren's neck. "Bird-footed? Ha!"

"Are you a man or a woman?" Idren asked aloud, determined not to fear this oddity. Qareens and ifrits and the djinn were tales told to scare children.

"So I have indeed come to a simple-minded fool? O My King, O Lord of Fire, what have I done to merit this punishment? Why am I left to care for a dolt?"

"I only asked so—" Idren tried not to think.

"You and I are bound to each other. Bound, not married." The unworldly thing sneered at Idren. "My private business is mine alone and none of yours. It doesn't matter in your world whether you think of me as a man or a woman. We shall not mate."

"Yet you intrude on my thoughts." Idren glanced at Silina, ashamed to be arguing with her spirit-thing, while also wondering if this was a trick she played on him, a dose of old-woman dream-conjuring.

"Not intrude. Not a trick. No conjuring," the bird-person said. "I listen to your foolish thoughts to keep you safe. Your life is the burden I am forced to carry in this world. Just like your burden is to do what your grandmother says."

"Do what?" This had to be a Silina's idea of a jest. Idren was a man, full grown. However powerful mothers and grandmothers might be, they didn't tell a grown man what to do.

"Whatever Susa tells you."

"Susa?"

"The ancestors called me Susa from the beginning." His grandmother broke her silence.

"What do you want me to do?"

"You are the oldest, child." Silina, her voice as dry and ancient as ever, caught Idren with her stern eyes, like when he was indeed a small child. Her blue-tattooed lips moved like a woman repeating prayers. "It's your work to carry our seed and our glory into the world and then make your way home, to close the blue door and keep everyone safe inside."

In spite of the bird-person strutting along his shoulders, marching from his left arm to his right, dragging its wings along the back of his neck, Idren could not accept this madness.

"Grandmother, we have no glory to show the world. We live in a mud-and-stone house, like everyone in this village. We tend our garden. Hunt in the right season. Keep our heads covered to avoid the attention of the Veiled Ones and their caliph."

"Our ancestors gave us power to bend the world our way," she said.

"The most I can claim," Idren pretended modesty, "is to be the best hunter when we're seeking red deer or gazelle for my aunts' stew. Not the business of changing the world."

"Didn't you and your brothers tell the recruiting man that you follow their prophet, that you're Berber?"

"Yes."

"Yet you can see the truth when you look at neighbors in other villages. We are too dark to be Berber. They stole many of our words, but we have our own voices." Silina drew her robe closer around her, disappearing into the folds of indigo cloth. "Our people lived here for generations upon generations before the Berbers came, but we bent their world to serve our needs. We were here before the righteous Veiled Ones came, and we still make the world serve our needs. Now it's your turn to shape the world."

"Susa," that bird-person said. "It's time."

"Yes, my friend. You can go now, Idren. Go shape the world."

"Grandmother, what have you done?" When Idren asked, the bird-creature tugged at his ear, as if impatient.

Her voice came from within the deep blue folds of her robes. "I do only what I must, child. My qareen needs to be in the world again. You will learn to obey."

"Obey? This nasty bird?"

"My maker called me…." The qareen-creature emitted sounds that Idren heard as Ar-ta-si-ra-ri, but he didn't see its mouth-beak move. "Susa and her ancestors call me Zirari."

"Whatever your name is," Idren tensed under the clutch of the creature's claws, "I am a man. I do what I choose in the world."

"You are welcome to think that." The creature whispered in Idren's ear again, like a lover. Then it scratched at his neck. "Creature? You heard my name. You may not say it aloud, but think of me as Zirari. We have a long way to go together. If we're lucky, we'll see the waters of Babylon again."

"Go now," Silina said.

Idren stood in the archway of the house. When he stepped onto the stoop, the blue door slammed behind him, nicking his heels and propelling him onto the pathway.

"You'll need boots," Zirari said.

"I don't wear boots. Only sandals."

"You'll need boots where you're going."

"What does a bird-person know about boots?"

"What does a Berber hunter who isn't even truly Berber know about Iberia?"

"What is Iberia?"

"Your fate, little brother." Again, speaking soft, alluring words like a lover murmurs in the night.

"No, we are only helping to lead barbarians into Dar al-Islam and bringing home silver."

Zirari pecked his ear, which felt like a lover's bite that time.

"O you headstrong fool."

2
Meri

NOW HE WAS CALLED Idris and his brother was Jamal, but no one could remember to call Meri anything but his own name.

The band of recruits walked down the familiar high mountain that held the brothers' home village, then they crossed a narrow valley and climbed more mountains. Some villages seemed happy to let macaques prowl near their gardens at dawn or sunset, which Idris's aunts never tolerated. Soon more than fifty men had joined the march, plus the Veiled Ones on horses, so they seldom saw the game that Idris's nose and bones told him roamed these peaks and valleys. Most of the animals they saw were birds flapping away in the same direction the men marched. And reptiles.

"Viper!"

Three times Zirari warned Idris, who grabbed his mates by the neck to keep them from wandering into a snake's nest.

Each time, his qareen seized Idris's ear, nearly bit it off to warn him. After three times, Idris offered his beast-companion a sincere thank-you. Foresight from his qareen, plus Idris's ability to identify a source for sweet water two or more times each day, gave him a reputation for being a seer. Men from their valley like Umar and Ali claimed Idris as a mate.

"Our friend Idris is known across the mountains as the best hunter and the finest friend," Umar told a group of men who had joined them from further down the mountain.

"He's the friend you want by your side," Ali said. "Not just because he has second sight."

A camaraderie developed over the days of marching, and a core of twenty men became strong friends with Idris and his brothers, setting up their bedrolls near each other at night, enjoying the music Meri played on his flute and the stories Jamal told. Only the captain and his four mounted soldiers remained standoffish.

Zirari purred in his ear. "You should thank me. These men look to you as a leader."

Idris rubbed at his ear. "I thanked you. But you never once were on a hunt with me. That's what Ali and Umar claim. Not because you sniff out snakes faster than I do. And they like Jamal for his jokes and Meri for his flute."

"If that's what you want to believe, O Child."

Yet gradually their quarrels transmuted, sometimes resembling a tussle between brothers, though Zirari never gave up one jot of his arrogance.

Idris tied a knot in a string for each day that they walked to their new work in the Veiled Ones' army. He didn't need to count the days ahead, because the man who led them—who was called Badr al-Malik—would never say how long until they arrived at their destination. Rather, Idris wanted to be able to count the number of days' walking for when he returned home.

As rocky as it was, the trail the recruits followed did not require boots, only the sturdy sandals of hunters. Each day was the same, beyond the new songs that recruits taught each other, which his brother Meri learned to play on his gazelle-flute. The flute made Meri popular with the others, but not so popular with their overly-holy captain, al-Malik.

Zirari pecked Idris's left shoulder to turn his attention to the fellow who had hired them and now shepherded them down the mountain and onto the plains. "You need to speak Arabic as well as that captain."

Silently, Idris argued, "It's a filthy tongue. A conqueror's tongue."

"No, that would be Latin."

Perhaps the most important thing Idris learned on this journey was to hide his surprise each time Zirari clawed him or nuzzled his ear. The first day, his brother Jamal kept saying, "Are you daft, brother? Or possessed?"

"Daydreaming," Idris said.

"Yes, I'm dreaming too," Jamal said. "I'm dreaming there'll be women at the end of this march, like that captain promised. It's what keeps me putting one foot in front of the other. They say the women of these plains are without fear and love men."

Meri said, "But they are paying us to fight barbarians and heretics and the devils they conjure. In a great desert, more immense than anything we can imagine."

While his brothers quibbled over the future they believed they'd been recruited into, the Zirari creature spoke in Idris's ear.

"You are very handsome."

"What do you know about it?" Idris had heard his sister say that, and also a milkmaid he'd met who lived in a neighboring village.

"That's what your captain al-Malik thinks about you and your brothers." Zirari hopped to the top of Idris's head and marched about. "I'm not used to being with a man. It's been generations. I've only been with women since I came to this part of the world. So I mostly can warn about what matters to women. If there's a viper on the path. If your robe is too close to the cooking fire. If the baby that's being born is turned the wrong way."

"That isn't useful to me." By each midday rest, Idris had grown tired of his bird-qareen's nattering.

"I'm trying to remember what a man needs to know. Except I'm positive you need to speak Arabic."

Idris said, "So at my grandmother's bidding, I must endure the life of a man who keeps a dog that forever barks at the neighbors."

"Yes, but to my way of thinking, Idris is the dog that I, Zirari, must care for. Do you know any tricks?"

If they weren't quarreling, Zirari whispered Arabic words in Idris's ear and recited poetry and taught about the world beyond the mountains. "The caliphs and people on the plains call them the Atlas Mountains. At least since I came here."

"Does 'Atlas' mean home? We call these mountains *adras*, which means home."

Idris wasn't sorry about asking Zirari that question, because he was learning about the different kinds of people who roamed the mountains over generations, the kings and languages that changed, battles fought by great kings with elephants and thousands upon thousands of men.

Idris tied the tenth knot one night. When he woke before dawn the next morning, Zirari was clutching Idris's hair to keep his perch while whispering Arabic poetry in his ear.

"Oh, you're awake. Want more stories about kings and warriors?"

It took that moment for Idris to realize that Zirari had been speaking to him in Arabic for days, and Idris had answered. Cautiously, Idris tried a few words with Captain al-Malik while the men were eating breakfast, and found that al-Malik understood Idris's Arabic.

And because of that, al-Malik made Idris give orders to the other men, the ones who spoke little or no Arabic.

"Tell your friends to quit their Berber tongue and learn to talk like your masters." That's what al-Malik said, and Idris started by teaching the men how to count and to recite old poems.

"Your captain will tell you about boots soon," Zirari said. "Maybe your brothers aren't the fools I think they are. Maybe they'll listen about boots."

Flocks of storks flew north, a mass of huge bodies that clouded the azure sky, headed for their season in the home of the old gods. Their black wing tips striped the sky overhead.

The recruits had passed from the cool comfort of home in the high mountains, through arid passages, and then into warmer, wetter lands, where farms lined the valleys that became plains. At last they crested a rise and before them lay the Great Sea, a shining azure-blue, the color of the door to Idris's home. In the green that rimmed the sea lay a city which Captain al-Malik called Maliliyyah.

"It's not such a big city," Zirari groused, answering Idris's internal exclamation about the number and size of houses crowded along the Great Sea. His qareen babbled the names of unknown places. "Memphis and Babylon and Persepolis were each fifty and a hundred times larger. Must still be. What you see here is a town, not a city." The explanation was in Arabic, citing cities from the fairy tales that Zirari told.

"We sail as soon as a ship is available," al-Malik said.

Idris didn't know about the Great Sea, or about sailing away on it. None of his friends did.

"A ship is a large boat," Zirari whispered, as if Idris were a child who'd never heard stories of the Great Sea.

Idris batted at that ear. "I know. I didn't know we were going to cross the Great Sea."

"How else would you get to Iberia? Fly?"

Al-Malik led the men through a maze of streets, skirting souks and anywhere that crowds of people might be. He now had seventy recruits, and the men's excitement grew as they followed the captain through the narrow streets. Children shouted from doorways, calling them Defenders of Islam. Old men on porticos praised them as brave, wished them great victories. The long file of hunters-turned-warrior fluttered like a large flock of birds in spring, flowing through the city with a shared, excited heartbeat.

"This is what the captain meant," Jamal said to Umar, "when he said we'd be working for more than silver."

"We are heroes," Umar said, patting his own chest, as if he'd returned from a victory, rather than just starting out. "The old ones in my village said it would be—"

The captain shouted for them to stop. They were near the sea, outside a large timber-and-mud walled compound, its great wooden gates many times larger than they'd seen at any of the forts they passed on their journey through the mountains.

"Why are we here?" Idris asked al-Malik, who lingered behind the recruits, instructing that they must all remain inside the compound until a boat was ready.

Al-Malik, as usual, seemed annoyed at Idris's question. "Our generals don't want to waste the cost of getting you here only to have you run off to Tunis."

The captain retreated with his four mounted soldiers while the recruits were herded inside.

Cost? Idris and his brothers wore their own sandals, carried their own blankets, and brought their own food, having only now come to the last of their weeks' old couscous and goat cheese. And now they didn't have even the air of the open road or freedom to scatter across an oasis to sleep without the unbearable stink of strangers nearby.

When that gate closed, they were locked inside high walls thick enough that armed men walked along the top. Inside, the scent of the sea was lost in the odor of hundreds of men crowded shoulder to shoulder.

Idris and Jamal tried to make friends inside, to learn about the place, but the men they greeted were taciturn at best and more typically silent and hostile. Their friends among the local recruits hung near Idris and his brothers, who managed to learn how food worked there. The last to arrive that day, Idris's band was at the end of the queue for that night's food, having to settle for the burned crusts of lentils pried off the edges of the cooks' kettles along with broken scraps of pancake, such food that any man's aunts would scorn to serve to an itinerant beggar.

Among all the different Berber dialects, Idris needed Zirari's help to translate.

"How long have you been here?" Idris asked one man.

"Since the full moon." The man, with face tattoos that said he came from the central mountains, spat in disgust. Another man took offense, that the spittle had landed too close to his foot. Idris stepped away from the dispute and continued to ask more questions of other men.

Then he gathered his friends from among the recruits. "The best place for us to sleep will be farthest from the gate. Men who have been here longest won't let newcomers near the gate."

"How long will we be here?" Umar and Ali asked at the same time.

"That depends on when our captain can find a boat. Some men have been here since the last turning of the moon."

Most men from their travelling band of recruits, fifty in all, settled in another corner, where people spoke a dialect similar to theirs. Idris's twenty friends settled in the farthest corner, complaining about the idea of the boat and the crowding.

"Did our Veiled captain ever mention a boat?"

"Stinks like a camel pen in here."

Though unhappy about how the day concluded, the men arranged their blankets, most deciding to sleep sitting up, back to back, shoulder to shoulder, not one of them trusting the strangers who surrounded them.

Idris and Jamal volunteered for the first watch, and Meri answered the men's nightly yearnings by softly playing his flute as if they were still on that long, lonely trail from home.

At least, the stars still shone overhead.

The mass of caged men writhed, groaned, and finally slept. Or at least quieted.

Then a shiver ran through the compound. Silently, other men around them rose. Zirari clutched at Idris's hair. "They're going over the wall."

"To find boats?" Idris began to rise, but Zirari clutched at his scalp, shooting pain through his head.

"No, to go home. Make all your friends stay."

"Why?"

"It won't turn out well."

The other men in the compound moved, black shadows in the dark of night, low murmurs like the voice of a waterfall. *No more. We're done. We're not slaves. More of us than them.* Men lifted makeshift ladders over their heads, nestling the crudely lashed-together spears and walking sticks against the timber-and-mud walls. Men began to climb.

Idris's friends woke to the mass movement. He moved among them, whispering in Berber dialect.

"Be still. Staying here is our only hope."

His friends all had the same thoughts and questions.

"But why?"

"We didn't leave home to live in a cage."

"These fellows have been here longer. They must know."

"What do they know?" Idris argued without passion, intending to sound like the most reasonable of men, though he offered insights from the qareen on his shoulder. "Those men don't know what's on the other side of these walls. They may be walking into slavery. Or slaughter."

The complaints and disagreements grew weaker.

"We didn't come all this way," Idris said, "to work for our families, only to throw it away. We don't know what's waiting outside."

Most of his friends nodded in agreement, or so Idris thought from the movement of shadows within the huddle.

Then screams echoed from outside the walls.

High, sharp shrieks.

Unlike any sound Idris had ever heard from human throats. The screams didn't cause the surging mass of men to halt. Seeming desperate to escape, they continued to scramble up their rickety ladders, a massive writhing shadow at the top of the wall, continually displaced as it tipped to the other side, replaced again, and more wriggling shadows topped over the wall.

The shrieks rose, along with the clash of wood on bone, a sound that Idris recognized from hunting. Horses and camels cried in the night, braying their terror and distress.

Then the drums started, as if all the old thunder gods from ancient times beat on their tambours at once.

"It's the drums of the Veiled Ones' army," Zirari whispered.

"I know. Silina told me how they marched into our village before I was born, beating drums and shouting how we must better serve God."

When the sky began to shed the darkness, turn from no color to the aged-tattoo blue of dawn, Idris nudged first Jamal, then Meri and their traveler-friends. Together they moved cautiously from their far corner of the compound, skirting any other bands who'd remained inside. None of those men roused from their fear to join Idris's band.

They stood before the massive timber gate, leaving room for it to swing open. Idris made only a few suggestions, again repeated in every man's dialect. The band collected together, travel packs and weapons tied on their backs, sandals lashed, as if ready to march the way they had at every dawn since leaving home.

"I don't like doing this," Idris growled silently.

Zirari sat stiffly on his shoulder, as if he too were a soldier. "This is the only possible tactic." The qareen gripped a pinch of tender skin near Idris's throat. "Like Ulises. Or Agis and the Macedonians. Or Hannibal when—"

"Stop. We aren't at war." Idris resisted fidgeting, given how long they stood in front of the gate. Quarrelling with his beast-companion substituted for fidgets.

"O Child. The Veiled Ones turned men into slaves and murdered people last night."

"How do you know? Can you see through the walls?"

"Surely you know the screams of death-throes when you hear them."

When the drums ceased and the massive gate creaked open, Idris's band stood still, just beyond the arc of the door's swing, each man's hands pressed in supplication, like their captain taught as the proper posture for prayer. Arrayed across the opening was a wall of shields, spears jutting from the narrow chinks between each shield.

Behind that line, another row of men with shields and helmets. Then another row. And another.

"Where is Badr al-Malik, our captain?" Idris asked in Arabic. "We are eager to go to work for our caliph."

"It's a short way across," said the man who sailed the boat. He spoke only Arabic, shouting orders to his sailors in that tongue. This very short man with hugely muscled forearms and a vicious scar on his face was also a captain. His men called him Abdullah. "Two days if the winds are kind."

The Veiled Ones had huge ships for carrying horses to Iberia. Those bands of recruits had been forced to wait for boats that had room for soldiers. But since al-Malik's band had lost fifty people the night before, it was easy to find a ship that might carry twenty men to Iberia.

Once Idris and his friends came onto that boat, their own captain left his recruits to fend for themselves. Al-Malik settled into a waxed canvas shell, out of the sun. Most of the sailors avoided the Veiled captain. Zirari made Idris watch and listen to the sailors, many of whom didn't speak Arabic. He listened hard, until he understood that some of the sailors were enslaved infidels.

The three brothers huddled together against the rail. Jamal became sick when the wind rose. Idris tried to comfort him between bouts of vomiting. Meri played his gazelle-flute. A long while after day turned to night, when the moon was high in the sky, Zirari straddled Idris's shoulders and pulled on his ears.

"Spears!" Zirari shrieked. "Too dark for arrows."

Idris leaped up, prodding his brothers. "Grab your spears."

The boat rocked wildly.

"Pirates!" Abdullah shouted, then cried for God's protection.

The attackers tried to board right where the three brothers crouched. Half the men crawling over the side took a spear thrust in their middles and fell back. The three brothers' knives finished the other pirates who tried to board.

The boat rocked again, when the invaders sailed away, abandoning the roped hooks that linked the two boats. The men who sailed the boat and Idris's friends all cheered. They stripped the dead and injured pirates and tossed them overboard, and then clapped Idris and his brothers on the back, calling them good fellows, all while Abdullah shouted repeatedly for every man to offer thanks to Allah.

In a quiet moment, men sat still enough that it was possible again to hear the water against the boat as it moved through the water. Suddenly Meri shouted thanks to Allah, which he hadn't done when Abdullah had commanded them all to pray. He blew three notes on his flute.

Then Meri fell against Idris, who caught his brother and held him. Idris eased his gasping brother down to the deck, cradling him. Meri's tunic was sticky and wet with blood from a wide, wicked gash at the crown of his head. Struck by a pirate, Meri had walked around for half the night before he fell.

"Susa would sing to him." Zirari sat astride Idris's shoulders, holding on with a strangling grip.

Idris began to sing. His brother Jamal sat beside him and held Meri's hand. He echoed the words that the mothers and sisters sang for half a day when any of the family joined the ancestors.

When the sun streaked on the horizon again, Abdullah squatted beside them.

"Is he dead?"

Idris nodded, not able to say it aloud, not remembering the words one is supposed to say when speaking with the overly righteous Veiled Ones about a man who has gone to the ancestors.

Meri still held his flute, floating in his open palm. Idris took it and slipped its cord over his own neck. Zirari lifted first one foot, then the other to accommodate the cord, standing on tiptoes, claws feeling along the cord.

"Poor bastard." Abdullah shouted a command. Four enslaved infidels jumped to the deck, barefooted like Idris and Jamal.

"¡Madre de Dios, sálvanos!" one said, words Idris didn't understand. Then the man said in Arabic, "Sorry, brother."

The four men wrenched Meri away and tossed him overboard.

"Aiieee!" Idris shouted. "His soul!"

Abdullah was saying the prayer for the dead, the one Idris couldn't think of a moment before. And then Abdullah, in a jolly mood, again thanked Idris and Jamal for resisting the pirates, and without a pause, he screamed for everyone to go back to work.

Idris gazed out at the too-blue morning sea. Not the proper blue for a house. Or a man's veil. Or a woman's tattoos. A man must be buried in the ground, so he can find the trail that leads through the earth to the ancestors. A man can't swim or float away to join his ancestors, who are of the earth, not the sea.

Meri was lost in the Great Sea. Not able to walk the trail to join the ancestors, the true old ones.

"What did that infidel say?" Idris dared ask only Zirari.

"It sounded like how Roman soldiers called on the goddess Cybele at Carthage, but I never learned their filthy Latin tongue."

Jamal wept, his head on Idris's shoulder, until the wind rose again, tossing the boat, shaking it like a camel race over rocky trails. Jamal again leaned over the side, retching. Idris grasped

Jamal around the waist, so the lurching waves didn't drag another brother over the side.

3
Casa Rodriguez

"HEY, HANDSOME BOYS!"

Two women across the docks called to Idris and Jamal while the boat was being tied to the dock. The women sat in the shade of a portico across the way, goods spread around them on carpets.

"You need what we have for you!"

Zirari tugged Idris's ear. "They are widows seeking husbands. Don't listen."

"They are selling belts and boots." Idris brushed at his ear, still mourning Meri. "Leave me alone."

"What you got?" Jamal called in the broken Arabic he'd learned from Idris. He poked his tongue to the side of his mouth in a teasing way that would make even their sternest uncles laugh.

The women did laugh, motioning the brothers over.

Idris nudged Jamal. "We lost Meri only two nights ago. How can you play with women?"

"We're still alive. Meri would want to play if he was here."

When it was their turn to leave the boat, Idris and Jamal imitated those who had gone before them, swinging both legs over and leaping to the dock. Jamal stuck out an elbow to bar Idris's way, and then stalked toward the women, who were vendors with goods on display under the portico of a house.

"Those women want husbands," Idris called to his brother in their village dialect. The warning was what all three brothers had agreed: they wouldn't be lured by women the way their father and uncles had been. The brothers came to work and then go home.

A youth leaning against a corner of the women's house watched Idris, the same way children in any village scrambled to stare, wide eyed, whenever Idris and his brothers walked past in search of comrades to join a hunting party. On the march from the mountains, though they'd skirted villages, clumps of children gathered to watch their passage. Twenty, then fifty, then seventy men carrying spears and shields, headed down the mountain. The older boys watched the recruits, wanting to be in that line—that's what Idris saw in the expression on that insolent boy's face, here by the edge of the sea, too old to play with children, too young to be with men.

And Idris wasn't so far from boyhood that he'd forgotten. He'd often stared at hunters as they walked out of the village, judging their strength, their grace—and how close he might be to joining them. Remembering, Idris shifted his stance, prepared to wait for however long it took Jamal to finish flirting with the women who sold goods from the portico.

Zirari tugged Idris's hair. "Don't show off your nice muscles to those women."

"I'm not. Those women are Jamal's business, not mine."

"You puffed up, then stepped so your thighs look their best. Then grabbed your spear to flex your shoulders. You want that woman to eat you with her eyes, while you stand here being beautiful."

"There's no woman devouring me." Only that boy stared, with blue eyes like a ghost and skin burned red across eyes and nose, though pale as a ghul around a wide mouth.

Meri stepped up beside Idris, spear in hand, face and torso painted ochre, wrapped in a loincloth, exactly as he'd appeared at his first hunt. Zirari shouted explosive, joyous greetings, first in the village dialect, and then in a tongue Idris had never heard.

Surprised, Idris nearly dropped his spear, quelling an instinct to embrace his lost brother, who smiled and reached to pet the qareen, scratching behind what might be the creature's ears. Then Meri ran a finger down the gazelle-flute that hung on a tether over Idris's neck. Confused, Idris bit his lip to keep from crying out to Jamal that Meri was here, alive, fresh from the sea.

That fleeting thought was punished by a searing yank of Idris's ear lobes and a beak-mouth biting his lip.

"You are bound to me," Zirari hissed in village dialect. "You keep your ancestors' secrets."

"Hey, friend." Abdullah tapped Idris's shoulder. Idris couldn't look away from his little brother. "Can you give your friends their share of booty? And you keep your lost brother's share." He offered a leather pouch, dangling it by its strings.

"Booty?" The word sounded filthy, like a boy's bad joke.

"What we took off those pirates you butchered." He pushed the pouch into Idris's hand. "Fair is fair. You saved us."

"Idris!" Jamal shouted. "These women will help us. They can sell us boots."

Meri smiled broadly, seeing the women. He took the flute and began to play. Jamal turned from where he'd been busy making those women laugh. He tilted his head, as if straining to hear something far away, and then shaded his eyes to peer out at the sun-dappled sea.

That was when Idris accepted that only he saw his little brother gleaming there on the waterfront, looking like the ancestors' own idea of the world's best brother. Forced to silence, Idris still wanted to embrace Meri, to touch his brother's shoulder in the way all three brothers traded silent messages with their fingers. But Zirari's beak-mouth at his ear froze Idris in place.

Meri played his gazelle-flute, that child's song he'd learned after carving it on the second day of a hunt with the uncles. Meri had carried home very little meat that day, but began to play music that pleased even the fiercest of their scolding aunts.

Jamal shook his head, and then returned to flirting with the vendor-women.

Men unloading the boats behind them shouted caution. Children's cries drifted from a nearby alleyway. Idris shifted his stance, again gripping his spear, spooked into wariness in spite of Meri's soothing flute. Then he grabbed his courage and began calling to his fellow-travelers to receive their reward.

"Save it," he cautioned as he counted out brass and silver coins. "Don't lose it."

That boy leaning against the corner of the portico still stared. He must have been watching the whole while that Idris twitched upon seeing Meri. Then the boy moved from where he loitered to whisper to one of the women, the oldest of them, who seemed least beguiled by Jamal's chatter. The older woman nodded.

The youth approached Idris. "We would like to hire you for the night, to protect our house."

"I work for the caliph." That's what Zirari warned him to say, since the nightmare in Maliliyyah.

"Surely not for every moment of the day that the Lord our God has given us." The youth's words were Arabic, but not in an accent that Idris had heard, nor had he heard anyone call the name of God in that way. "I heard what your captain shouted. You and your friends are free until he takes you to Granada tomorrow. Come earn silver pennies, just by sleeping at our house for tonight, when so many savages have come to our town."

"Savages." Zirari repeated the word in village dialect, then nestled as the back of Idris's neck, like a cat hiding.

The sun blinded him when Idris glanced down the street that ran along the waterfront. While Meri glowed brightly beside him, Idris saw his friends the way that boy must see them.

People of the town walked along the street in immaculate white *sarawil* trousers, long tunics, and tidy turbans, their soft leather boots slapping silently on the stone-paved passageway. Many men wore no turbans, the hair on their uncovered heads oiled and combed, shining in the sun. The women, not one with even a single tattoo, wore wool robes of yarns spun finer than the thinnest wool his aunts could spin. They tied their robes closed with wide belts, beautifully dyed and embroidered, displaying more colors than Idris ever knew could be harvested. However wealthy or poor each woman might be, her boots were painted in elaborate designs. The women's veils were soft colors or white, though none seemed to be in mourning. No one wore either the indigo or black that all of Idris's aunts and cousins wore.

A pair of the caliph's soldiers passed, laughing behind their hands, pointing at the newly arrived recruits. In addition to boots, the soldiers wore leather coverings laced up over their shins and vests of boiled leather, metal studs pounded in to create a brass sheathing across their chests. They wore swords longer than any dagger or weapon that the men from the mountains carried.

"Just like the Romans who ruined the good life in Cairo."
Zirari seemed to muse on a memory. "Except for the turbans
wrapping their helmets."

Idris's band of newly-arrived recruits scattered along the
paved street. Half wore no shirts at all, like Jamal. The others left
their thin tunics open to the sun. Many like Idris wore thin, dust-
colored *sarawil* trousers, the linen edges dropping over ashy feet.
Others wore the familiar loincloths that freed mountain hunters to
stalk through bush and rocky valleys. They all wore sandals,
different only in the braiding or dye of the thongs that tied them to
those ashy feet. Feet that had walked through mountains for half
the turning of the moon.

Idris's friends—this many days on the road, most were friends
now—spat in the street while haggling with vendors. A pair
trotted over to the docksides, loosened their loincloths, and pissed
into the watery gap between two moored boats.

Another pair stopped dead in the street to watch two veiled
women pass, staring open mouthed until the women's servants
shoved them aside, snarling at them in Arabic. "Savages."

"No shame," Zirari whispered what must have been meant as
comfort. "You didn't know. How could you?"

"You could have told me, you filthy beast!" Idris shouted
silently.

"You might remember that I said you'd need boots." Zirari
resented the scolding. "You'll have to spend that pirate-booty.
And tell this little friend yes. Take the work offered for tonight.
You need the silver."

Idris gritted his teeth, glaring at that insolent youth who'd
waited patiently for an answer, showing a childish propensity to
smirk and judge. When had Idris given up foolish smirking like
that? After his father marched away as a mercenary and was never
heard from again?

"Yes." Idris bit off the word. "My brother and I will work for
you. Only for the night."

The sole blessed event of that day, aside from Meri's arrival,
was that those women dealt in second-hand armor. He and Jamal
bought boots and leather vests—cuirass, the women said in that

odd accent—and swords that needed sharpening, along with belts and half-rotten leather-and-wood scabbards and sheaths.

Then Idris coaxed Jamal into staying with him while he convinced their twenty-odd friends to spend pirate-booty to outfit themselves, so they looked more like the caliph's men. The arguments lasted until prayer time, when Jamal drifted away again, calling back to the woman who'd laughed most heartily at his teasing jokes that he'd see her later.

4
The Rooftop

"COME INSIDE."

The youth motioned Idris forward where a serving man had swung open a heavy wood-plank door.

Idris glanced back to the darkening street, making sure his brother Jamal followed. Meri stepped aside so Idris could see. Yes, Jamal was there. The women who'd been selling goods on the portico never reappeared after the call to prayers.

"We have our usual guards at the gates and on the streets." The youth waved them on. "We want added protection if the walls are breached."

The brothers were led down a narrow, dark passage. Idris resented his new boots, since the leather slapped on the tiles in ways his bare feet never would. It meant learning to walk in a new way. Only Meri padded silently along the passage.

That youth, their employer, disappeared around a corner.

Which opened onto a magnificent inner courtyard, with palm trees and flowers and a fountain in the center. Intricately carved plaster and bright tiles decorated the arches and the wall of the upper gallery. Wooden doors on two levels stood guard over hidden interiors.

The air, perfumed by flowers and spices, felt as cool as dawn after the heat of the dock-side streets.

"This is my house."

"But the market arcade on your portico…" Jamal spun around in the courtyard, gaping at the galleries.

The youth said, "Those women are of the Rodriguez clan. Distant, but my clan never forgets anyone. The clan makes sure they have work here, and a safe place."

"Clan is like family?" Idris asked. He could scarcely hear the youth's soft words over the buzz of Zirari's indistinct comments.

"Yes, family. Only bigger, more complex."

Servants appeared and received instructions for offering food to the *guàrdia*, which was a word that Idris didn't know. The servants were to lead Jamal to the upper gallery and Idris to the rooftop.

The roof proved to hold another garden, with smaller palms, more flowers. Left alone, Idris walked along the edge of the roof, seeking where it might be possible for invaders to scale the walls. At each portico along the streets below, two armed men stood chatting; one man looked up the street, one watched the other direction. The sprawling house, with several connected rooftops, had been built like a fortress, with no possible handholds for scaling the stone and plaster walls.

"What does your new friend really want from you?" Zirari stirred a circle on Idris's collar bone.

Puzzled, Idris chose a corner of the roof that gave a broad view of the street and sea. Cushions and carpets indicated that others before him had chosen this place for its view. He set his new sword, bow, and spear close to hand. A breeze wafted from the sea, the air smelling the way it had in the peace of the night on the voyage from Maliliyyah. Before they lost Meri. Who now sat on one of the rooftop carpets and stared out at the sea, the same way that Idris did.

The moon had risen high enough that it reflected on the huge expanse of water that separated this land from home. A cry echoed up from the interior below. Two children called to each other and then giggled, their joy trilling in the night. Jamal's voice resonated for a moment, then fell to a murmur.

Meri played a tune with only two notes.

Idris's belly felt stitched with hunger for home, a desire deep in his muscles to toss his laughing nieces in the air, to lift a young nephew into the village tree, so the boy could scramble up to where all the cousins hid while the aunts and mothers sat on their stoops, gossiping and spinning. He heard the old men chatting over the tap-tap rhythm of the village coppersmith, making bracelets to trade. But the sound proved to be the sea below, knocking boats against the dock.

He wanted to step into the cool interior of his grandmother's house and close the blue door. That muscle below his heart, at the end of his ribs, clenched with longing to go there now.

Zirari hopped off his shoulder, interrupting Idris's private reverie, and joined Meri, who abandoned his flute and set up to play a *naqala* game, motioning Zirari closer, shaking pebbles in his hand.

"You can't win when you play with Meri," Idris said. "Unless your fire lord taught you to cheat."

Over its feathered shoulder, the qareen said, "Susa is weeping for Meri. I want to help."

"You aren't helping." Idris said it aloud, just as two servants appeared, one bearing the promised food, the other kindling coals in a brazier and setting an iron pan upon it.

Idris stood, bowed to the servants, and said thank you, the way his aunts taught him, except he spoke in Arabic. The servants backed away. Behind them, that youth appeared again.

"Sweet accent." The youth sounded friendly, though Idris only guessed that word meant sweet.

Zirari tossed a pebble. "More like delicious than sweet. Ask why you're really here."

"Will cakes and lentils do for you?" the youth asked, the way a warm, eager friend might offer. "Do you drink wine?"

"No," Idris said. "Only infidels drink wine."

"Oh, you're one of them." His host sounded dejected. The moonlight glowed bright enough that those blue eyes seemed even more ghostly.

"One of what? I'm with the men who came from—"

"The Veiled Ones. Who came to steal away our world."

"No, we came only for one season. To pay our taxes. And then go home."

"*¡Madre de Dios, sálvanos!*" An exclamation, the same words that enslaved sailor shouted when Meri died. "What's your name?"

"Id—" He couldn't get the rest out before Zirari whistled a warning. He said, "I'm Idris ibn Musa. What's your name?"

"A good Arabic name for a Berber man. Where are you from?"

"The top of the *adras* mountains, which hold up the sky in the south." He counted the knots on the cord wrapped around his wrist. "Thirteen days' walk west and south of the Great Sea. Now, what is your name, please? And why did you ask us here? You do not need protection."

"You should eat your supper." The youth settled on the cushions beside Idris, dishing food onto a smooth pottery dish and then offering it, a thin hand grazing Idris's, causing a lurch in his muscled knot of loneliness, perhaps at the youth's simple offer. "I first saw you in a dream, Idris ibn Musa. Then today I knew you from how you take care of the men with you. My grandmother insists that I must trust you, because you will save me."

"A dream? My grandmother warned me from the cradle not to trust dreams. You never know what creature carried them to you in the night." Idris scooped up lentil stew with a portion of thin bread, but when he took a bite, his tongue found crispy lamb meatballs, and then pepper and spices burst in his mouth. Didn't the youth say it was lentils?

"You like the *mirkas*?" The boy sounded pleased. "The cooks make it spicier here than we have at home."

"It is a pleasure," Idris said, "but not like anything I've known. Now, tell me your name, O Dreamer. I shared mine."

The boy spoke words as strange as when Zirari announced its name.

"Oro Vida de Jai Yen del Casa Rod Reego?" Idris tried to repeat the unknown words. Zirari muttered, "It means 'gold life' in the Roman invaders' tongue. Maybe those bastards are still here. Ask."

The boy continued explaining his name. "People here, in clans like mine, are called by their native city and mother's clan name."

"Which part is your city name?"

"Jaén." The boy repeated the word again. "It's across the Sierra Nevada and north of Grenada on the road to Toledo. Our clan name is Rodriguez, from the line of an ancient Visigoth king."

Idris took another bite of mouth-burning stew, regretting how little he'd learned from his qareen about this new world. He hadn't heard of any places the boy named. "I've never been in these lands before."

Zirari sounded its usual arrogant self. "You could help by asking about Caesar."

The youth offered more food. "Try the *isfiriya*. One bite takes me back to childhood. I don't mean mush for babies. My sisters and brothers and cousins ate *isfiriya* on spring days we spent together at the farm." The nostalgic notes in his voice tugged Idris into his own memories of childhood. "Eggs and saffron and cinnamon, and so soft, it's like eating a cloud."

"My aunts make cakes like these," Idris said. One bite proved that these cakes were sweeter than he was used to. "My great-aunt says cousins who eat cakes together must never quarrel."

"Perhaps we can be friends like that, ibn Musa. That's what I saw in my dream." He offered more bread and another scoop of the stew. The copper spoon scraped on the pottery dish, sending a vibration up Idris's arm that felt like a touch among intimate friends. "Tell me about your village and your family."

A moth flitted between them, its wings catching and reflecting the moonlight. The boy sat unnaturally close by. Another nugget of knowledge, how this world differed from Idris's, that strangers sit so close to each other. The noise of the Great Sea, slapping against the docks and beach below, sounded as loud as the whistling winter wind that pierced the blue door, seeking entrance to their little house. The warmth of that boy pulled Idris even closer, like the boats rubbing the docks, like when he sat with his brothers, at peace in a hunters' blind, waiting.

"My homeland is beautiful, but hard to describe," Idris said. "You need to see how the sun burnishes gold across our mountain, even on rare days after snow in winter."

"You have gold in your lands?" The boy perked up, his thigh brushing against Idris when he shifted on the cushion. "Yet you joined the caliph's army to earn silver?"

The boy's curious note caused Idris to hesitate. "I've heard of gold in stories. But I only meant that it's how I imagine gold must appear, a substance so beautiful that kings kill and die for it."

"Did you leave a wife behind in your village?" The boy probed, but seemed so innocent when he asked.

"No. In my country, a man usually goes to live in his wife's village." Which was why Idris couldn't marry until another man came to the village and took his place, since there weren't other uncles and cousins who could serve as hunters and helpers. "You might say, a good hunter is his own bride-price."

"My grandmother would have liked that, staying in her home. That's one way you and I are alike. We both want to stay with our family. Tell me about your grandmothers."

Idris began first with his mother's mother, surprised that telling this story eased the loneliness in his belly. But that made him pause. "This isn't what I talk about with strangers."

"But we aren't strangers now. I hope we are friends." The boy asked more questions, until Idris had described every aunt, cousin, grandmother, and even his sister's new husband, who'd lost his foot in a hunting accident. Idris described what was in their houses, what they ate, what the women wove while they gossiped on their stoops, how the old ones gave judgment and advice under the great cedar.

Then a lingering silence, with only the nagging splash of the treacherous Great Sea while again Idris felt the yearning for home gnaw at his belly. He wanted Meri to put aside the *naqala* stones and play his flute again.

"Too few uncles." The boy's tones were more a sigh than spoken words, his breath passing close by Idris's ear like when Zirari was busy teaching. "Too many aunts left alone. And too few children."

"We are the first people in those mountains. We are—"

"Please, your story is the same everywhere among the poor of Al-Andalus. Men can't afford to stay home. You go to war to claw back silver pennies that the caliphate takes and takes and takes."

Idris brushed a finger to his lips, signing the need to whisper, since such words shouldn't drift on the wind.

"No one hears us." The youth leaned even closer. Idris reached to pull him even closer, but stopped, surprised at that impulse. "Anyone who might hear will only shake his head and smile sadly at the future of villages like yours."

"The future is—" Idris wanted to repeat Silina's words about the days that came after this one, which was called "the future" in Arabic. But that space between his heart and his belly lurched at the sensation of that boy so close.

"Your village's future is decided," the youth said, his voice muted with sadness. "When your people can't pay the taxes, because the uncles and sons have all gone away, your aunts will be driven from their houses. They'll travel to the next village. And then the next, until they come to one of the caliph's cities, where they'll live as servants."

"No!" Idris spoke too emphatically.

"Or worse, I'm very sorry to say." The lad leaned close again as he spoke.

"The ancestors will guide the aunts and mothers while we are absent," Idris said, as if Silina spoke through him.

"And if any one of you speaks of your ancestors that way, you will all be in chains, slaves forever, as..." The boy said a word that Idris had heard before but didn't understand.

Zirari called to Idris. "It means 'not Islam.' What the Veiled Ones scolded about when they first rode their horses into your village."

"We know how to make our way in the world." Idris felt hectored, by both Zirari and the Rodriguez boy. And bewildered.

"Do you? Do you know how your family will get the silver you earn? Are there people from your clan here who will carry your silver across the Great Sea to your home?" The boy leaned quite close, whispering in Idris's ear. "Or do you summon an ifrit to fly through the sky?"

Idris's heart quickened, those lips so close to his ear. Yet something wanted to hide in that empty space under his heart, like a fox hiding in the rocks. "Why are you saying these things?"

"Because the Veiled Ones are destroying my world too. It's why you and I saw each other in my dream. My clan needs..."

"I didn't see you in a dream."

"My grandmother thinks you will. Or remember that you did." The boy fell silent as if listening to the boats knocking down by the sea.

Idris couldn't remember any dream with a blue-eyed ghul, or a warm, insistent youth. His hands wanted to reach out, but they obeyed him. That lonely muscle below his heart would not obey. But he was the oldest brother, the tallest uncle in the village. He mastered himself and spoke in the same stern way he did when his brothers went astray. "Your clan needs what from me?"

"To be bound as partners."

"I work for the caliph." He hoped he spoke with the same strength as he had at Maliliyyah.

"You made that promise when you had no other choice." The youth moved the plate of food from where Idris had left it, setting it back on the serving tray. "My grandfather was among those who warned the *taifa* emirs not to hire the Veiled Ones as mercenaries. It'd be better if our grandfathers had simply paid *parias* to Castile and Barcelona. The Veiled Ones have made life worse for everyone, from Zaragoza to Cordoba. Far worse than border raids by *cristiano* kings, even the ones that follow the Roman way."

Idris knew most of those words, except the place names. He wished Zirari would explain *parias* and *cristiano*, but the qareen was silent. What Idris did understand was the boy's passion, an over-boiling kettle between them.

Heat. Turmoil. Spluttering on open coals.

"Ask. Ask about the Romans." Zirari hopped, scattering unplayed *naqala* pebbles. "Who is Caesar now? A conqueror or debauched fool?"

"Who is your..." Idris didn't know the Arabic word. "King?"

The boy slapped both hands on the cushion, fingers grazing Idris's thigh. "We have a caliph across the Great Sea, who sent the warrior Yusuf ibn Tashfin with tens of thousands of men like you. We have a dozen *taifa* emirs. Clans in the north have their Sanchos and Alfonsos, kings who stab their own brothers and invade their cousins' lands. We hope that we have Rodrigo Díaz on our side, now that Valencia is a tributary to Rodrigo." A pause. "If Rodrigo doesn't once more change the king he serves."

Ask. Ask.

Idris waved to silence his qareen. Too many names he didn't know. Instead, Idris prompted the youth again. "You didn't finish saying what you want. What does your clan need?"

"Honest warriors who can fight. For the clans. For all the *dhimmi*, whether *judía* or *cristiano*, whether Roman or Visigoth. Even for the Muslim farmers and traders who lived here in peace until the too-holy Veiled Ones came."

Ask. Ask.

"The Veiled Ones and the *cristiano* kings seek to destroy my world and yours." The boy put his hand on Idris's thigh. "Come work for our clan, instead of the caliph."

It felt like being touched by a woman, or what Idris imagined that might feel like, from what Jamal told him. That sensation must come from the boy's fiery passion. Instead of withdrawing, Idris rested his hand on the boy's.

"What do you really want from us, little friend?" He couldn't say the boy's unpronounceable name, for fear of being laughed at. "You called us savages today, out on the street. Because we don't wear fine clothes or painted boots."

"And you told me how your family and village are more human than all of the rest of the world. I hired you for tonight because you are a good person. I saw that in my dream and here, right now. Work for our clan instead of the caliph."

Aiieee! Dreams!

Idris repeated what Zirari said was true in Maliliyyah. "It's dangerous for my village if I break my promise to work for the Veiled Ones for a season. When we finish this season's service, we'll go home."

"My clan will give you horses." The boy's hand tightened on Idris's thigh, which felt like fire. "Your captain won't give you horses, will he?"

Confusion burned through Idris's veins, from both that boy's touch and those words. "Horses? Why would he give us horses? We're bowmen and hunters and—"

"Because in Al-Andalus, if you don't ride a horse to battle, then you are the same as enslaved infidels."

"Now you call us slaves?" Idris lifted his hand away, but the boy grasped it, wrapping it in both of his hands, fingers flashing pale in the moonlight against Idris's much larger hands.

"Don't you see, ibn Musa? The Veiled Ones bring boatloads of men to send to battle half naked with painted faces and spears, only to frighten the enemy for a moment. When the enemy's knights reclaim their courage, they slaughter that front line. Those men from the mountains and desert die only to protect the Veiled knights, who all ride horses." The boy squeezed Idris's hand again as if pleading or begging him. "So, did your captain promise you horses?"

Idris called silently to Zirari. "Is it true?" But Zirari didn't turn from the game with Meri.

After the silence grew too long, the boy said, "Do any men from your village ever return from fighting for the Veiled Ones? Is that why your village has too few uncles and cousins?"

Hissing, Zirari swiveled its hideous head to glare at Idris, its eyes burning red like the coals on the brazier. "Susa was right."

Idris's mother refused to speak Musa's name for years, while Silina insisted that Musa was a good man, that he hadn't left his wife for another woman, that he'd never abandon his family.

Perhaps there's a reason...

A coal popped on the brazier. A tiny white flame flared up.

Idris's father, his lost uncles. They had died.

Another pop and flare.

They had died here, on the wrong side of the Great Sea, far away from the trails they must follow to join the ancestors. Lost in this world, like Meri, who needed Idris to take him home.

"Oh, I've hurt you!" The boy put his hands on Idris's face, like Silina had done. Idris liked the sensation, and feared it. The boy whispered, "Forgive me. My thoughts race away with my tongue. Please forgive."

"You hired me to ask me to break a promise? Or to insult me?"

"No, no. Because my grandmother says you will save me. As if you were the hero I should love." Then his hands were in Idris's hair and pressing their faces together. The boy was kissing him. Idris's mouth opened in surprise, and he kissed too, instead of tearing himself away.

The boy leaned back, the late-night moon shimmering in his ghost-blue eyes. "Is that allowed in your world? Or only in my dream?" Rather than wait for an answer, he kissed Idris again, lingering, then softly biting Idris's lip before letting him go. "That was nice. My sister said it would be." The boy whispered, like a conspirator. "But I'm not like her. I'm not about to play love-beast with this audience."

Idris still felt that kiss, and he wanted to ask what a love-beast was, but the lingering sensation kept him from speaking. When he finally forced words, his voice scratched. "We are alone here."

"I mean your ifrit." The boy waved at the corner of the rooftop where Zirari and Meri played *naqala* with pebbles. Zirari was indeed losing badly. "The shades of our house all came too. I think they like its company."

"You see…" Idris smothered surprise.

"Yes, but I don't understand. Does your ifrit speak the Berber tongue?"

"We aren't Berber. We only live among them." Idris said what Silina would, but Zirari cast a demanding glare over its shoulder. "And not an ifrit. Those are children's stories told by people who have no home and wander the desert."

Still close, a finger's breadth from Idris's face, the boy pursed his lips. "Well, obviously not a djinni, or you'd be a general instead of bound into service as a mercenary infantryman."

Zirari whirled around, agitated, hopping across the pebble game.

"This is my family's business and not yours." Idris folded his arms the way his uncles did when his aunts were to understand that the discussion had closed. Which put more space between his own heart and that boy's burning heat.

"Only a dear little qareen, then?" The youth titled his head, curious. "But how will it help you in Al-Andalus? Lower-world spirits can't live here. My grandmother says the *cristianos* in the old times cast spells that diminished the ancient bound spirits."

Meri reached out and stroked Zirari's head, calming the creature.

The horizon had lightened. Idris stood to watch the sun carry in the day, feeling like he might be in jeopardy yet wanting to stay close by the blue-eyed youth. "I don't need the help of spirits to travel mountain roads, to hunt or fight. It's no different on this side of the Great Sea than at home."

"If only that were so." The youth's name was being called from within the house. He stood, pausing in the doorway, one hand lifted in farewell. "Perhaps when we meet again, my grandmother will tell us what you and I are supposed to do. Outside of dreams."

When Idris was alone again, Zirari hopped up on his neck. "She cried *Madre de Dios* like a boat-slave. Skin like a bone-ghul. Big nose. And yet you made her feel sorry for you, so she'll be in love with you. Why didn't you choose a beautiful woman, like your brother did?"

"Not a woman. A boy. Perhaps a scholar, like in your tales of Persia. I learned more from him than you've taught me."

"¡*Madre de Dios, sálvanos!*" The qareen repeated the youth's exclamation. "Don't know what it means, but I'll say it whenever you're as stupid as a pickled turnip."

"What is a turnip?"

Zirari spat on Idris's shoulder, then rubbed a bird-foot in it. "You wouldn't ask about Caesar and the Romans, so I'm not telling you what a turnip is."

Idris tasted pepper and coriander on his lips, a tang of spices still coating his palate. It tickled when his tongue sought more of that flavor.

5
The Captain

ON THIS SIDE OF the world, the sun rose out of the middle of that vast expanse of water. The white-washed town gleamed as blinding-white as the sun rays on the Great Sea.

Zirari began hissing as soon as the great wooden doors closed behind them.

"Disgraceful. Using *pity* to make a kind woman fall in love with you," the creature said the word as if it were blasphemous. "That's what first carried me away from civilization to live in your golden mountains. I've heard it too often before. 'O my true love, I long for your touch in the night. You make me whole. ' It's reprehensible, planting pity in order to reap a good woman's love like—"

"Not a woman," Idris repeated, not meaning to say it aloud. He rubbed his face, still feeling that kiss.

"Certainly not like any women we've ever known." Jamal said, catching up from behind, rubbing his hands like an overexcited child. "Her sister, the one who kept me for the night, is called Cristina, which sounds like something good to eat. And she was indeed delicious."

"Whose sister?"

"That woman Aurovita. Cristina is two seasons younger. They are both off to marry *cristiano* lords in Valencia." Jamal, blinded by his morning memories, didn't notice Idris's confusion. "Which is why Cristina was so curious. That's what she said when she brought me into her room. 'I'm curious.' Then she cuddles against me like a house cat."

"¡Madre de Dios, sálvanos!" Zirari stomped about in Idris's hair. Meri, amused by Jamal, played an infant's counting song. *One kitten, two kittens, three.*

Idris felt like he was reliving that time he'd tracked a panther, walking in a circle for two days, only to find the panther tracking him. Except that time, discovering the scats of his own stupidity hit him hard in the breastbone.

This time, it hit his groin. And that void between his heart and his ribs. A woman kissed him, said she saw him in her dreams. "And she was kind," Zirari whispered dreamily, "and wise. If not beautiful."

"Let's go, Jamal. We need to find our friends and join our captain."

"O Serious One!" Jamal's laughter made Meri play faster. "You won't tell me how it was, being kissed by a woman? It was your first time, wasn't it?"

"I have nothing to say." Idris walked on. He licked his lips, tasted spices, and clenched his fists while mastering his thoughts.

His qareen droned, "Truer words were never spoken by prophets or kings. Nothing to tell."

"You won't share what it's like to remove trousers from a woman who dresses like a man? I'm curious." Jamal shook a finger playfully.

Idris batted his brother's hand away. "I didn't take off her trousers."

"Then how—"

Idris flicked his brother's ear. "Remember our uncles' chiding? Men don't tell what they do with women."

Which stopped Jamal. So Idris didn't have to confess…to nothing. To being the most ignorant man to ever walk out of the *adras* mountains.

"Is this what happened to our father?" Jamal mused. "Getting paid to spend the night with a woman while pretending to protect her." He pinched Idris's arm. "These women need protection like a gazelle needs goat cheese." Then Jamal noticed at last that Idris wasn't laughing. "So serious, brother? You didn't like that sister? Or she didn't like you?"

"I spent the night learning how it really is in this world for men like us." Idris explained about Berber infantry on the front lines of battle with only spears against mounted knights. "Do you understand, Jamal? Our father is dead. The Veiled Ones used him as a shield against their enemies, to protect their knights."

Zirari scratched at the tip of Idris's ear. "And that's what they want you for, too. Tell him."

Idris rubbed at his ear.

Jamal slapped his brother's arm. "You're scratching your ear. Second sight? Are you about to tell me that our father came to you in a dream to warn you? Silina taught us not to trust dreams." He stretched again, still happy with memories of the night before. "Let's find our captain. While we march you can tell me what you learned from your lover."

Zirari nestled in Idris's headdress. "*Aiieee,* the eldest brother learned that the difference between women and men is more than their clothes." His qareen talked and talked as they walked. "Did you know that? How women are different?"

"I can't think about it right now." Though Idris couldn't stop thinking about it, while Jamal walked alongside in a daydream, not seeing Meri with them.

Zirari persisted. "When we met, was that why you asked if I was a he or she? Because you can only tell trousers from robes?"

"Look." Idris pointed with his elbow where he wanted to direct both Jamal's and the qareen's attention, where the captain was gathering the men to travel. "Our captain is a cruel man and those four horsemen are just as bad. We have to pay attention."

There were no horses for Idris and his friends, only for the four Veiled soldiers and al-Malik, who hustled the recruits through the town, onto the road to Granada.

When they began the journey out of Al-Mería and into the countryside, Idris couldn't look away from the captain's petty cruelties, having to decide each moment whether to distract attention or intercede, and having to dodge lashes swung by the Veiled Ones on horseback. Jamal, still dreamy eyed, caught the lash twice for clumsiness.

Al-Malik had acquired a servant, a northman called Viggo, the only man in their company who was taller than Idris. His face was burned as red as a bald ibis, but wherever the man's tunic lifted to show his torso, he was whiter than a ghul. He spoke Arabic, but Idris caught the man exclaiming in his own language, which sounded like a song a man might sing with a mouth full of couscous. It was the first midday break before Idris understood the man was a slave. After the soldiers had hobbled their horses, al-Malik clipped a chain to the brass bracelets Viggo wore, handed the chain to Idris, and warned him not to let the bastard escape.

Close by where Idris and Jamal had tossed their travel rolls for the midday rest, Viggo sat stiffly on a boulder, hands folded before him. He murmured words in that mush language.

"What, friend?" Idris was not comfortable being responsible for that chain. Meri settled between them and began to play, the kind of mountain songs that calmed everyone at night time.

"I said, where am I going to escape to?" The man spoke in Arabic. He seemed to relax a bit. "I'm Viggo Torbjornsen. My father was Torbjorn, which means thunder bear."

"That is a good name," Jamal said. "My father gave me the name of an ancient king. But here I'm called Jamal."

"We are from the *adras* mountains," Idris said, "which hold up the sky in the south. Where is your home?"

"The Dane land, by the North Sea. I work for traders, to protect them. But on our way home we were attacked by pirates, who sold me into slavery." The big man raised his hands, which rattled the chain that Idris was supposed to guard. "The gods do not make men to be slaves."

After midday, al-Malik humiliated Umar and Ali, who were ill and tarried too long in the bushes by the road. They had to carry Viggo's chain and walk directly behind the horses, which always required extra care.

At supper, the recruits had cold couscous that never met spice, with bread that had been fried in oil too many days earlier.

Come breakfast, Idris wanted only to eat his food, even though it was rice porridge without spices, and rice isn't a fit food for humans. Jamal squatted to eat beside Idris, and murmured imprecations between mouthfuls of porridge, decrying the haphazard ways of this world which led to Meri's loss.

"If this is supposed to make us believe—"

Idris stopped Jamal's tirade, lifting a finger in warning, nodding toward al-Malik, their captain, who ate his breakfast with his four horsemen. Idris said the words that they were taught good Muslims must say, speaking in Arabic so al-Malik heard.

"When evil afflicts us, we can call on—"

Meri squatted beside Jamal and began to play his gazelle-flute. Jamal blinked, looked around, his eyes wide, yet never seeing Meri right there before him. But Jamal stopped condemning the ways of the world and began to recite Meri's fine attributes, the same way their aunts chanted at dawn on the spring equinox, begging the ancestors to remain with the family always. Then Jamal told all the funny and sweet stories that the aunts loved to repeat about Meri as a child.

Idris listened, laughed, brushed at his eyes, grateful for this, the only funerary oration Meri would have.

While Meri softly played his flute and never said a word.

Zirari rustled in Idris's hair. Idris had forgotten about his qareen while thinking about Meri.

"You have to ask about the promised silver," Zirari said. "It's the only way with men like that captain."

"You said you only remembered the ways of women, because it's so long since you've been companion to a man."

"I've asked around." A serious note rumbled in Zirari's throat.

"Who did you ask? Are there qareens all around us?"

"No matter. You must demand the silver due from that captain. He's out to cheat you."

Zirari scratched at Idris's scalp, trod along his shoulder, nipped at his ears and neck, so Idris no longer enjoyed the peace of Jamal's oratory or Meri's music. Idris scratched where it hurt most from Zirari's pecking.

Jamal said, "What, brother? You're rubbing your ear again. Do you have new wisdom from the ancestors?"

Idris set his cup beside Jamal and approached al-Malik.

"We are owed Amir ibn Musa's death portion. My family, that is. And I am my family's leader. You must give it to us."

"Death portion?" Al-Malik frowned, but Idris couldn't tell if he frowned at his porridge or Idris's demand. "Who is Amir ibn Musa?"

"My brother, who died in battle. We are due his death portion."

"That pirate attack was the boat-man's problem. You work for the caliph."

"My brother died saving this whole band."

"Which he could have also done in a tavern brawl or at the compound in Maliliyyah. Not the caliph's battle, so no death portion."

He turned his attention away from Idris, adjusting his travel goods. That's when Idris saw it, the same leather pouch the captain had raised over his head back in Umar's village. Still as plump as when he'd jingled it to get the village men's attention.

No silver had gone home to their villages. No taxes had been paid. Zirari dug into Idris's scalp, urging him to answer the captain, but Idris was so amazed that he couldn't find words.

Al-Malik said, "You should be grateful for the sensible ways of our caliph. There's one less portion of travel provisions to be taken from the silver due your family."

"We pay for our food?" Idris, surprised, didn't mean to say it aloud. Zirari hopped madly on his head, agitated.

"Changed my mind," the qareen growled. "Don't rile this man."

Al-Malik laughed. "It was plain as that big nose on your sad face, in the contract you signed."

Idris bowed to his captain and went to join Jamal and prepare to travel again.

Zirari tugged at Idris's ear and swore softly. "O blighted flames. I haven't taught anyone to read since Cyrus invaded Babylon." The qareen made a sound that might be a chuckle though Idris had never heard the creature laugh. "However, writing is writing and..." Zirari's thought trailed off. "I know Persian, from the old days. I could teach you to read that."

Idris silenced the qareen. "Better I kick you back to your fire lord's lair."

With Meri gliding beside him, the trail passed quickly. Idris wanted to learn more from Zirari, since he'd caught several black glances from the captain, which indicated that Idris had asked questions he shouldn't. Idris whispered his thoughts, unreasonably angry with Zirari as well as al-Malik.

"How are we paid? Why didn't you tell me?"

"If you recall, I wasn't there when you signed up to fight infidels. I was busy keeping rats and cockroaches out of Susa's house and making sure the milk didn't go bad before it cured to cheese, and—"

"How do we find out? Do they send the silver to our families? Or pay us? If we send the family our silver, how do we know it gets there? How much silver do we need to go home again?"

"You didn't ask the recruiting man? Now you want me to find out?" Zirari then went silent, standing still where he perched on Meri's head.

"Hey, qareen?" Idris prompted for an answer.

"I'm trying to remember from when Darius hired mercenaries."

"Who's he?"

"A king, well, he started as just the son of a satrap from Bactria, then he ruled all of Macedonia and Persia and—"

"Is that at the east end of the *adras* mountains? Or in the southern desert?"

"It's on the far end of the Great Sea." Zirari used that tone when he wanted to pretend that Idris was an unschooled fool. "I was with a prince in Persepolis then and—"

"How were his soldiers paid?"

"The mercenaries' families became wards of the king. Food came each week on the day after worship and prayers. Men who couldn't march in war defended the king's villages and helped with the harvest."

"How did families get the mercenaries' silver?"

"The men shared war-booty when they came home."

"If they didn't come home?" Asking for Meri's portion spawned many thoughts. For the first time, Idris considered the possibility that he too might not return home.

A gaping pit opened before him. He stepped back, as if the gulf were actually there, a canyon across the mountain trail.

Zirari trotted to the back of Idris's neck, not seeming to notice the canyon that opened in Idris's thoughts. "Then their families became King Darius's permanent wards."

"Why did my father's pay never come to our family? Or his death portion? Will the caliph take care of our family? Relieve us from the taxes that forced us into service?"

"We shall have to ask."

"Ask who? Your blasted fire lord? Does the djinni-king of bonfires know how the caliph does his business?"

Zirari raked a talon along the soft flesh behind Idris's ear. "Do not blaspheme my lord."

At next midday break, al-Malik again charged Idris with holding Viggo's chain. Which felt filthy in his hand. While the other men rested, Idris whispered to Jamal about Meri's death portion and that they had to pay for provisions and passage to Al-Andalus.

"We didn't know we were coming to Al-Andalus," Jamal said, after he finished cursing.

"Worse, brother. In the captain's pack is that bag of silver he promised for our families. He has it, as full as when he rattled it while we signed to come fight infidels."

Idris had looked around to ensure no one else heard, seeing only Viggo nearby, who had listened in silence. Yet when Idris finished his story, while Jamal gaped, slow to believe, three of their friends appeared from where they'd been pissing in the bushes.

"So the captain stole our silver?" Ali asked first, with Umar and Tariq beside him, angry enough to catch fire. They began murmuring among the other men.

The whole while, Meri played his gazelle-flute, the way he did at the last feast-day, when he'd whipped the young men and women of all three villages into a circle dance, where they spun until they dropped exhausted late in the night. Or maybe Meri didn't provoke the wild dance; maybe he just played along with it.

As if answering to a signal, the way al-Malik had been teaching them since they first walked down the mountain trail, the men rose and each picked up a spear, a rock, a knife. Idris stopped Jamal from joining them. And dropped Viggo's chain. The men moved into a circle, fifteen of them surrounding the four veiled horsemen, and the rest closing in on al-Malik. Who looked up from where he lounged on his blanket.

"If everyone's awake, then we best get on the way."

"When will you pay that boy's death portion?" Viggo asked, his Arabic easily understood by every man there. He bashed the brass bands on his wrists together, the clang ringing out across the camp.

Al-Malik laughed. He stood, reaching for the chain that now dragged on the ground, motioning for Viggo to kneel.

Then al-Malik's hand lay in the dust, and he stared at the blood pouring from the stump. Before he could scream, a spear was thrust in his middle, and rocks rained on his head. Viggo pushed through the men, snatched up that chain, and choked the captain with it. Al-Malik fell to his knees, then pitched forward, his fall stopped by the length of the chain that Viggo still held. Behind him, the others jumped on the horsemen, taking them down with knives. Only one had time to scream.

All while Idris pressed on Jamal's chest to keep him from joining in.

Meri's song quavered, then dropped again to the soothing songs he played when men wanted to sleep. People breathed heavily and stretched, the way men do when they rise from a night spent on hard ground, loosening the kinks and stiff places. No one spoke. The men didn't look at each other, just began packing their gear, retrieving their weapons, stripping the four horse soldiers.

Zirari breathed so heavily by Idris's ear that it stirred his hair.

Ali, from the next village over, eased his knife from the belly of one of the horsemen. He glanced over his shoulder at the silent band of men.

"Idris ibn Musa is our captain now. We can trust him. He knows what to do."

"But I'm just a hunter." Idris's shock at what these men had done passed quickly. What they asked now was more disturbing.

Zirari tugged Idris's ear. "¡Madre de Dios, sálvanos! Who else can do it but you?"

"Not me!" He barked silently at the qareen. "No one in this part of the world will believe Idris the son of the milkmaid is the captain of Berber mercenaries."

"No one in this part of the world knows Idris al-Makkzan," Jamal said, as if he'd heard that thought. "Badr al-Malik al-Makkzan. He carried a letter to give to his general."

Umar and Tariq searched al-Malik's body, stripping it. Tariq tossed that bag of silver to Idris.

"Idris ibn Musa should hold our silver. We know he is an honest man."

The band murmured assent while two other men searched the captain's travel pack. One offered Idris a packet of parchment. Another offered the badge that was pinned at the top of the captain's tunic.

"We'll find someone to read these when we come to Granada," Umar said. "To learn where our captain is supposed to take us."

"We should take the silver and go home," Jamal said. The men all stood straighter, glancing at each other, considering the idea. "We can be back in that town by tomorrow. Find a boat and sail home."

Zirari pulled at Idris's hair. "Yes! Go back!"

"Is that a magic bag?" Viggo pointed to the pouch Idris held. "It cannot possibly hold enough silver to buy passage for more than two or three of you."

"What do you know?" Tariq challenged. "You're only—"

"A slave? I spent ten years guarding merchants. I've seen how much gold trades hands when a man hires passage from one port to another." Viggo had taken up a broken blade and a rock, and was working with Idris to break the hinges of the brass bands that bound his wrists.

"We can sell the horses, too," Umar said.

Idris smashed open one of Viggo's bands. Viggo said, "And how to explain that your Berber band has returned without your captain but with his horses?"

Idris began to work on Viggo's other band. Jamal and many of the others disputed Viggo's argument, declaring that they could go to another port city, while Zirari kept hissing. "Yes. Yes. Home. We can take care of Susa."

Idris batted at his ear, hoping to silence the beast in his hair. "We need to purchase food, too. The northman is right. We need to go on. Do the work they hired us for and then go home when they pay us."

Jamal grabbed Idris's hand, as if pleading with him, but then nodded. "My brother is right. We can't return to that town without our captain."

Meri took up a soothing song again. Zirari quit scratching. Idris freed Viggo's right arm of its brass band.

Umar said, "We still agree. Idris ibn Musa must be our captain."

After they moved the bodies of the Veiled knights far off the trail and covered them with enough stones to keep away scavengers, the men picked through the supplies and ate a second meal, while Idris prompted them to think about how they might work together. They decided to divide half the silver equally among them and have Idris hold the rest, to purchase provisions. Viggo taught them to stitch coins into the hems of their clothes, the way merchants do.

"And the horses?" Viggo prompted. "Who knows how to ride and care for horses?"

"My uncle had a camel once," one man said.

Zirari stirred again, as if waking. "I do. I know."

Jamal said, "Captain Idris! You're rubbing your ear again. Is there another surprise down the trail?" Then he slapped his knee, laughing. "O Idris ibn Musa, the seer from the *adras* mountains. Can you teach us to ride these horses?"

"We are hunters, not children," Idris said. "The animals will tell us what they want if we listen."

Five men agreed to go with Idris to deal with the horses. Idris followed them, rather than leading. Viggo the thunder-bear north-man came up beside him.

"Your ghost-brother plays beautiful music. The gods in this country must be happy to have him here." He clapped a hand on Idris's shoulder. "Is your bird a *nisse*? Does it sing?"

"¡*Madre de Dios!*" Zirari croaked. "Never!"

6
Horses

"THESE HORSES SPEAK ARABIC." Zirari adopted his best teaching tone. "You have to call them lover in their own tongue. Tell them how sweet and beloved they are."

The horse Idris first approached, his hand outstretched, shied away. Zirari hopped on the animal's head, whispering in its ear.

"Wrong side," Zirari said to Idris. "Only come to him on the right side. His name is al-Hassan, the Beautiful One. He's from the desert and sad to be so far from home. You have a lot in common."

Viggo was showing another man, Tariq from the next village, how to sooth and talk to the horse whose reins he held. He began in Arabic, but then switched to another language. It wasn't his mush-tongue. It sounded more like the enslaved sailors on the voyage over the Great Sea. But Idris was too busy talking to his horse to listen closely.

"This horse isn't like the others," Viggo said. "It must have been captured on the frontier. See, it doesn't like how the Veiled Ones harness their other horses."

Like an uncle teaching boys who long to hunt but haven't mastered their bows and spears, Viggo showed them how to harness the horses, insisting just like a teaching uncle that they must show the animals nothing but confidence.

When the horses were calm and ready to travel, Idris said, "Each of you must teach another man in the morning, and another man at night. Until we all understand the horses."

When they returned to camp, everyone had packed their gear to travel.

"We can't camp here," Jamal said. Overhead, bearded vultures circled, curious.

Mostly the men walked. But every man took turns riding for a ways on a horse, after listening to Viggo and Idris about how to talk to the animal, how to climb on, how to show no fear.

Jamal watched Idris teaching one of the smallest of the Berbers from the valley. After that man and his horse successfully rode down the trail, Jamal joined Idris to walk alongside him.

"Did you get second sight from our grandmother Silina? Is that how you conquer surprises like a king in this new world?"

When they left Al-Mería, Idris had begun tying knots a new way, to keep track of which direction they turned at each fork in the trail, so he'd know not just how many days to travel, but which turnings to take when they returned, headed for home. He'd just tied a knot when they reached a fork, about six fingers before sunset, which seemed to be the place where they'd learned in one village that they must turn if they wanted to go to Granada.

A grouse hen and her chicks scattered into the underbrush. Idris looked up at the sound of a whistle overhead. A kestrel dove and its mate followed, then both were lost out of sight, whistling again. He kneed his horse forward, the way Viggo taught him. Those who were taking a turn on horseback, keeping behind the men on foot so as not to overwhelm the hikers with dust. That meant frequent pauses along the trail, with every opportunity to study the forest and scrubland, to learn what kinds of animals roamed here.

And to listen to Zirari's endless chattering with bold guesses about which plants and flowers might be good to eat.

"It looks rather like an onion. Pull it up and see. And I'm sure the leaves with purple flowers are rocket. You can eat that."

"The horses avoid it," Idris observed.

Zirari huffed. "It's a spring plant. You eat it when it's young. It's bitter this late in the season."

Idris shut a door on his thoughts so his qareen couldn't hear or quarrel or remind him that he woke that morning drenched in bitter sweat, reaching for a dream he couldn't remember. The choice had been made, the only choice. To go forward.

A flock of birds, fifty or more, burst from behind the next ridge over. Idris shaded his eyes to see: bustards, followed by a mist of songbirds.

"Savages!" Zirari chirped, dancing in alarm, nipping Idris's ear. "Stop now."

With hand gestures, more like pleas than orders, Idris got the others to halt, demanding silence. He and Jamal, with Viggo close behind, loped silently up the ridge.

Below, where the road traveled through a narrow gorge, a band of merchants had halted, their unharnessed mules braying in distress. With their wagons drawn up for protection, the merchants stood in the center with spears and bows, facing perhaps twenty other men who descended in a circle from the sides of the gorge.

Like the trap you'd lay for unwary animals, in a low dip, no room for escape up any hillside.

"We can take them," Idris and Viggo whispered at the same moment. Jamal glanced between them and nodded.

"Not your fight. Just bandits." Zirari tried to scold, its bird-feet snagged in Idris's hair, holding on while they ran back to the others.

"That's just it. They're not Veiled Ones. Just bandits harming those travelers."

The strategy was simple. They stripped and painted the way they would for a hunt, and then came down in the same circle as the bandits had done, but with bows first, spears and swords in reserve.

It takes only moments, and quick bird calls, for mountain hunters to find their positions, whatever beast they hunt. The same way as on a hunt, the men hailed silent arrows down on the attackers, but then the number of arrows increased, whistling. Then Idris's men screamed, ululating, twenty-some voices echoing in that gorge as if it were a hundred men.

The twenty Berbers plus Viggo and Musa's two sons, all naked, sprang into the clearing, each with a spear and a knife, pulling the remaining bandits from their horses. And ending it.

Immediately, Idris's friends began retrieving arrows and spears. Viggo jerked at the tabard one of the bandits wore.

"*Cristiano.* Must be caliphate mercenaries, this far south."

"Like us? But infidels?" Idris frowned. The dead captain al-Malik had described *cristianos* as an especially evil breed of infidel, the ones that the recruits had been brought here to battle.

"The caliphate needs warriors. Mercenaries need to be paid. A convenient wedding." Viggo glanced back at the merchants they'd rescued. "Tell these people that we won't attack them."

"Why not?" Zirari croaked. "Darius would hold no quarter."

Idris gritted his teeth, thinking words his uncle used to silence rude children.

The merchants who'd taken cover within the barricade of their wagons now called out in Arabic, then in a language Idris didn't know. "You can have our silver. Please spare our lives."

"We aren't here to rob you," Idris called in Arabic.

"Who are you?"

"We work for the caliph. I am Captain Idris ibn Musa, and we mean you no harm."

One of the merchants leaped up onto a wagon, arms folded in defense, still holding a sword while studying the Berber spearmen and the so-very-tall northman beside Idris.

"Caliph's men? With no veils?"

It was that blue-eyed youth, Aurovita, dressed like a man in brilliant white *qutun sarawil* trousers and an embroidered tunic, a blue head cloth swathing half her face.

"Though even a turnip can see she's a woman," Zirari sang out. "And pretty enough for the queen of bone-ghuls."

Which made Idris excruciatingly aware that they all stood naked, dripping sweat, and painted for a hunt.

"No veils for our faces, but we do have horses," Idris said. He clenched his spear and kept the same stance as when he'd been commanding the men. No use hiding anything now. "And since we conquered your bandits, we have enough horses to be knights of the caliphate."

Jamal had noticed the other sister, Cristina, and called his surprise to her. "You didn't tell me you were traveling."

A man had crawled up beside where Aurovita stood on the wagon and was remonstrating with her. She dismissed his concern with a wave of her hand.

"Captain Idris, get your horses under control, so we can calm our mules." Aurovita's blue eyes flicked past Idris to where his men had begun to take the bandits' horses in hand. "The men you killed spoke a *castellano* dialect. Their horses likely do, too."

Viggo called softly to the nut-brown horse he was coaxing into friendship. *"Hola, chica buena."*

Idris had a firm sense of what must be done first, and second, and next after that. Sending his men back up the road for their own clothes wasn't immediately important, even when he discovered two more women in the merchants' caravan, ones who dressed like women.

While some of Idris's men worked with the merchants' mule drivers to capture and calm all the animals in the gorge, and one pair recovered spent arrows, other men stripped the bandits, shouting with great joy that they had chainmail and helmets for everyone. Some got better boots. Under the chainmail, they discovered bright-colored, quilted surcoats, which were shared around, with the nicest ones set aside at Jamal's suggestion.

"We should draw lots for the best," Jamal said. "That will make it fair."

Viggo slapped Jamal on his back, then hugged him. "You'll make a soldier yet."

"The ever-holy Veiled Ones don't gamble," Idris said, recalling how al-Malik had criticized the recruits for simple games of *naqala* when they camped at night. It seemed that Idris spent every moment trying to decide the next right action for these men, hoping for sensible advice from Jamal and Viggo.

Zirari, who was often not useful in this new land, whispered, "You must take the best for yourself. Otherwise, men won't respect you as a leader."

"I won't do that." Idris rubbed at his ear. He hadn't meant to say it aloud.

Jamal, still naked, held the bandit-captain's chainmail and surcoat. "Then don't lower yourself to gamble with us. You're the captain. Take this captain's clothes. They are finer than al-Malik's, which never fit you."

The bandit-captain's coat was deep indigo blue with a red-and-white embroidered band. His like-new head cloth was a pale blue. Best of all was the captain's sword with its polished wooden scabbard and brass fittings, and a belt of leather so soft it must have come from a very young animal.

"Definitely *castellano* mercenaries." Aurovita watched Idris as he dressed, her arms folded over the brilliant blue-and-red embroidery of her tunic. "Their captain didn't know how to wind a turban properly. You definitely can do better."

Zirari breathed in his ear. "See how's she's trying not to smile? She thinks you're pretty."

As much confusion as there'd been in that narrow gorge, the sun moved only three fingers' breadth in the sky before Idris's men were leading the merchants' caravan out of the gorge in search of a better-protected place to spend the night. The mules, calm and back in harness, seemed resigned to their work. The horses seemed to agree with the mules that it was best to go forward, whether or not they believed the promises of the men who rode them.

The wide trail wound up a ridge and then rounded a sharp bend. When Idris came around that bend, the other men had all stopped on the trail, staring out to the north and west.

On the northern horizon, mountain peaks jutted up from rolling hills, peaks so high that they retained a dusting of snow, with a pleasing shape like those at home.

However, below those peaks lay farmland unlike any of them had ever seen. Nothing like the sun-blasted vegetable patches at home or the gardens they'd passed on the edges of Maliliyyah. These farms roamed over the hills as far as anyone could see, until traces were lost in the indigo blue of the mountain sides. Some hills were terraced, with neat rows of crops between ditches and streams. Hills rising from the valley floor held orchards, again in tidy rows, many trees blooming white or as rose-colored as the dawn. And everything was green, like grasses on the mountains at home after snow melts, which stayed green for only a single turn of the moon, but these unending fields were brilliant green amid row upon row of darker green trees. In the distance, farther than they could travel before dark, an enormous whitewashed house stood on a high hill, shining in the late afternoon sun. Lower down that hillside, small houses nestled in the shade of olive and cypress groves.

"Like the gardens of Babylon," Zirari trilled, "when Etana ruled in Kish. Or the flood plains at Memphis. I remember—"

"*Silenci!*" A useful Catalan word he'd learned from Viggo.

Idris got off his horse to stand and stare like the others, and then found Aurovita close beside him, glancing between him and the landscape he studied. Zirari hopped to Idris's shoulder, as if it wanted to be closer to the woman.

"Is it like your country?" she asked. "The same way you claimed these mountains are familiar to you? Are the plains of Tunis and Maliliyyah like this?"

"No," Idris said, "not from what I saw on our journey here. I haven't seen Tunis."

"Sand," Zirari muttered in Idris's ear. "Tunis is sand. And grain fields and palms. And more sand."

"What does this look like?" she asked, her hand sweeping across the length of the horizon.

Zirari nuzzled at the back of Idris's neck, as if settling for a nap. "It looks like the reason why the Veiled Ones decided to stay in Al-Andalus. Instead of going home like good mercenaries should."

At camp, Idris's men chose to stake themselves in four corners surrounding the caravan, seeming timid about mixing with the merchants' guard. Everyone spoke Arabic, but with different accents and unknown words so that it was hard to be understood.

When Idris sat by a campfire to eat his supper—lentils and bread from the merchants' camp kitchen—Meri settled too, leaning against the same rude, rock bench as Idris. He began to play sweet songs, which he hadn't done since calming the men after they discovered al-Malik's betrayal. From across the openings among people, Idris's friends began to call to the merchants' guards, inviting them to join in *naqala* or dice games.

Jamal and Viggo sat by Idris at his small campfire, where Idris was talking with Diego, the Rodriguez clan steward responsible for the travelers' safety and provisions. He was a little man, thin as a sprite and no taller than Umar and the men from that village. Diego had been a provisioner for an emir's army on the Jaén frontier, but he claimed to be quite happy to be called home to work for his clan.

"The caliph's generals have taken up every spare man that the emirs haven't claimed. We couldn't hire sufficient guards in Jaén or in Al-Mería." Diego threw up his hands, as if appealing to the higher spirits. "Can we persuade you to come to work for us? At least as far as Valencia."

"Our captain has a letter that sends us to Granada," Jamal said. "My brother Idris thinks we should go there."

"If you're headed to Granada," Aurovita appeared in her boy's clothes and sat between Diego and Idris, "you're on the wrong trail. This is the road to Valencia. You need to go back a half-day's ride if you want to go to Granada."

"Perhaps our new friend might show us that letter," Diego said, which Idris understood as a friendly diversion from the embarrassment that he'd led twenty men in the wrong direction.

Idris tugged the letter from inside his tunic. The animal hide was rolled tightly, tied with a leather thong. He unfurled it and set it before Diego, who bent forward to read it.

Zirari popped on top of Idris's head, nearly toppling forward in its effort to see, though it wasn't writing that the qareen knew.

"This says Badr al-Malik al-Makkzan is to bring seventy men to join the caliph's general in Granada to serve as infantry." Diego paused. "Seventy men?'

Idris said, "There was an incident at Maliliyyah. Al-Malik abandoned fifty recruits who tried to escape, to return to their homes. The man our captain reported to, before we sailed, said

that al-Malik must make do with what he had. Because infantry
was needed in Al-Andalus now, not weeks from now."

"And your captain al-Malik?" Diego asked.

Jamal said, "He died in a tragic accident."

"We could change the letter here. And here." Aurovita pointed
to places in the letter, indicating that she possessed a witch's
ability to read men's writing. "So they are sent to Valencia."

Diego laughed, jostling Idris with his elbow. The people here
seemed to like to stand and sit so close. And touch each other
more. At least his new friend Viggo left enough room between
them to move and breathe. "*Ai*, Captain Idris, see how easy it is to
come work for us. I can add even more to your purse just for the
extra safety this letter means for us."

Diego named a sum greater than Idris's purse would hold.

"Payable as soon as we are safe in Valencia, where El Campeador rules, in practice if not in name."

"Yes!" Jamal exclaimed.

Zirari leaped down to Idris's shoulder. "Yes! And you can stay
with this kind woman instead of only your twenty Berbers."

Idris leaned back. "El Campeador?"

"Rodrigo Díaz," Diego said. "El Campeador means great warrior in the *castellano* tongue. He fought the Veiled Ones in
Zaragoza and is now defeating them all around Valencia."

Jamal bounced his knees, where he sat folded on the ground,
as if he were ready to go now.

"Muslim or *cristiano*?" Idris asked.

"He's worked for both the old emirs and the kings of Castile
and Aragón." Aurovita spoke with that same sureness that had
persuaded Idris on that rooftop in Al-Mería that he was listening
to a young man. And once more she named a string of people and
places that Idris didn't know.

"He began as a mercenary," Diego said. "He fights for
territory and peace, not religion."

"How far to Valencia?" Jamal asked.

"Fifteen days from here," Diego said. "If Jesus our Savior
continues to protect us."

Zirari wiggled as if startled, then nestled for comfort within Idris's new head cloth.

Aurovita touched Idris's shoulder, though perhaps she offered comfort, which was the song that Meri had been playing. "Fifteen days if our horses and mules are cared for, and no more bandits."

"Let me show you." Diego had a stick from the heap gathered to feed the fire. He held it now like a scribe about to write. With his boot, he smoothed the dust lit by the flickering campfire, then drew a jagged line. "Al-Mería is here. Then Cartagena, and Alicante. And here's Valencia."

Aurovita took the stick and drew more lines, covering ten times the space that Diego had, her arm repeatedly brushing against Idris while she drew. "Here's the rest of Iberia. Jaén is here. And Toledo. Galicia is here. Leon. Castile. Aragón. Am I correct, Diego?" She didn't wait for an answer. "It takes more than a full month to ride your new horses across it, Captain Idris."

"A month?" Idris asked, wondering how long that was.

"At least," Diego confirmed.

"A full course of the moon," Viggo whispered, guessing what Idris asked.

Viggo reached for the stick next and drew lines half way across where they sat in that circle. "Up here is the North Sea. And my homeland. You sail for two months to go there." He leaned back and drew lines in the other direction. "Here is Barcelona. And Narbonne. Two weeks' sailing from there, you come to Rome."

Zirari hopped into the dust, walking through the map as if measuring with its bird-feet the distances that Idris's friends described. Idris caught both Viggo and Aurovita following the qareen on its walk, but Diego and Jamal didn't notice the bird-beast. Zirari glared over its shoulder. "I'm not a bird or a beast."

"Where's my homeland?" Jamal asked. He frowned, an unfamiliar worry line deep across his brow.

"It's south of Al-Mería," Idris said, because he knew at least that much.

Viggo drew a line near the edge of Iberia. "I believe your mountains are here. A few days' ride from one of these ports."

Idris knew already that the silver in his purse wouldn't buy him passage from any of those ports. And certainly wouldn't buy passage for even one horse to ride home.

"We'd best help you get to Valencia," Idris said.

"Perhaps her grandmother can show us more dreams." Zirari nestled in Idris's head cloth.

7
Al-Broma

DIEGO THE STEWARD WAS the kind of man who couldn't tolerate silence and so filled every peaceful moment with words. He rode beside Idris, talking endlessly about the battle strategies of local emirs and *castellano* lords and the Veiled Ones.

Usually Idris preferred silence, but on this journey he liked the distraction of Diego's speeches. Besides offering more than Zirari's stories about generals from a thousand years ago, Diego's stream of words stopped Idris's thoughts from drifting amid the lull of riding on horseback along this trail. If he rode in silence, Idris spent too much time wondering where his father had died in the midst of all the lands Viggo and Aurovita had drawn in the dust. Or considering what that blue-eyed woman had to say about her dreams while she hung too close by him, too often.

"Ask. Ask." Zirari muttered again, in the midst of one of Diego's tales.

Diego had spent that morning telling stories about Rodrigo Díaz, the *castellano* general who controlled Valencia after many confusing rounds of serving one count or emir, betraying another, trading loyalties again, and making promises to one king only to betray that king's son to another lord.

"Rodrigo says he serves Alfonso of Castile," Diego said. "But with the tribute he receives from the Muslim ruler of Valencia, Rodrigo now controls more land than Alfonso. Most believe he'd declare himself king if it weren't for the pope and the Veiled Ones. He needs to stay united with both Aragón and Castile."

"Who is Caesar now?" Zirari muttered again. "Ask. Ask."

"Where are the Romans?" Idris finally mentioned it to Diego, only to stop Zirari's nagging.

Diego seemed surprised. "Mostly far to the north, in Barcelona and beyond. Most of the *castellanos* and their cousins still abide by the Visigoth rites, not Roman. Like our clan does."

"Visigoth rites aren't the only ways *cristianos* here pray." Aurovita rode up beside them, sitting astride her horse like a man, which tore at a hollow space inside Idris as much as the qareen nagged at his ear. "But no one in Al-Andalus wants Rome dictating to us."

Zirari pecked. "Romans don't care about rites. Their soldiers devour everything in their way, like fire ants."

"I mean the Roman soldiers." Idris resented being the bird-beast's go-between. He had better control of the twenty Berber spearmen than he did of his qareen.

"Rome doesn't have its own soldiers," Diego said.

Aurovita said, "That's why the pope has to threaten the immortal souls of kings to get any war to go the way he wants. At least Castile and Leon still resist the pope's meddling. Aragón, does not resist the pope as much as others do."

Zirari yelped. "¡*Madre de Dios*! Pope? What's that? No Caesar?"

In Idris's thoughts, he opened a box bound with metal straps and placed Zirari inside, closed the lid, and shouted through the gap at the hinges, "No more Caesar!"

"Are you all right, my friend?" Her voice warm with concern, Aurovita seemed to notice the storm raging between Idris and his qareen. She touched Idris's arm, reaching across from where she rode beside him on the trail. He didn't mean to rub that spot when she took her hand away, but it hurt, as if she'd grabbed a tendon tied to his heart and pulled him close to her.

"I'm just struggling to understand your world." He did indeed have his own questions, besides Zirari's. "What does all this mean for your clan?"

"Rodrigo Díaz's success offers great hope for the house of Rodriguez," Diego said.

"His wife Ximena is my aunt," Aurovita said. "She found a husband for me, so we can strengthen ties among those of us who have lived in Al-Andalus since before the old king Rodrigo."

Idris straightened in the saddle, building another box in his mind to tuck away the unwanted tremors from when she touched him or sat close by the fire or when she spoke with kindness.

Over fifteen days, Diego continued to tell stories about lords and cities he knew, and about the strategies in battles fought in the decades since the Veiled Ones came to Iberia. Viggo taught Idris the Catalan tongue he'd learned in Barcelona (with Zirari murmuring, "Sounds like the Roman tongue if you ask me..."), and he also described in great detail how merchants from the Dane land traded in the Great Sea and the North Sea.

Meri sat astride the saddle behind Idris, playing women's songs during the day and soothing desert and mountain songs at night.

"You're in love with her," Zirari said, "And now you want to be a great hero so she'll love you back."

Idris kept building new boxes to hide his thoughts.

When the merchants approached Cartagena, Diego hailed several passersby, dismounting to ask questions. At midday he led them on a detour up a trail, then declared that those who wanted to could accompany him to mass. He pointed to a squat, square stack of stones with small, high windows.

"This church is left from the time of the old kings. They have no priest now, but we can say prayers and give thanks for our deliverance so far on this journey."

Perhaps ten of the Rodriguez party went inside with Diego, including Cristina and her maid, trailed, of course, by Jamal. Diego reappeared at the door, beckoning to Idris.

Aurovita grabbed Idris's arm—the only time she'd touched him in daylight—stopping him before he could follow Diego and Jamal into the church. "We can't go in there."

"But Diego invited—"

Viggo held him back too. "No, brother."

Meanwhile Zirari had dived deep into Idris's head cloth and murmured thank you thank you thank you.

"Why?" Idris felt that hot passion wafting from Aurovita again, while Viggo felt cold as a mountain stone in winter.

"My grandmother says not to go in places like this, the ones People of the Book call sacred." Aurovita folded her arms, taking a stance that she must think imitates a brave man, but Idris was staring at her mouth, which had white lines at the edges. Like fear.

"Why?" Idris queried again, though what Zirari begged him to ask was *What book?*

"Ah," Viggo looked past her, back toward the trail. "Your grandmother. Of course."

"Yes," she said. "You see her?"

"*Ja.*" Viggo nodded vigorously. "How long?"

"She died ten years ago." Aurovita spread her hands. "But she's still here, for however long I need her."

Caught once more wrong footed, Idris glanced between his friends while rubbing at his ear.

"If you go in there, Captain Idris, it will hurt your qareen," Aurovita said. "My grandmother says Viggo and I can't go in because we can see your qareen. We don't belong there."

"It's not a *nisse?*" Viggo raised his bushy brows in mild surprise.

Aurovita tossed her hands up. "I don't know. Companion creatures never tell us what they're really called, do they? Or their true names?"

Instead of finding out what it meant to pray in a church, Idris took a midday break with his men, while Aurovita and Viggo sat talking on the far edge of the travelers. Idris was still deciding about his thoughts, when Zirari said, "Her grandmother is a significant and kind soul. And she teaches kindness. Doesn't it make you happy?"

After that midday break, whenever Aurovita was nearby, his qareen curled up deep in Idris's head cloth, humming the same tune Meri played, becoming a small, warm comfort, like a kitten sleeping in your lap. If Aurovita was far away, and the sound of her voice carried to where Idris rode his horse or did his chores, then Zirari crawled deep in his tunic, above that space between

Idris's heart and belly, and then softly thumped the beat of an unknown song that had the same rhythm as Idris's pulse.

Diego wanted Idris, Jamal, and Viggo to sleep near the women.

"Because we're handsome?" Jamal asked, not quarreling with the assignment.

"Because you're stronger and bigger and better fighters than anyone else." Diego perpetually tolerated Jamal's jests and showed no irritation over Jamal's persistent flirting with Cristina.

Jamal spread his blanket, folded his *burnus* for a pillow. "Who knew we'd find ourselves living beside the most beautiful women under the sun?"

"I don't know. I don't look at them." Viggo's voice sunk in the night, like a man who wanted to sleep. "I have a wife at home."

"A wife?" Jamal sat up, upsetting where Idris still checked for stones and sticks before spreading his blanket. "I thought you'd been in Iberia for ten years."

"My merchants go home for the winter. You can't sail the seas in a storm." Viggo sighed. "This is the first time that she's had to shiver through midwinter without me. I want to sail to her as soon as we come to Valencia." Another heave of the northman's breath. "Every morning I get on my horse and think, I could ride across Iberia. I want to go to her."

Jamal settled down again. "The women here glow like sunshine from inside. Like honey flowing from the comb. But I suppose every man thinks his wife is most beautiful."

"If he's lucky," Viggo said. "Mine is."

"My idea of a beautiful woman," Idris said, "is one who keeps to the old ways."

"A protective eye tattooed in blue on her forehead?" Jamal teased.

"Or better, a moon-tree," Idris said, serious. "Her lips tattooed blue, like the ancestors taught us. A lion's paw on her chin, showing her strength." He rubbed at his eyes, knowing that he described his grandmother Silina when she was young, a swash of ochre across her cheeks and nose, like a woman sending her man off to a great hunt. That vision had to come from his qareen, who nestled silently in Idris's hair.

"My wife is the color of moonlight," Viggo whispered. "Her hair is the color of flax in the fall, and it's so long, it covers her bum when she lets it down. Only I get to see that, because she binds it up in braids, to let everyone know she's married. And she has—I don't know the word in Arabic." He said a word in his mush language. "So beautiful, even when she isn't nursing a child. When I go home, I shall lay my head down on them, and she will hold me close, and I will not rise from her care for a week. No, an entire month."

Jamal breathed deeply and evenly, like a man asleep. Viggo sighed again, and then again, like a man who couldn't sleep. Idris thought about women who tattooed their lips blue, the same indigo as their robes and shawls. Meri played that song Silina liked, the one about the little bird that never flew from its cage, though the cage had no door, and the house had no door, and the village opened to wide indigo skies.

In all that silence, Jamal spoke again. "But I won't marry the most beautiful woman. Another man already paid for that. I'm just a camel in the caravan taking her to him."

In the morning, Jamal carried breakfast to Cristina, who sat at the edge of one of the wagons, the dawn light caught in the gauzy veil she wore loosely over her head.

Jamal offered his portion of honey for her morning gruel.

She pretended it was too great a gift for a humble being.

Idris sat on the other side of camp, done with his own breakfast, arms folded like one of the old ones delivering judgment under the village cedar. Meri played a song Idris last heard when his youngest aunt married a man from three villages away.

He felt his friend the northman nearby and said, "Diego should lock up those women."

But it wasn't Viggo. It was Aurovita, dressed in those infernal boy's clothes. She folded her arms, not in imitation of Idris but instead indicating that she was annoyed.

"My clan doesn't lock up its daughters and wives. Neither do any other people in this part of the world. Only the Veiled Ones insist we live like your women do."

"We don't lock up women," Idris said. "Not my people, my village."

"You said the uncles have all the power."

"For the hunt," Idris said. "They own teaching us strength and skill. The women own our hearts and souls. The aunts and mothers teach us to be worthy. The old ones who offer judgment include both men and women."

"That must be wonderful for you." She was still annoyed.

Which annoyed Idris, since he spent every day trying to protect her. That led to him saying what he thought. "If your people don't lock up women, how is it that they sell you into marriage?"

"No one sold me." That wide, beautiful mouth formed a hard line. He'd made her angry. "My aunt arranged it to unify significant clan interests in Iberia. If my future husband knows my aunt Ximena, who runs much of Rodrigo's business, he knows this contract is only business."

"What business?"

"My clan thinks I'm valuable because I understand how trade works in Al-Andalus. How gold and silver flow, and how it's buried when people are afraid. Most of the *compadors* and merchants between Granada and Jaén and Toledo and Valencia have known my clan for generations."

He held his bare hands to her, palm up, to show that he surrendered, that he didn't want to quarrel with her.

Aurovita glanced at his hands, her nose wrinkling, still unhappy with him. "I shall be my clan's best agent amid the world's chaos."

He'd never heard a woman boast like that. He admired it. "A proud claim."

"I'm only proud that I can serve my clan so well." Turning away, she hailed Diego, calling out that it must be time to travel. Then she started to walk away, but in ten steps, her shoulders rose, then relaxed. She stopped as if listening, her head tilted. Finally, she came back to Idris, her hand out the way men here greeted each other.

"I'm sorry. We must be friends." She grasped his hand and shook it. "This adventure is new to me and when I'm uncertain, I try to be brave, but just end up being ill-mannered."

Diego called, and she went to join the steward, giving Idris a small wave.

Zirari moaned. "You make her happy and sad at the same time. Her grandmother can't read your heart, so she's no help. You'll have to tell the blue-eyed woman how you feel."

At night, when Idris had guard duty, Viggo and Aurovita sat with him, each whispering stories about how it had been in their villages when they were children. The games they played. The scoldings their great-aunts and grandmothers delivered. The food they missed from home. He'd watched Jamal making friends with the other men in his band, which had ceased for Idris when they made him the captain. With Viggo and Aurovita, who also seemed to be outsiders, Idris felt again what it was to make friends.

Since his qareen had proved useless with this question, Idris finally asked. "Tell me about *cristianos*. The captain who brought us to Iberia said they are the worst of infidels. They believe in one God and the ancient prophets, but they refuse to follow the laws as taught by the last true prophet."

"No, that's not right," Viggo said. "They believe in three gods. My grandfather said they made up new names for our Hanged god and Thunder god, and for the god of sprites and spirits. They also believe in a goddess who is a virgin mother."

Idris couldn't put those last two words together in his thoughts in any way that made sense. In its teaching voice, Zirari said, "Artemis of the wildland," which didn't help. Instead, Idris asked about words he did understand.

"What is your Hanged god?"

"That's the one they call Jesus," Viggo said. "He hung on the tree at the center of the world for many days, to save the world."

"From what?"

Viggo said, "Their priests say that if you don't believe their story, you will go to a fiery pit under the earth when you die, where devils will torture you."

"But under the earth is the trail to the ancestors." Idris was deeply puzzled. "The earth is the earth. It can't contain fire. The sky holds fire."

"Viggo." Aurovita spoke at last. She'd been wrapped in her own arms, as if cold, her head down, listening but not speaking. "You are a good man, but your grandfather didn't know what he was talking about. Most cristianos believe in one God, who takes three forms. A father, a son, and a spirit that sparks life."

"Like how a caterpillar makes a pod, and then it's a butterfly?" Idris regretted asking about cristianos.

"No. They believe the three exist as one God at the same time."

"Like I'm here, and in my homeland, and somewhere on the Great Sea at the same time?" Viggo started laughing, then put a hand over his mouth to stop himself.

"Yes, if you really were in all three places." She didn't mind him laughing. "Some cristianos believe there are two gods, the God of Light and the God of Darkness, and that Jesus was only an apparition who taught truth. The Roman cristianos call those believers heretics."

Zirari stirred. "Mani the prophet taught that. I heard him preach in..." the qareen shrank, as if sad "...when I was last in Babylon."

"Two gods?" Idris felt like the time he'd pursued an injured gazelle into a mud pit. Surprised. Confused. Trying to get free of the muck. "When the Veiled Ones came to our village, they condemned the old ones' prayers to the old sun god and our ancestors. They forbid how women pray to the moon god."

Viggo spat over his shoulder. "My grandfather said he learned from his grandfather that if their sword is at your throat, you pray the way they tell you. Even though you know it's the Hanged god and the Thunder god who stir trouble and then save the world."

"That's the Veiled Ones, forcing laws with their swords at our throats." Aurovita seemed to be thinking more about that. Then she said, "At least the *cristiano* priests don't threaten us with the sword."

"In your land, perhaps." Viggo slapped his thigh. "In my homeland, their priests built their churches over our sacred springs and in our groves. The kings farther to the north, they're just like the Veiled Ones. Take the Cross or get a sword in your gullet."

"The Cross?"

Before either friend could answer Idris's question, Cristina called, and Aurovita left them. It felt good to halt that talk of gods and swords and prayers. After a long silence, Idris took the chance to ask Viggo about his real worries.

"How much silver does it take for my brother and me to get passage on a boat from Valencia?"

"Back to Morocco?" Viggo whistled, then named a sum a hundred times what al-Malik's purse held.

"And if we're truly mercenaries," Idris spoke slowly, hating to admit the foolishness that brought him to this land, "how long does it take to earn that much silver?"

"You have to pay for provisions and horses and arms. So two years. Maybe three."

"That long?"

"Unless a border tiff heats up so that lords are forced to pay more for the fighters they need. Of course, then you risk dying or being crippled."

"Or being sold into slavery if we're caught."

Viggo sat utterly still in the night, the only man Idris had met who could match Idris's ability to wait. No one could hear even their breathing. Zirari seemed to be asleep. Meri sat near Idris, his head resting on a boulder, his flute silent. Only the singing of the infernal jumping bugs rang through the night. So when Viggo spoke again, his voice gave Idris chills.

"And your friends from your homeland? You'll leave them behind?"

"They aren't from my village," Idris said. Zirari stirred, as if listening. "I can tell them to save their silver. But they'll have to earn their own passage. I want to go home. I can't wait for them."

"*Ja.* Just like I will leave you as soon as I find my friends in Valencia."

Idris's hands felt like something had been snatched from them, violently, painfully. He rubbed them together, feeling pain in the hollows of his palms.

He spent the rest of that time on guard thinking about those coming two years, a future full of loss.

They had ample warning, since the scouts who rode ahead that day were Idris's men, who possessed the sight and silence of great hunters. The *castillo* where they intended to stop for the night, Al-Broma, was a possession of the lord that Aurovita was to marry, a count called Gonzalo Garcés. But that lord wasn't presently at Al-Broma, which was under siege by a small troop of mercenaries paid by the Veiled Ones.

"*Castellanos* and Arabs," Umar said. "No Berbers."

Idris let the men discuss what to do about those pressing the siege. Diego believed the merchants' train and Idris's men should retreat and choose another road closer to the Great Sea.

"We can take them," Jamal said. All of Idris's friends nodded.

When Idris proposed to Diego how they'd attack, it was a combination of tactics that Diego had described in the history and battles he'd shared on the journey. Diego finally agreed and went with the merchants' guards to keep the women and the wagons out of it.

Idris and his men ended the siege that day, with only one of them injured—a crossbow bolt to the shoulder, which was these hunters' first introduction to the crossbow. They recovered five such bows left behind when the siege ended.

Their attack on the siege army wasn't very dangerous or worthy of retelling around firesides for decades to come. It was only remarkable because Idris, conscious of the Rodriguez women watching from a distant ridge, persuaded his men to drive off the mercenaries rather than ending their ability to fight for all time.

"We can't spend the night here," Diego said. "We need to continue on to Valencia."

"The people at Al-Broma need our help," Idris said. He'd paused for water and a bite of bread at the merchants' wagons before returning to work alongside his friends. "Their animals have scattered. The women and children fled for caves in the hills and need to be led safely home."

What he'd learned, which he didn't repeat to anyone except Viggo, was that Count Gonzalo had left only six men to guard the *castillo*. They didn't have sufficient men to send scouts out, to know if enemies were advancing, or to help get people and animals inside the *castillo* when attacked. The *castillo* didn't have a decent supply of food to withstand even a week's siege.

And Count Gonzalo wasn't a real count; he just called himself that. The frontier here was claimed by three true counts who were variously sworn to serve Castile, Barcelona, or Aragón.

Gonzalo Garcés, the *cristiano* lord that the Rodriguez clan wanted for its ally and protector, wasn't a very good lord here. Perhaps the captain of the men at the *castillo* was right. "Gonzalo Garcés is busy fighting alongside El Campeador. That's what will save us all from the Veiled Ones."

Idris learned one more thing in the countryside that Count Gonzalo allowed to be ravaged. Al-Broma was where his father and uncles had died.

Alone except for Meri, Idris had climbed a hill when the sky was still midnight blue and the moon's little sister shone above the horizon, the one that Viggo claimed people here called Venus. The hill was crossed only by sheep trails, so he took care not to stumble in the blanket of *matorral* weeds and grasses. He walked beside a small creek and passed a place where three standing stones, as tall as men, guarded the spring where it first bubbled out from the ground.

He came to the hilltop when the first pin-pricks of light pierced the night veil. His father Musa and the uncles sat in a circle, legs folded, arms akimbo, the way men sit together when planning a significant hunt. They recognized Meri first and embraced him, which left Idris filled with longing, as deep and wide as the hole in the sky between that hilltop and Venus, though he wasn't sure what he wanted. But then the uncle and his father Musa turned from Meri, arms around each other's shoulders, jostling each other like happy hunters come home. They followed Idris back to camp.

So Gonzalo Garcés could not take care of his own people, and some time ago, that false count had gotten Musa and his brothers killed. It was the first and only time Idris felt what it was to hate another man.

8
The Compadors

VALENCIA WAS SO LARGE, with warrens of streets, that Idris had to calculate direction continually from the sun. He tried to guess how many people lived within the walls, while also guessing how many people from the broad plains around the city would need to be sheltered if an invading army came. What Idris refused to do was offer a positive answer to Diego's many questions. He wasn't in the mood to appear stupid, since Aurovita walked with them through the city.

"It's astonishing, isn't it?" Diego asked.

Zirari muttered, "He means, isn't it astonishing to you, you savage."

Aurovita said, "Do they have cities like this in your land?"

No answer from Idris. Zirari still muttered about bigger cities. "Persepolis was more magnificent."

They burst out of the shadows of an alley into one open square that bathed in sunshine. Narrow walkways ran between large open vats that otherwise filled the square. A few vats were as scarlet as the beak of an ibis. A few were as burned-brown as Idris was. Other vats held small seas of indigo.

"It's the dye works," Diego said.

"Not so large as our family's in Jaén," Aurovita said.

Another waterfall of words poured out of Diego, explaining. All Idris heard was, "Don't you see?"

What Idris saw in the sunshine was that her skin, after so many days on the road, was the color of honey from a bees' nest, except for the streak of sunburn across her nose, between her blue eyes and where she'd wrapped a veil to protect against dust on the trail. Her poorly wrapped white head cloth allowed a lock of hair to escape and drift across her cheek. That lock was the color of cinnamon, when it's still only peeled bark and not ground in a mortar; ruddy and delicate.

"Idris?" Diego looked at him, curious. "Gathering sheep's wool from the thorn bushes?"

"My people aren't herders."

"I meant, you seem to be daydreaming. We've arrived."

They'd turned into an alley where the sun could shine only at midday. Diego had hold of the iron bar on a massive wooden door. He tugged with no result, so Idris reached to grasp the bar, and they dragged the door open together. Inside, little light streamed through from the alley, and they stood in what felt like a dank cave. He could hear water dripping, and the scant light showed ferns growing at the joint between the stone walls and the timbered ceiling.

Diego tapped at an inner door. A hatch burst open.

"*Qui és?*"

"Rodriguez clan," Diego said.

"*Hola,* Diego."

The door swung open, and they entered a wood-paneled room, drier than that dank foyer. Oil lamps and beeswax candles lit the room so that Idris could see the two men he was meeting. The taller man, in spite of being as old as a grandfather, reminded Idris of Meri because of his nimble spirit and the way light reflected in his eyes. When Diego introduced them, speaking Arabic, the man beamed.

"You are the son of Musa? I have the same name, Moshe."

"For the ancient prophet?" Idris asked.

"One of the greatest," Moshe said. He pressed his hands together, dipping his head, showing honor to Idris. "I'm happy to meet you, ibn Musa."

At that moment, it came to him that his father had left the village without telling Idris his true name. Now he couldn't ask. But the man's open, smiling greeting brought the shades of his uncles and brother out of the corner where they'd lurked.

Benito, the younger man, was thin as a stalk of grain in the aunts' cereal fields. He spoke Arabic with an accent, and he hurried to say he was from Barcelona, to please excuse his clumsy tongue.

These men were *compadors*, and Moshe accepted Diego's request to explain how they'd manage the business if Idris accepted work as a Rodriguez mercenary or chose to work for any other lord.

"We hold your agreement when you sign. For private mercenaries, most houses agree to pay every two months, so you can buy food and arms and equip your horses." Moshe was explicit about how arrangements must be regarded, how any breach of an agreement could be judged by the local *al-cade*. The details that mattered to Idris, after understanding how he'd be paid, was to learn how to protect himself, how to know when to trust any lord.

"Or how to trust your *compador*." Moshe smiled, seeming even more like Meri. "In a city like Valencia, all men need to know that business will continue no matter who rules the city. We have honored promises for generations, proving that you can trust us with your silver."

Moshe began counting out silver for the work of guarding the Rodriguez merchant train. Benito explained more about mercenary rewards among these *cristianos*. "In addition to your pay, the general Rodrigo and his captains distribute shares of booty every six months." Benito had a warm, open smile, the kind that Idris had been used to in his homeland. Which made him too aware that he hadn't trusted any man other than Viggo since he'd walked out of his village.

Benito continued. "The generals don't distribute booty after every battle in order to keep men from deserting."

"It also keeps men from gambling away their booty with the first sharp they meet on the street." Moshe left Idris feeling as confident as he did when the best of the old ones passed judgment under the cedar.

"You'll go to work for our clan, Captain Idris?" Diego asked. Aurovita had remained silent after the initial hellos.

"Will you dispose of this for me?" Idris handed Moshe the commission letter that had belonged to the original al-Malik al-Makkzan. "I no longer require its protection."

Moshe read the letter at a glance. "You came here to work for the Veiled Ones."

"In truth, we didn't understand what they brought us here to do. Fate, and meeting new friends, has changed what we are doing."

Blue eyes darting between the letter and Idris, Aurovita said, "You are disregarding Diego's advice to keep the letter in case you need it later."

"I'm not going to push the Veiled Ones' idea about God on other people, the way it was pushed on my village."

"Ah, you see the predicament of our lives here," Moshe said. "Under the old emirs, my people were free. Nowadays, it's very much more complicated."

"At least with Rodrigo lusting after the Kingdom of Valencia," Benito said, "we have protection from the Veiled Ones."

"At least," Moshe said, "our new friend ibn Musa will have no trouble finding mercenary work. But I'm going to save this letter for you. Who can tell what the future will hold?"

Diego had been fidgeting for several moments, his attention distracted. "Captain Idris, can you see our senhóreta safely home?" he asked. "I have more business in the city." The steward scarcely waited for an answer, making for the door, calling farewells to Moshe and Benito.

Aurovita was busy with Moshe. "If it's not me who comes, it will be another woman from my clan. You'll know from this sign." She had Benito's piece of charcoal and was scribbling on the desktop, but Idris couldn't see what she drew. "Not a man. Only a woman."

"I understand, senhóreta." Whatever she handed to Moshe, he had already made it disappear.

The two *compadors* bid them good day in elaborate ways, allowing Idris to learn several honorifics in the Barcelona tongue. Then he led their way out, into the counting house's dank foyer where no oil lamps burned and scarcely any light sneaked in from the street. His boots squished on the damp floor. Idris let the inner door close, and then leaned against the outer door, the shades of his uncles surrounding him like bodyguards.

"What was that you gave him?" He had no right to ask, but did anyway.

"My grandmother's gift." She didn't push past him to leave. In fact, she seemed to be in no hurry.

"What kind of gift? Why don't you keep it with you?"

"Gold." She shivered in the dank room. "In case I ever need to rescue myself."

Zirari burrowed beneath Idris's head cloth. "You are a turnip. Stop her."

"Don't do this," he said. "Don't marry that count. He isn't a good man."

"You've never met him."

"I saw how badly he cared for that sad *castillo* we rescued."

"I have a duty."

He took hold of her hand, as lightly as you'd hold a baby kitten, and pressed it over his heart. "There's a place, between my heart and my belly that tells me an ancient god, a good god, created us to be bound together."

"For the sake of my clan, I need to be bound to a lord or a general," she said. "Not a Berber spearman."

"I'm not truly Berber. And I'm not an infantryman or slave. I'm a captain. I have warriors. I will protect you to—the grave and beyond."

"However, you aren't a *taifa* general or *castellano* lord. You don't have land and warriors to fight the Veiled Ones. My duty to my clan requires—"

He embraced her, not like hunting brothers do, but like he'd seen Jamal with Cristina in secret, and even more like capturing a bird in your hand and hoping it won't fly away.

"If she wants to run," Zirari warned, "you have to let her."

Idris whispered in her ear while he tugged that wretched head cloth free, so her hair cascaded over his hand, smelling of lavender. "Viggo says the old gods still decide who should be bound together. Brothers. Lovers. Whole villages are bound together by the gods. Stay with me."

"I can't. I have to take care of my people."

"Is that what your grandmother says? I thought she liked me. Is she here now?"

She hadn't resisted his embrace, but then she did. A tiny ridge of tension along her spine. So he let her go.

"I will still rescue you." He called after her when she rushed into the street. "Perhaps your grandmother will tell you when it's time for me to come."

"*Aiieee,* turnip." Zirari screamed in his ear. "Diego told you to take her home."

Idris walked a spear-length behind her the whole way, like an enslaved man.

The messenger recited his piece: Idris ibn Musa al-Makkzan and his brother were commanded to appear before Rodrigo Díaz and Gonzalo Garcés, whose *castillo* Idris had rescued from a Veiled Ones' siege. Jamal, however, had followed Cristina to her aunt's house, pretending to be a bodyguard. Meri had stayed with Jamal, which meant his brothers were safe together, even if Jamal didn't know.

Idris called after Viggo, who had shouldered his pack and was on the way to the wharves to search any northmen-traders who might be found.

"Do this thing with me, brother." Idris begged, unashamed of his need. "This isn't my world."

Viggo looked him up and down, like a horse to be judged before riding. "Of course. But the baths first."

Then Viggo led him into another new world, out of the bright sun into the tiled interior of the baths. Overhead, star-shaped cuttings in the arches let in beams of light that filtered through steam rising from the pool.

Viggo laid out silver so both of them were shaved, then demanded silver from Idris to send a bath-servant to fetch new *sarawil* trousers and tunics for them both. When they were being shaved, Viggo insisted on keeping his braid, but Idris let the servant do it all, the sharp blade taking away both beard and the hair on his head.

"Sorry." Idris felt Zirari traipsing across his shoulders, shifting as the servant worked.

"It's a gift," Zirari squealed, as if happy. "The vermin kept interrupting my thoughts."

Emerging from the bath clean, hairless, in immaculate white and ready to meet Rodrigo, Idris repeated for Viggo the directions that the messenger delivered to him earlier. "It's the finest palace here, the messenger said."

"Does that make you uneasy, brother?" Viggo asked.

"No. I've heard stories." From his qareen. "About how such men surround themselves with gold and silks and fine carpets. Even their dogs and parrots wear gold collars. They live in enormous rooms that make you fall to your knees in awe. I'm not afraid of that."

"What then, my friend? You're the bravest man I know."

"Appearing as al-Makkzan, of the Veiled Ones." Idris presented his empty hands, which is what he thought he had to offer the general.

"Ah, yes." Viggo rested a reassuring hand on Idris's shoulder. "We shall bluff our way through the meeting together. Any other worries?"

"Only," Zirari cautioned, "meeting the man who gets to have his one true love."

Any shock or worry was forestalled and numbed by the extraordinary long time that the two of them spent in a cold, bare foyer, sitting on a carved cedar bench, waiting to be summoned. Stupefied by the wait, Idris was more disappointed than surprised when the room they were led to was like the foyer: cold stone, dull wall hangings, rushes across most of the floor, with well-trodden carpets only where benches surrounded a rough table.

No gold. No silks.

"So, not a king." Zirari dragged a wing across Idris's neck. "The Romans must have looted this city. It's their way."

"You've come!" A hearty voice hailed them in Arabic. "The hero who saved the *castillo!* And rescued the bride of Gonzalo Garcés! The poets will sing songs for generations."

A small, wiry man sprinted across the room to greet them, his hand out like *castellano* knights greet each other, aiming for Viggo, who stepped aside, pointing to Idris. The man grasped Idris's hand and began to pump it, his long pointed red beard bobbing as he shook his hand. The man stood only as high as Idris's breastbone. "I see your mother made a couple of very different choices."

Zirari whispered, "Every woman should."

Viggo next grasped the little man's hand and answered in that Roman-sounding tongue he'd taught Idris. "This is Idris, and I am his brother, Viggo Torbjornsen."

"*Ai,* I know that accent." The man switched to speak the same tongue. "You are Barcelona men. Am I right?"

"*S—si,*" Idris said, stuttering in surprise. He'd escaped being seen as a Veiled One who'd wandered into in the wrong place.

"So you two brothers are the Count of Barcelona's men? Count Ramon Berenguer will do great things for Barcelona. When my daughter married him, she promised she'd make him a better man." Rodrigo elbowed his companion, a lump of a man with a round face, a face too big for his round head and already wrinkling like a summer melon wizening in the sun. "You're about to find out what that's like."

In the midst of this exchange, Idris recognized that the little man was the famous general. The big-faced man was—

"Your enemy." Zirari growled. "He wants you dead."

9
The Bride

DONE SHAKING VIGGO'S HAND, Rodrigo had Idris by the elbow. "But this a surprise. We heard you were wild Berber slaves, run renegade from Yusuf ibn Tashfin."

"Not Berber." Idris always said it, despite the qareen tearing at his earlobe.

The little general looked over his shoulder. "Isn't that what we heard, Gonzalo?"

"*Sí.*"

Idris liked Rodrigo, but he despised Gonzalo even more than he had after seeing the sorry state of the man's undefended *castillo.*

"Now, tell me." Rodrigo dropped his voice to a more intimate pitch. "What is the truth about you two?"

"Our men paint themselves like wild mountain men before battle," Viggo said. Idris never loved his friend more, for saving him in this cold room.

"It puts the chill on even the most righteous Veiled knights." Idris found his courage and spoke.

"A warrior and a philosopher of war?" The little man barked what must be a laugh. "Whose strategy do you most favor?"

Zirari yelped. "Fabius! I taught you this. Tell him."

Idris rubbed at his ear. "Using time instead of force. How Fabius defeated the Carthaginians—"

"Fabius Maximus's strategy!" The little man was thrilled. "Though Fabius only helped. He wasn't the actual victor!"

"We'll never have the advantage of numbers." Idris smothered disappointment that Zirari had not been exactly correct. "It's what we did at the count's *castillo.* Lured the Veiled Ones into hilly terrain where their cavalry isn't useful."

"You read from the same book that I do." Rodrigo turned to wag a finger at Gonzalo. "I've seen you laugh when I make the captains listen to strategy from the Romans."

"How do you do it?" Idris asked. Gonzalo's face made him sick in his stomach. "You have many more men than I do."

"Same principles." Rodrigo nodded at the question, as if Idris offered sage words instead of changing the subject and turning toward Rodrigo so that he didn't have to look at the despicable count. "Your veiled Berber cousins depend on their supply train. We cut them off, pick away at their foraging parties."

"How the Saxons fought my ancestors," Viggo declared.

Idris wondered if a faulty shave of that count's face might prick it like a bladder, so everything inside would run out. Red like an animal? Or green like an ifrit or a demon?

Zirari growled. "My cousins do not bleed green."

Rodrigo Díaz was saying, "The more we deny the Veiled Ones victory, the more their mercenaries desert in search of better booty."

"The strategy works best," Idris ventured, "when villages have scouts and so know to take their livestock into the *castillo*." Which hadn't happened at Count Gonzalo's remote castle-village.

Rodrigo said, "We want to reward you for your heroics. Before we met, I'd thought to offer frontier land near here. But since Captain Idris is Ramon Berenguer's man, then it must be on his frontier. What do you think, Gonzalo? What have you got for Captain Idris?"

"Morella." The count sulked, answering with a scowl.

Idris tried to pin his qareen in place, demanding what Morella was, but with a single squeak, Zirari went still, which meant it didn't know.

The little general laughed. "Well, our hero won't go broke paying tribute to the Count of Barcelona." Just as suddenly as every other move he made, Rodrigo turned solemn as a stone. "I want to give you something personal, Captain Idris, because the women you saved are my wife's cousins. This is family business."

Rodrigo snatched up from the table a short sword in a nicely carved wooden scabbard with a painted leather belt. Then he dragged his own baldric over his shoulder and offered his dagger to Idris. The leather had been embroidered with crimson string.

"It'll never keep an edge, however hard I work at it." Rodrigo leaned even closer to Idris, speaking confidentially, in that too-intimate way of *castellanos* that Idris couldn't get used to. "But my wife put a spell on it."

"Can't you keep your wife from such foolishness?" Gonzalo's voice, as well as his face, made Idris's stomach turn. "Magic? And what other Visigoth nonsense? Pure heresy?"

"Oh, you can laugh, Gonzalo. When your wife wants to put a spell on you, then you'll see it my way." He was jesting with Gonzalo, who was a stump instead of a man. "Give a good woman whatever she wants, and accept her magic if she offers it."

"That's true with my wife," Viggo said.

"It won't be true of mine," Gonzalo said, still sulking.

Zirari huffed, "Inside his lumpy shell, that man is the size of your little finger."

Rodrigo tapped Idris's chest. "Are you taking your reward to find a wife?"

"No, I came here to work as a mercenary." Idris resisted pushing Rodrigo's hand away, feeling that he'd been mauled since the beginning of this meeting.

"Yusuf ibn Tashfin is back. He sailed to Iberia with ten thousand men. The Veiled Ones want him to seize all of Iberia." Rodrigo clapped his hands. "So Captain Idris, the don of Morella, you have employ as long as that prince of fierce Muslims is biting my tail."

Idris was forming proper thanks, in the Barcelona tongue, but the energetic Rodrigo blew right past that, like a gale wind when the door is left open.

"Eat dinner with us, you and your brother. Gonzalo here will give you a bed for the night, as a hero's reward."

The count nodded, but from the expression on his too-big face, he didn't like having to agree.

That dinner was spent listening to stories about battles fought in Zaragoza and Aragón and wherever Rodrigo chose to roam. It seemed unending, but finally Rodrigo left for his own home and Count Gonzalo excused himself. Then Viggo said good night, off to search Valencia for merchants from his homeland. A servant showed Idris to a sleeping chamber in the count's villa.

"When will others return here for the night?" Idris asked the servant.

"No others, master. This is only for you." After lighting oil lamps and a branch of candles, the servant left him.

Alone, for the first time since he'd left his village, Idris prowled the room, feeling like a stray cat let loose in a stranger's house.

So this was the kind of bed that rich men in Al-Andalus slept in, high up on posts, with carpets on the surrounding walls, and covered with cloth softer than his new *sarawil* trousers.

On the table, someone had left a platter of fruit and soft cheese. A pitcher of water. Bread, salt, and a small urn of olive oil. After the night's spicy feast, he didn't need more food. But he decided to finish what had begun earlier at the baths.

Stripping, Idris sat on that high bed and rubbed the olive oil into his ashy feet, his hands, his hairless head. Enough remained on his hands that he rubbed his legs, his arms, his torso. It must be what the kitchen-garden feels when aunts water in the dusky light at the end of a day. The high overhead window let in enough of the warm summer night air that a breeze brushed over him, standing on end the tiny hairs of his arms and legs, whispering across his scalp and shaven cheeks.

Meri was playing a dance song, the kind that starts a night's festival, when men are still shy. But Idris rose and, barefooted, danced in the room, circling the table the way he would a feast-day fire, arms up to catch the breeze from that window, feet slapping the wood-plank floor, happy to be free of boots. His shades drifted into a circle, one arm on another's shoulder, following him in that dance around the table. After three turns, Susa joined them, dancing more like a hunter than how women dance. Meri picked up the tempo, until Idris and his shades whirled around the table. His qareen, adding to this moment of freedom, sat on the table, tipping its head to Meri's music, seeming content to let Idris and his shades spin, leap to touch the rafters, crouch to touch ground, like one does when offering thanks to the ancestors, then leaping again, more free than—

She appeared in the room, though he hadn't seen the door open. It was a woman in a gauzy indigo robe, veiled, but he knew it was Aurovita, even if he'd never before seen her in woman's clothes.

His arms were still high overhead, reaching for the rafters, while his dancing shades retreated to a corner, farthest from the lamps or the high window, arms once more around each other's shoulders.

She spoke before he could choke out words.

"When I was weeping this afternoon, my grandmother stopped me. She says I must do what I want at least once in my life." The night breeze rustled her veil. "And what I want is that for one time, you think I'm beautiful."

He dragged away that veil, and the night wind pressed it against him, so it stuck in the oil and sweat on his chest and arms.

She'd drawn delicate indigo outlines on her forehead and chin, and painted her lips the same indigo. The sunburn across her cheeks, just below her eyes, shone in the lamp light like a maiden's ochre swash. She reached toward him. Her sleeve slipped up her arm, revealing the same delicate blue outlines climbing up from her fingertips, then lost in the sleeves at her elbows.

"Idris?" Her eyes wide, she reached for the veil, then drew back. "Say something. You're frightening me."

He didn't release the veil. Tugging it caused her to stumble closer. He embraced her again, not imitating Jamal this time, but holding all of her close, like holding the first warmth of the sun after winter.

"How'd you come here?"

"The guard at the kitchen gate is a Rodriguez cousin."

"Ah."

"Is that all you want to say, Captain Idris?"

"I love you."

He whispered into her uncovered hair, which flowed over his arms, sticking in the oil. But he said it in Susa's tongue, and Zirari started a quarrel. Idris flung his qareen into the corner where Meri and the shades had retreated, and silently warned, "Toss dice till you've lost all the pebbles in Iberia!"

The motion of throwing off his qareen stirred the breeze over his bare body. She studied him.

He offered his open hands. "You know everything about me. How can you not know that I think you're beautiful?"

"But the right kind?"

He untied the embroidered belt that clinched the waist of her robe, then the tie at the neck of her linen undershirt. The robe and shift drifted open in the evening breeze, revealing that the delicate indigo design covered her torso. He slipped the cotton and linen from her shoulders, then stepped back in awe.

But stumbled, falling back to sit on that high bed.

She followed as if that breeze made everything stick to his oiled, damp skin, his arms folding around her. Like in a dream.

As if he knew what he was doing, Idris lifted her onto his lap, her legs bent as she kneeled over him. Then she did what she had that first night, kissing him until he had no choice, but to open his mouth and accept deep kisses, offering back his own.

She whispered in his ear, "This is the last night, for this time on earth, that I can be selfish." Then she pressed him back onto the bed and kissed every part of him, her breath warmer than the night breeze, her lips softer than anything that had ever touched him.

He did know how it was done, and didn't resent that she asked whether he did. The filigree of indigo lines on her body had already smeared onto his when he finally entered her.

"Yes." She sighed, but he didn't know which language they spoke.

The night was as long as an entire childhood plus seasons learning to hunt, like a long walk home in the consoling light of dusk. When at his core he felt dawn coming, he couldn't push it back. For every beautiful word she'd uttered, every sigh, he still couldn't stand hearing what she said.

"I have to go. The sun is coming. My selfish night is over."

"It doesn't have to be."

"You know that's a lie." She brushed her fingers over his shaven skull, along his eyebrows, touching his ears. "Just like you, I was made to serve my clan."

"How can you know that? Your ghost grandmother says so?" It sounded bitter, though he hadn't intended to.

"It's why we are both on this earth. It's how you and I are alike. God placed us here, where both the Veiled Ones and *cristiano* kings threaten our families, our world."

"Which god?"

"I don't know. But I'm sure that what I'm intended to do means more for the world, for the future, than whatever you and I feel."

"What do we feel?" He stroked the place between her eyebrows where she'd painted a sign like a god's eye for protection. (*"Madre de Dios, sálvanos!* You feel love, like in poets' songs. Tell her again!") He closed his thoughts to his qareen, like tossing a rug on a parrot's cage to silence it.

"Perhaps we want to feel like old-time heroes." She wiggled away from him, fetching her robe from the floor. "But that's not what we're in this world for."

"I think what we feel is love, like in a song." It didn't sound as good when he spoke the qareen's words aloud. "We should stay together."

She pressed a finger on his lips, like how you silence a child. "Don't beg me."

"I won't."

"We won't see each other again. I have to do what I must. And you and your brother and your shades should go home."

She was already running away when he said, "I love you," but again saying it in the wrong tongue.

He kept her veil, which had covered her face before she revealed that she'd painted blue designs across her chin and forehead, dyed her lips indigo. To please him.

The veil smelled of her. Sandalwood. Spices Idris couldn't name. And here, at one edge, a print of her painted blue lips, as if she again blew warmth and perfume over him.

Thinking of the way she folded her arms whenever she was determined, sure of the next thing, Idris folded the edges of himself around the warm space she'd left, that hard muscle between his empty belly and his throbbing heart.

His qareen remained silent. No movement or whispered warnings.

When Idris went out at dawn, intending to greet the sun at the edge of the Great Sea, Zirari murmured, "My friend Susa has joined the ancestors."

So unexpected, it came like lightning and sudden rain when you hadn't noticed a cloud overhead just heartbeats earlier. Instead of the morning light rising from the sea, a chasm appeared that might swallow the world.

The shades of his uncles, who clung near him, became a weight Idris wasn't strong enough to bear. Meri played on his gazelle-flute, but it sounded more like tears.

"I must go home." Idris said it aloud, in his own tongue, so that people along the trail to the sea stopped and stared. But it felt like the only truth.

Zirari's hum sounded more like a sob. "The blue door stands open with no one to close it. Your sisters are gone. You might call them married. They'll be in those men's houses forever. Your mother journeyed to her sister's house and has no way to come home."

Idris ran back into the city in search of Jamal, who was, of course, lingering in the kitchen of the Rodriguez villa.

"We have to go home."

"That was the plan," Jamal said. "But we're needed here now." He swept his hand, the way Idris signaled men to follow him. "We're working here until there's passage for everyone."

"I'm going. Today. Please, brother, come with me. We're needed at home."

Jamal followed Idris back out to the road that led from the city to the docks down by the sea. Jamal seemed to sing a chorus with

Zirari, to that whirling song Meri played, begging Idris to stay for all the others. Jamal and the shades had to hurry, though, to keep up with Idris, who ran down the long road to the harbor.

At the same moment that Idris spied Viggo on the wharf near a merchant boat, Jamal stopped, crossing his arms. The shades of his uncles and Meri huddled close by Jamal. "I want to stay here. I don't want to leave what I've found."

Idris wanted to drop to his knees and beg. "My second sight shows me that Silina is dead. Our village is in danger. My heart says—"

"Our great-great-grandmother is as old as the mountains. If she's with the ancestors, it's where she has wanted to be." Jamal thumped Idris's head with his knuckle, nearly banging into Zirari, who strutted in distress. "What your heart is telling you is that Cristina's sister is marrying another man today. Stay here, brother. The world can still turn your way."

Jamal remained stiff as a standing stone on the edge of the wharf, while Idris greeted Viggo, who'd found merchants preparing to sail for the Dane land. They rapidly agreed that Idris could work his way with them, and they'd leave him in the south, where he'd find passage across the straits to home.

Jamal didn't call to him when Idris got busy helping the sailors push off into the sea. The uncles clung to Jamal, but Idris still felt them as a weight, so his muscles couldn't work with any grace. Meri wasn't playing music, just waving, like you do when you want the person to come back. Zirari screamed in that tongue Idris never understood.

At the same moment that the boat's captain called orders, first in Viggo's mush language and then in the Barcelona tongue, Viggo nudged Idris.

"You can't go, brother." Viggo pointed back to the wharf.

Susa appeared beside Meri, but not the old grandmother Idris had always known. She was young, as beautiful as a woman could ever be, painted ochre, glowing in the sun like Meri, carrying a spear like a man. The uncles and his father Musa, all of them no older than Meri, embraced her.

Viggo heaved Idris's pack over his head, throwing so hard that the pack landed on the wharf. "I love you, brother. But you can't come with me. The others need you."

He pitched Idris into the water, calling goodbye in the Barcelona tongue.

"Go with whatever gods will have you. Farewell."

10
Shades

AT THE MOMENT WHEN the sun rising over the local hills chased off the shadows and early light washed over him and turned the men below golden, Idris understood what to do.

The only logical next action was to serve the men who had made Idris their leader. He watched them break camp after the first night on their journey to work for one of Rodrigo's allies. The men were harnessing their horses, with all of the great care they'd learned. Idris's horse, still hobbled, looked up frequently to watch its friends.

Idris said, "I shall show my horse all the love it deserves. You are right, Zirari. Horses are truly amazing creatures."

His qareen, sitting between Meri and Susa, didn't answer, having not spoken since the dunking at the docks, which Idris didn't want to be reminded of, so he enjoyed the silence.

Jamal climbed the hill looking for him, and sat when Idris motioned the place by his side.

"We need to be a village on horseback."

"Your second sight tells you this?" Jamal teased.

"No, just common sense." Idris explained what it would mean to work as mercenaries, since there was no way to go home.

Bake bread daily.

Dig night-soil pits far from where they slept.

Maintain their own arrow factory, so they weren't trading silver for the weapons they needed.

Find pastures with sweet grass and water for their horses.

Hunt the local wild creatures in season, and learn to live at other times on the smaller creatures creeping out of rock piles.

Mend and make new leather harnesses, belts, scabbards.

Create a portable smithy to shoe the horses and keep their sword blades and spear points sharp and shiny.

"The sound of whetstone on steel will be our night music."

Jamal listened closely as Idris described how they could make the world work for them.

"A village?" Jamal picked a stalk of cheatgrass, blew on it between his fingers. The splat of the straw-horn echoed in the hills. "Will we have wives?"

"I won't," Idris said. "That was never my path."

"Why should this new village on horseback be our lives?" Jamal tickled Idris's arm, making him shiver. "Your second sight tells you that we should live with a band of Berber savages in a strange land?"

"No." Idris snatched that piece of cheatgrass to stop the tickling. He spoke his brother's ancient name. "Juba, I can't bear being alone with what I know. I have to tell you a secret."

Over every screeching complaint from Zirari, Idris told his brother everything.

That Meri walked beside them, and when he played his gazelle-flute, it made the men happy, or calm, or wild to fight.

That their father Musa and the uncles had been killed at Al-Broma, but because Idris found them on that hilltop, they now walked beside him everywhere.

That Silina had died, but instead of joining the ancestors, she now rode behind him with Meri. Young again, painted for battle, carrying a spear.

That when Silina died, their aunts and sisters had left the village, so there was no home to which they might return.

The only secret that Idris kept was the fact of the qareen pestering him, nipping his ear, scratching the back of his neck with its wing feathers, snatching at soft places near his throat with its bird-feet.

A ragged flock of expressions flitted over Jamal's too-handsome face. Now puzzled, now laughing. Afraid for two heartbeats. Doubting. Then, along with Meri's music, Jamal laughed.

"Are they here now?" he asked. "Where?'

"Meri is right beside you, with Silina. He's playing that song about the rascal husband, the one that always makes you laugh.

She's tapping silver finger cymbals with the music. Our uncles and Musa are over there, where the shadows still fall on that cascade of broken rocks."

His brother studied that point, where the early morning light glimmered on the edges of their family's shades.

"Idren?"

"Yes, Juba?"

"Why didn't you tell me?"

"It belongs with…" his ears rang from Zirari's screams "…other secrets. Secrets that Silina asked me to keep. But now you know why we have to turn this army into our village, to make a new home for all of us." Idris swept his hand in a circle, encompassing all the shades on the hill, as well as his living brother.

Jamal had rested his chin on his hand, thinking, but then pressed his hands over his ears, as if he didn't want to hear Meri's music. Meri changed to play that child's song again.

Idris tugged Jamal's hand away. "You hear the music. I know you do. I've seen you look around, trying to find where it's playing. You can tell me what Meri is playing right now."

Jamal sat listening. His chin trembled. Then he began to sing in the dialect that only people from their village spoke. "*One kitten, two kittens, three.*"

"Yes, so you know what I'm telling you is true, brother, even if you can't see them."

"Do they talk to you? Can they hear us?"

"They never speak. I don't know if they hear us. But instead of following the trail to the ancestors, below the earth, they follow me." After unburdening his secrets, Idris felt that space open again, between his heart and his belly. Like running free and easy in the sunshine. "That's why we need to make a village here, you and I. Since we can't go home."

"Fine. I understand." Jamal started to rise, then sat again, sprawling, so that Meri had to hop out of his way, scrambling to hold on to his gazelle-bone flute. "But I'm in love with a woman. You are too."

"I don't know what 'in love' is, except in songs."

"Yes, you do. It's why you wanted to sail away yesterday, isn't it? Because your heart's on fire."

That space in Idris's core turned cold. Idris folded his arms over his torso, like when the old ones rendered judgment, but he was rendering judgment on his own foolishness. "When she kissed me goodbye, Silina insisted that it's my turn to shape the world, to bend it to be what we need." Idris stood, ready to join the men on the road.

"Then why don't we bend the world to include those two sisters? Ask them to come away with us, to live the way Viggo lives with his wife."

"I did ask. It turns out that I can't bend the world to suit what a woman needs. I only know how to shape the world by leading these men."

Jamal kept staring at the rock fall where the shades huddled.

"I'm not giving up on Cristina. That lord she's marrying is old as a rock in a mountain stream. I'll outlast him." Jamal picked another stalk of cheatgrass and blew a single note. "Use your second sight, Idren. You can figure out a better plan than mine."

From the start, Idris let the men decide who did what in the daily duties, who stood guard while others carried out food and armory chores. Umar from their old neighboring village proved to be best at keeping the decisions in memory, and Jamal showed unusual ability to settle any squabbles. From some *castillo* along the road, Jamal picked up the title *al-calde*, which Zirari said meant "the judge," though to Idris's knowledge, no one but the old ones had ever before done the work of sitting in judgment.

Idris continued to tie knotted cords around his wrist, until the band ran up his forearm, though he no longer counted backward for the number of days to the nearest port. Instead the knots recorded the time spent working as mercenaries and tracked what they were owed by the lord who currently rented their services.

While Idris taught everyone how to make daily life go well, he and his qareen quarreled less. It started when Idris and Jamal were discussing which spurs they liked best among what they'd captured from *castellano* bandits.

"Darius rode Nisean horses." His qareen was in its most ponderous teaching mood. "Without stirrups, without spurs. However, you want—"

"Not useful." Idris batted at his ear, which always distracted Jamal and caused him to stare while Idris blinked and twitched.

"Fine." The qareen paced across his skull. "But I'll bet all the silver in Iberia that future knights will wear *castellanos'* spurs."

"You don't have all the silver in Iberia. You don't have pockets or a purse. You gamble with pebbles."

"I have two millennia of experience with horses and armor." His qareen huffed and strutted.

"You're guessing about the spurs."

"I'm helping. It's what I do for you."

"It doesn't help. When you don't know something, let me figure it out."

"You only want warnings about vipers and whether the food is turning bad?"

"*Si, mon amic.*" Idris answered in the Catalan tongue that Viggo had taught him, which he knew the qareen had not yet mastered.

Their first employment was to guard a merchant train on its way to Alicante. In that town, they found similar employment that, unfortunately, sent them back to Valencia, for which Jamal was eager, setting off immediately to find Cristina, while Idris trudged over rain-slicked cobbles to collect booty at Moshe's counting house. He passed Count Gonzalo's villa on his way. There were guards at every door and on the roof. Idris picked at the colored bands at his wrist. Zirari was silent. The shades surrounded Susa and Meri, who held up his gazelle-flute but didn't play.

In the *compadors'* counting house, Benito prompted for the kind of rumors mercenaries hear in the field. And Idris asked what rumors Moshe and Benito had heard about who might be hiring guards for the winter season. "Anything with the Rodriguez clan? I liked working for Diego."

Zirari sighed. "You turnip."

Idris rubbed his ear.

"Diego's gone back to Jaén," Benito said. "Count Gonzalo took over the clan's affairs here."

"And he won't hire Berbers," Moshe said.

"What about Rodrigo and his captains?"

Moshe wagged a finger, a kind smile warming his stern face. "We heard what Rodrigo promised Captain Idris ibn Musa. Go ask any of his captains for employment."

Walking out of the cave-like counting house, Idris encountered Rodrigo Diaz himself, the only time he'd been near the general since they first met. But Rodrigo recognized him.

"It's the Morocco man from Barcelona! Captain Idris, isn't it? The don of Morella!"

Idris acknowledged his name, and didn't confess that he had not yet visited Morella, the frontier land he'd been given. But Rodrigo was, as usual, a bundle of energy, his eyes bright.

"Where's that giant Viking that's your brother?" He nudged Idris. "Or so you said."

"He's gone home." Idris paused, distracted by thoughts of Viggo, another reason he didn't want to remember that day. "He has a wife. He didn't like mercenary work."

"So why is a Muslim man like you working for *castellano* lords, eh?" Rodrigo nudged him again, in that way that knights here jostled and joked with each other. "Not that I'm complaining. We need good men. Just that—"

The general's question was about loyalty, or so Zirari whispered.

"I'm not Muslim."

"Ah." Rodrigo took it in, then frowned. "Usually when Roman priests get their paws on Berber men, they give them a new name. A saint's name. Didn't you get a new name when you were baptized?"

"I'm not Berber," Idris said. ("And your name isn't Idris," his qareen muttered.) "And I'm not a Roman *cristiano*."

"¡*Madre de Dios!*" Zirari shrieked, biting Idris's ear. "Shut up, turnip! Shut up!"

"Oh, one of those heretics, eh?" Rodrigo again slapped Idris's shoulder, like *cristiano* comrades-in-arms do. "I've got a house full of them at home. If they aren't still claiming Visigoth magical powers, they're talking about the God of Light and the God of Darkness."

"You don't mind?" Idris ventured. "What they call heresy?"

"It's better than sending our gold to the pope so he can rule Jerusalem." Then Rodrigo uttered a blasphemy that had "Rome" as part of it, though Idris didn't understand.

I agree! I agree!

Idris rubbed at his shoulder, where bird-feet scratched.

"What do you pray, Captain Idris?" Rodrigo continued to jostle and jest, but Idris didn't trust questions like that.

"As commanded," Idris replied, ready to change the subject. "But I don't find prayers useful in battle. I still prefer strategy, as you and I discussed early in the summer."

"Good man." Rodrigo's pointed red beard waggled in agreement. "You and I decided Fabius was a genius, didn't we? That first day I met you?"

Idris nodded, not because Fabius meant anything to him, but because Rodrigo had a reputation for detailed memory. And Idris didn't want to remember his first days and night in Valencia.

"Yes, Fabius. Delay and tire the enemy." Rodrigo seemed quite cheery with that thought. "You can do worse than to gain a reputation like Fabius. It's why I'm happy to let Alfonso and the Veiled Ones go at each other, fighting over Toledo. When they tire, I gain the Kingdom of Valencia."

Idris paused. "*Si.* Many generals say that Castile will pay best this year."

"Indeed!" Rodrigo clapped his hands again. "Because Yusuf ibn Tashfin has a passion to take back Toledo. It's more important to him than Valencia."

"Perhaps." That wasn't what Idris and Jamal heard from the Veiled Ones in Alicante a month earlier. "Or perhaps ibn Tashfin is drawing *cristiano* forces away from Valencia to make this city easier to conquer." He repeated what he'd learned on the road.

Rodrigo had a hand to his chin, thoughtful. "Perhaps stay in the area this year, Captain." Then he clapped his palms together and became that spirited host he'd been the first time Idris met him. "Come to my house. We have a farewell feast for some guests."

Zirari stood on Idris's shoulder, looking about. Rodrigo had Idris by the elbow once again, steering him through the alleys in a way that didn't invite refusal, all the while retelling stories about summer raids and probing for more of what Idris had learned while in Alicante.

In front of the villa, wagons were lined up, and an armed guards milled about, waiting to travel; none of them were Berbers.

Rodrigo held Idris's elbows still. "My wife's relatives are volatile. I'd say capricious, but I love my wife. I do." He'd stopped to watch what was happening in front of his house, his hand on his chin, thoughtful again. "

A tiny woman stood at the door, arguing with people who were inside. She talked with her hands, a few words in *castellano* escaping into the streets. *Blessed Lord Jesus. Faithful vows.*

"Give her a chance to see the true way," the woman shouted.

"*Aiieee*, Ximena, dear heart," Rodrigo muttered. "Why tell the city we have a house full of heretics?" He turned to Idris. "Do you love your wife? Oh, I forgot. You don't have one. Let me tell you. It's complicated."

The false count, Gonzalo Garcés appeared in the door, shouting. "I can't get her to walk into a church, much less confess. I want my children baptized."

The count dragged a woman from the door. The woman—yes, it was Aurovita—clung to the door frame, resisting. Cristina pushed past her sister, shoving the count with both her hands, shouting bad names in *castellano*.

Ximena screeched at Aurovita. "Just walk into the church and confess to the priest, you silly girl. It doesn't matter what you believe. If you're determined to waste time with heresy, then learn to lie. Otherwise, what good are you in the world?"

"We're going now!" the count shouted.

Aurovita faced Idris, but wasn't looking into the street to see him. No veil, but she wore women's clothes. Her face was bruised. She shouted at Ximena, "You promised me shelter. You promised me protection."

"Your husband is your shelter," Ximena said.

Count Gonzalo shoved his wife into one of the wagons, quarreled again with Cristina, who then climbed into the wagon with her sister. Shouting orders at his guards and the drovers, the count mounted a horse. His party departed, the count riding close by the wagon with the two Rodriguez sisters.

Rodrigo slapped Idris's shoulder. "The feast will go so much better without that betraying bastard. Let's see what Ximena plans to lay on her table in celebration."

That night, Idris dined well, at a table where Gonzalo and his business weren't discussed. Inside, every muscle seemed to have its own thought, and that thought was to run after those wagons, to save those sisters from the foul count.

Zirari paced across Idris's shoulders, stopping occasionally to peck at his earlobe. "Perhaps things are not as they seem."

Idris batted at his ear. "Time has to be made to work, when the force isn't strong enough."

He hadn't meant to say it aloud, but Rodrigo again slapped his shoulder. "We are like twin sons of different mothers, Captain Idris. We only wait for that betraying Count Gonzalo to organize his own doom."

He poured wine into a goblet for Idris, but Idris never drank.

Later Idris found Jamal, who was tossing dice with the kitchen guards behind Rodrigo's house.

"I was right," Jamal said. "That I'd live longer than her ancient husband. He died weeks ago. But—"

"She's left Valencia with her sister."

"So we have to go fetch them." Jamal settled up with his dice mates and departed with Idris into the dark alleys of Valencia. "Unless your second sight suggests a better idea."

Zirari thumped its head against Idris's skull. "Your second sight agrees with your too-handsome brother. In my experience, it can take years to turn enemies into worms. You might want to speed things along."

In the morning, Idris went to find information at the best source, Moshe's counting house.

"Count Gonzalo threw in with Alfonso," Benito said. "Took his servants and family to his holdings at Al-Broma."

"But he—"

"Promised Rodrigo to help protect Valencia?" Moshe shook his head. "There's been a rift. Rodrigo's wife is furious, since Count Gonzalo took a pile of her clan's wealth with him, including what that one niece inherited when her antique husband died."

Moshe was reserved as usual, commenting on allegiances, which mercenaries were in what lord's pay. Since his business and his honor were built on the preservation of promises, Moshe didn't approve of Count Gonzalo's change of allegiance.

"A promise is a promise," Moshe said, as if repeating holy words. "So naturally Rodrigo will take compensation for that betrayal. I predict that he'll seize a great deal of the land Gonzalo held from the king of Aragón."

Benito then repeated what Idris's aunts called gossip. Count Gonzalo was a bad husband, which did not surprise Idris.

"When Gonzalo took his wife out the city, she didn't have time to—" He stopped, because neither of the *compadors* was capable of revealing a secret.

Except Aurovita had told Idris that secret. Zirari moaned. "She left without seizing her rescue gold."

11
Siege

THE PLAN WAS PERFECT, Jamal claimed.

His qareen placed more faith in the plan than Idris did.

The first disagreeable element of Jamal's perfect plan was how much dust they had to eat, traveling roads after fighting season had ended, before the late-fall rains drenched the landscape. Of all the ways these mountains might resemble the mountains of home, the dust here tasted foul.

The plan was supposed to begin with attacking Al-Broma while dressed as Veiled Ones. The first complication came when they met another band of Veiled mercenaries, all of them Mozarabs, who were on their way to employment at Al-Broma.

The pretend-count Gonzalo had betrayed not only his allegiance to Rodrigo but also Alfonso. Gonzalo Garcés now hired and fought only for the Veiled Ones, who had been picking off villages and *castillos* throughout the region. Idris had the additional tasks of sending messengers back to Rodrigo with this information.

In Jamal's revised plan, the mercenaries who attacked Al-Broma were *cristianos* decrying the betrayal of Alfonso. After that siege lifted, and the *cristiano* mercenaries disappeared, Count Gonzalo decided to move himself and his household to Alicante for safety. On the road, in spite of the count's new alliance, a band of Veiled Berber mercenaries swooped on Count Gonzalo's train, and the wild Berbers proved too much for the count's Mozarab guards.

After that raid, the captured women and children were left at a crossroads, soon rescued by *cristiano* mercenaries who delivered the captives to safety in Valencia.

Idris didn't join in the close work of the rescue, only watched from a hilltop. His qareen nestled close by the pulse in Idris's neck, like a purring kitten. "You performed as well as any prince in Persia."

Jamal, astonished that Cristina heaped wrath on his head instead of the gratitude, consulted with the Rodriguez cousins who guarded the Rodrigo kitchen gate.

"It's sad for you, *amigo*." The cousin was small like Ximena, and russet-headed. Jamal always let him win when they tossed dice. "I don't know what Ximena and my cousins planned, but you interfered and destroyed it."

Idris did not have to endure wrath, because through the whole adventure he never encountered either sister. The only reason they knew the sons of Musa had rescued them was because Jamal came to Cristina on her first morning in Valencia and bragged about it. Idris resolved to be content with knowing that Aurovita was safely inside the city.

However, due to miscalculation, given everything Idris had learned over the summer, it should not have been a surprise when the Veiled Ones laid siege to Valencia, a major effort in their passion to push *cristianos* out of Iberia. The sisters were safe from Count Gonzalo, but not from starvation.

"And if you and Jamal were paying attention," Zirari yawned, "you wouldn't be caught inside any city under siege. When I was in Persepolis once—"

Idris tossed his qareen into the box at the back of his mind and stayed busy working inside the city, where the siege presented a host of chores for keeping the city clean and taking any opportunity to foil the attackers.

When taking duty atop the city walls, Idris spied Count Gonzalo's banner in the distance among other renegade *castellanos* who fought with the Veiled Ones. Zirari again repeated stories from ancient times, about how weak men choose whichever side appears to be winning.

During the siege, many Rodriguez clan people and their business partners were sheltered in Count Gonzalo's villa, and Jamal was captain of their protectors. He declared that he'd no longer tolerate being separated from Cristina, who'd quickly lost her anger about being rescued.

During the long months of the siege, Idris often saw Aurovita on the balcony of that villa. She was starving to death, like everyone else in the city.

Aurovita came to council meetings, where city leaders and captains of the guards gathered to make decisions for enduring the siege, like how to protect and share the food supply. The council meetings were in an open-air plaza, under an olive tree. Yet there wasn't enough wisdom shared for Idris to compare it to how the old ones held judgment in his village. There was too much despair and fear, too often expressed as anger.

At the meetings, Aurovita seldom spoke, except when the talk wandered off into distant fields. Then she'd call people back to the work. Sometimes she sat near enough to Idris that he could see the flecks of gold in her blue eyes, the fine lines around her mouth and eyes. She'd become more beautiful, even while starving. He was starving too, like everyone else, yet he still felt the jittery trepidation in that empty space where he hid all thoughts of her. Meri still liked her. Whenever she had to settle a quarrel at a council meeting, Meri played that soothing song that calmed even wild men.

"She's kind," Zirari whispered in one meeting after Aurovita quietly persuaded her aunt Ximena not to demand all the cats be killed.

Idris had missed most of the discussion, because like every meeting he watched the light filtering through the olive tree, dappling the veil Aurovita wore. Faded indigo and, like the rest of her clothes, in tatters.

Two full seasons since they parted, and now Idris wore a magnificent tunic stolen from a Veiled Ones' raiding party, and he commanded one hundred of the men who stood atop the city walls sending fire arrows into the siege lines. Yet whenever Aurovita was present at the council meetings, Idris sat in silence, a naked savage in the presence of the most confounding creature the gods ever made.

Although there was unending work in the siege city, the women became discontented with their assigned jobs. Perhaps it was because there wasn't enough food to cook, nor firewood to keep the cook-fires burning, and no one had patience any more, having been frozen in place with nothing to do for months. Cristina and Aurovita and the women from their household were the first to appear and request different work.

"We want to do more than just deliver arrows to the men on the wall," Cristina said. "Teach us to shoot."

The consensus among men willing to teach—some felt that God's laws forbid close contact with women—was that teaching the long bow would waste too many arrows. If any woman showed she was strong enough, she'd be taught the crossbow. But, the captains agreed, no woman was to string a bow because it was dangerous. Teaching women seemed like a new kind of heresy, and there had to be limits.

Idris walked the top of wall, listening to lessons in several tongues.

"Keep your fingers out of the way if you want to keep them connected to your hand."

"Check the bolt. Make sure it's straight. We've been picking up what they shoot at us. It might be bent."

"Make sure the stirrup is steady. And get your foot on there."

"Make sure the bolt lays true on the groove."

"Check your target. Use your eyes. Don't just be shooting."

Idris could not claim to be happy looking down the line at women in chainmail and old-fashioned helmets scrounged from their husbands' war chests. But if he glanced back into the heart of the city, he was less happy about children crying in the streets, sick or sobbing that their dogs and chickens had all disappeared.

"Captain Idris!" It was Umar from his old homeland, hailing him urgently from further down the line. Idris joined him. "I have to go. Can you take my place?"

The only answer was yes, though Idris had vowed he would not teach women to use weapons, not because God's laws forbade touching women, but because his own laws stopped him. This pupil, however, seemed to have mastered Umar's lessons. Idris began repeating the usual reminders in Arabic, since that's what Umar spoke.

"Check the bolt to be sure it's—"

"*Si*," the woman answered in *castellano*. "It's straight as an arrow."

It was Aurovita, standing closer to him than at any moment since she left him holding that blue-stained veil. He wasn't about to touch her to make sure she held her weapon correctly.

"*Hola*, Comtessa. I heard from my brother Jamal that you pray with the goodwomen. Don't your heretic friends hate war?"

"Do you like war?" Her voice from inside that helmet sounded ghostly.

Zirari thrashed around inside Idris's head cloth. "Where's her grandmother?"

"It didn't end up being a choice," Idris said.

"How is your qareen?" She sounded kind, like Zirari said she was. "The *cristiano* curses aren't causing harm?"

"I followed your advice and stay out of churches. And I avoid those odd men they call priests. How is your grandmother?"

Aurovita fired the crossbow. It bashed against the attackers' shield wall and fell to the ground. It'd be fetched back in the night, straightened, and fired back over the walls of Valencia the next day.

"You have more shades about you," she said, staring out where that bolt had fallen. "Though I can't count them. Are they men you lost in battle?"

"No. My father and uncles." He couldn't mention Susa without his throat knotting up. "I found them that day we saved Al-Broma. It's where they died. They were with me when you and I last… talked."

"Tell me if I'm doing this properly." Her foot in the stirrup, Aurovita prepared to knock another bolt in the crossbow.

When he approved, she took time finding a target.

"I know what you did," she said, her voice echoing inside the iron helmet. "Jamal told Cristina. Though I asked you to stay away."

"Jamal did most of the work. We thought it answered your grandmother's prophesy, that we'd save you." Then he asked, "How is your grandmother?"

"She went away when my baby died, to help his soul find a new form." She seemed intent on her target. "Though he didn't have time to become a real baby. My husband screamed at me that it wasn't his child, punched me until my grandmother had to take the wee thing, to save us both."

"*Aiieee!*" Zirari clawed at Idris's skull. "She's been alone this whole time."

How far into the heavens can a man's soul fly in the two heartbeats after he hears he might have had a child from the woman he loves, but he doesn't because of another man's cruelty?

As high as an imperial eagle circles on the wind?

Or as high as the moon god that women pray to in secret?

Dust clotted in his throat.

"I'm so sorry." He heard the rasp in his words before hearing that he spoke in his own tongue, saying what Susa would. He wanted to wrap his arms around her, like you do for a child, but his qareen kept warning, "Don't touch!"

She was still intent on her target. "It's in the past. Losing my son and grandmother led me to the goodwomen and their teachers, to learn about where our souls go next when we die."

She fired the crossbow. This time it hit the top edge of a fixed-wooden barricade, striking with enough force that it chipped into the wood and hung there for a moment, before the weight of the bolt caused the wood to give away, so the arrow again fell to the ground.

"Do you want me to kill him for you?" He didn't know what else he could offer.

"To save me? No. And Rodrigo will take revenge on his entire family for betrayal. I'm fine, though my aunt Ximena is still angry that I returned to Valencia instead of serving as the hidden agent that she and Rodrigo asked me to be."

Aurovita had already stepped on the crossbow's stirrup and knocked a bolt in place before he formed words in the proper tongue.

"Your sister Cristina insists that I should not have let Jamal steal you away. That we behaved like savages."

"Or like heroes in famous songs?" Again, she took time finding her target. "I did what I could to keep my clan safe amid chaos. It didn't turn out the way we planned. But I might still have a chance to save my family in this life."

The arrow sang out as Zirari shrieked and Meri blew one note in alarm.

"Took ten tries." She thrust the crossbow at Idris, causing him to fumble while he stared where she'd fired that bolt. "Now I'm done."

The so-called Count Gonzalo Garcés sprawled over a fixed wood barricade, his big face caught forever in surprise, that iron bolt shot through his throat. His men struggled to haul him down.

"Guess I'll live my next life as a dog. Or a crow." She forced the crossbow into Idris's hands. "It's worth it."

Famine during the siege meant sick and dying people everywhere. Rodrigo sent a messenger to find Idris and bring him to his villa, where the general began repeating instruction before Idris had time to shake the dust from his boots.

"You'll need to take perhaps three dozen men," Rodrigo said. "Four if you can find them. It's a month's ride with wagons to Barcelona, which we can't afford. You'll have to take them on horseback."

What Idris was being instructed to carry was a passel of Rodrigo's children and their cousins out of the siege. Rodrigo had lost his oldest son in the siege; now, almost too late, he wanted a dozen children carried to safety.

"The Count of Barcelona has offered to hold them, as a sort of hostageship, but really to protect them, no matter what happens here." The siege, and the loss of a son, had quieted Rodrigo. He too had been ill from the famine, and his restless energy had not yet returned. "And you'll take their older Rodriquez cousins with you."

Idris said, "We can manage children without imposing on women to endure the journey."

"*Aiieee*, ibn Musa, you understand strategy. The Rodriguez clan requires more work of those sisters, in another city. You know how it is with families."

"I'm not sure I do," Idris said. "My family had needs, but I chose what to do." His qareen pecked at him. *Didn't choose me.*

Rodrigo, listless, lifted his hands to the sky the way men did here, as if pleading with the heavens. "I married a Rodriguez woman. I learned to choose my battles. In this battle, I'm asking one of my best warriors to tend to these children. I want my family safe."

Idris, surrounded daily by his silent uncles and father, could not argue with that desire.

In the siege city, messengers found ways out at night to communicate with fighters outside who aligned their hopes with Rodrigo. These fighters ran distracting sorties behind the Veiled Ones' lines, successful in part because the siege had lasted so long that the Veiled mercenaries were bored and dissatisfied. Other fighters formed a cordon to shelter the women and children who would flee in the night.

While children and scant baggage were being sorted among the men, Ximena appeared outside her villa gates to say farewell to Cristina and Aurovita. However she managed it while starving, Aurovita glowed. She stood, nobler than anyone in the courtyard, while Ximena called on her to be useful *this time*. Aurovita stood there, as if her clan wasn't sending her into the wilderness with nothing, though she had already sacrificed her safety and happiness to protect that clan. Ximena continued hectoring her nieces, focused for the moment upon Cristina.

Idris came up behind Aurovita. She must have known it was him, because she didn't stiffen; she seemed to relax against him.

"Ride hard now," Ximena said, "before the Veiled Ones catch up to slaughter you like lambs."

Aurovita held out her hand to her aunt in goodbye. "Words to kindle courage in every heart, aunt."

"If courage is what you need to succeed this time, I wish that for you." Ximena barely touched her niece's hand in farewell and was quickly through the doors of her villa, and her guards swung the gates shut while the goodbyes still echoed.

Idris cleared all the dust of Iberia out of his throat so he could speak. "As your grandmother foresaw, the don of Morella is here to rescue you."

She laughed, and Meri turned it into a song.

In one last stop before the night's work began, Idris accompanied Aurovita to the *compadors,* where he also gathered the silver he stored there and retrieved the letter he'd left with them for safekeeping.

Then Idris's warriors mounted their horses, women and children astride the saddles behind them or wrapped in the warriors' arms, and rode away, taking children out of the city through the cordon and finding the road to Barcelona.

In the morning, after they'd found a safe place to rest, Jamal grabbed Idris. "The sisters we love are being exiled by their aunt. Let's take them back to their home."

"To Jaén? Twenty days' hard ride with sick children?"

"It's where Cristina wants to go. There's at least ten men who will come with me. Who've never been comfortable living among *cristianos.*"

"Go. It's the best idea for you."

"But not you?"

"I'll take these children to Barcelona first."

Idris and Jamal grasped hands, whispering. "May the ancestors guide you home, Juba."

"And you, Idren."

Idris and his men worked like madmen to scavenge food while scouting ahead and behind to check for Veiled Ones pursuing them.

Most everyone was sick from no food and the filth of the siege, so it was slow going, however much they wanted to take wing and fly over the *matorral.* They couldn't conjure magical wings, like storks or eagles, to conquer the plains and mountains; instead, tired and dispirited, they moved more like quail, fleeing in the brush, unable to take wing to protect the smallest and weakest among them.

Meri and Susa still rode with Idris, and his shades served as guardian spearmen, though he only heard their warnings through his qareen. He could carry two shades without tiring his horse, but he also had to carry two children, singing the songs that Meri taught him until he was hoarse with dust and exhausted from offering comfort. Then at night, he went out with Umar and Tariq to hunt animals that roamed in the dark, performing hasty field dressing, and hurrying home to the cooks, who woke long before dawn, kindled their camp-fires, and did what they could to feed everyone.

Each day, when riders traded off the children and women they carried, Idris ended up with one or more children who smelled of sunshine and dust while he held them perched on his saddle, showing them how to clutch the horse's mane without hurting it. And singing Meri's songs until the raw hole in his throat swallowed all loss, and left him content to chivvy starving children into pretend happiness.

One morning the horse Aurovita rode came up lame.

They had no horses to spare, and no tiny village they passed had a horse to sell. Dressed again in boy's clothes, Aurovita swayed, pale under her sunburn, while Idris proposed she ride with him. Rocking in his arms as they rode together, Aurovita clutched her youngest cousin close. Meri and Susa clung on behind Idris, and the shades of his uncles and father ran alongside. It was no burden for Idris or his horse, because Aurovita was scarcely more than bones dressed in faded indigo tatters.

"We'll rest in Morella," he said. "I believe it's a day's ride from here. We'll stay there until everyone is well and the dust settles."

"What if the Veiled Ones attack Morella?"

"Then I, Captain Al-Makkzan of the Veiled Ones' mercenaries, have a letter that declares I'm here in Iberia to help drive God's laws into men's hearts. We shall tell them you are al-Zarqa, the blue-eyed woman."

Too tired to talk, she settled in, no burden in his arms, while he did the work he had to, making sure everyone who travelled with them was safe, secure, then halting when anyone in the dusty train needed to rest. The children, whenever they woke from fevered sleep, sang the songs that Meri played.

The sun had traveled close to the western horizon when the scouts reported how close they were to Morella. His tired arms and aching thighs must have responded, because he felt her thin shoulder blades pressing against his belly. Susa and Zirari pressed at his back.

"Stay with me."

He spoke into her thread-bare veil, while Zirari cried, "There, you said it! Didn't hurt, did it, turnip?"

"I can take you home to Jaén, or stay with you in Barcelona, whichever you choose." he was sure she was awake, though she didn't answer. He could feel her breathing, even through his chainmail and surcoat. "You'll be at least as well off as if you'd run away with a savage Berber spearman to begin with, instead of waiting so long."

"Except you aren't a Berber."

"Just a savage."

"I'm sorry I ever said that."

"There's a place inside me," Idris said, "between my heart and my breastbone, where that savage hunter lives. I should have let him free. He'd have come for you before this."

"You were there," she said. "Or perhaps it was your shade from the future. After we said goodbye that night, I learned to watch the sun rise every single day. You were always there."

12
Babylon

MORELLA DIDN'T PROVE TO be much, having been razed a few decades earlier when Rodrigo was first working here, hoping for the Kingdom of Valencia. Nothing like the glorious orchards and gardens Idris had seen near Granada or outside Valencia.

But the countryside had the barren, sunbaked beauty that Idris had been used to in his old home. And the people were nice, perhaps more welcoming than in other villages where they'd been persuading people to shelter the refugees from Valencia. They understood Idris's accented Barcelona tongue. They liked the breed of horses that he and his men rode, and seemed happy to put them to pasture, since the horses needed as much succor as the travelers they carried.

She came to him at the first sunrise, when Idris was on top of the broken *castillo* wall, greeting the sun.

"Let's live here and make the world new." She folded her arms, the way she did when she'd made a decision.

Before he could reach for her, Aurovita seemed to notice more, looking past him while the horizon brightened. Perhaps the dawn light caught at the gauzy edges of the shades of his family.

"All of us," she said. "We can make this a good place."

After everyone was well, Idris's men delivered the children to the Count of Barcelona, with the letter from Rodrigo, and another that Aurovita helped write, with Idris submitting himself to the count as the protector of Morella.

It didn't take hard work to rebuild a town that had been devastated in a battle. Or to help smaller local villages fortify and rebuild their walls and food stores. It just meant getting up every morning and starting the next task. Idris wasn't a farmer, but he did persuade some of the farmers to grow hard wheat, which lasted longer in silos. He didn't intend to live in a town that couldn't both resist a siege and protect its neighbors.

Ten of the men who'd started out in the *adras* mountains stayed with Idris, homesteading in the nearby valleys. Those that wanted wives found them among the widows and sisters and aunts between Olocau and Vallibona. It proved easy for most hunters to turn shepherd, the men agreeing that you just talk more to tame beasts. However, the sheep always smelled the hunter on Idris, so he bred horses.

And he learned what a turnip was, because the women of Morella grew them in their kitchen gardens. He did not believe, however, that it was a kind of food that a man should have to eat if he wasn't starving.

After the first year, a package found its way to Morella, carried by a merchant caravan that went out of its way to reach the village. Since nothing ever happened in Morella, the arrival of the merchant train caused most work to halt in each household. Opening the package was delayed until everyone returned for *migdiada,* since the midday break brought each man and woman in from the fields. It wouldn't be fair, not to wait for everyone.

Idris pried open the crate. By the time he prepared to unseal the ceramic jar, he had a fair idea what it was. Yes, a jar of pigment from his brother Jamal in Jaén, with a message that declared Idris was the uncle of a fine boy named Rashid.

Idris didn't wait for the end of *migdiada*. He mixed the pigment with slaked lime and glue, and painted the door of his house blue. The color of the tattooed lips of a beautiful woman.

Not long after the message came from Juba-who-was-now-Jamal, Musa and the uncles departed. Idris believed that the way to the ancestors' trail was near the spring on the east side of a nearby ridge, where he liked to go to watch the sun rise. Perhaps others thought so too, because there were three standing stones beside the spring, plus a flat rock where women left flowers and hunters left a portion of their game on those special days when the sun was turning season.

On the midsummer day that Idris and Aurovita greeted their first child—a daughter!—Meri and Susa departed. Idris expected to be sad, but found he wasn't. And instead of going into a decline when Susa left, Zirari continued its house-and-yard protection duties, often while humming one of Meri's songs. Children in Morella never wandered into the wilderness and didn't seem to suffer cuts and falls and contusions, though many mothers ascribed that to Idris's second sight.

Certain names found their way into the village marriage records, but not true names. Neither Idris nor his one true love entered the stone shack that people built on top of the burned-out mosque. The secular priest who came once or twice a year was as much a heretic as Aurovita, or so she claimed. Except each time she mentioned it, she laughed so hard tears formed in the corners of her eyes.

Each fighting season, Idris and his men took mercenary work, which Idris decided was not as interesting as hunting. At first, Idris believed that battle was like hunting, where you prove you're smarter than your quarry. Then he gradually understood that in battle, you had to prove to be most ruthless.

Laying siege—the preferred notion of attack among the *taifa* generals Idris worked for—was played like *naqala* or one of the gambling games that Viggo the northman had taught them. Messengers rode back and forth, while most fighters spent their days felling trees, hauling the timber and stones from the hills, then helping to build the siege engines.

But it was honest work and brought home silver to the village.

Acknowledging Zirari's teachings from history, Idris never volunteered tribute to the Count of Barcelona, sending silver only when asked. Or he sent silver when demanded by the emir who held Valencia. Or if the king of Castile demanded tribute. Idris had no inclination to argue about whom the lord of Morella owed tribute, because Morella was most often forgotten by everyone. The buried silver and gold lasted more than a generation.

And Aurovita saved all of her grandmother's rescue gold to give to her daughters and granddaughters, not that they'd ever need it.

Most people said that Rodrigo prevailed that year of the first siege. The Veiled Ones retreated at the end of the fighting season and the siege was lifted. But in a year the great general was dead, and his wife Ximena ruled Valencia. That must have been a grand victory for the Rodriguez clan, to have a woman from their family ruling an important holding for the king of Castile. However, eventually the Veiled Ones laid siege again, which ended with Ximena and her court fleeing for Toledo.

What little Idris knew of the fortunes of the Rodriguez clan, he learned from the *compadors* who still paid him. Sometimes he worked as the Count of Barcelona's mercenary, sometimes working for local Muslim lords and clans like the Banu Hud who continued to resist the Veiled Ones. Eventually Zaragoza also fell to the Veiled invaders. It took the king of Aragón a few decades to claim back the territory and advance Aragón's rule and laws through the countryside, as far as Morella and beyond. By then, the Almohads arrived from Tunis and pushed the Veiled Ones aside.

Also by then, the sons and grandsons of men who fought the Veiled Ones had crusading on the mind. The first wave of *cruce-signati* had seized Jerusalem, so pilgrims could once more walk freely on the streets where their prophet Jesus had walked. But holding the land proved as difficult for the crusaders as it had for the Veiled Ones in Iberia.

Tales of glory about fighting in the Outremer spread from the North Sea to the Great Sea. Priests talked about gaining salvation for your soul by putting unbelievers to the sword. Men also heard about the glorious booty earned in the Holy Land—and ever since the Roman pope had cried the Peace of God, no joy could be had from raiding and fighting one's neighbors. Most of all, young men felt the call of adventure like a demand from an organ deep in the body, the way your lungs demand air.

"I'm going." Idris's grandson appeared for a last goodbye. He'd persisted in arguing his reasons for leaving, though no one in the village quarreled with him. The lad never seemed to remember that most of the older men there had once picked up and left their former homes, or that Idris had never begged a daughter or son to stay when they wanted to leave.

"Off to crusade for your soul's salvation?" Idris prompted.

The boy didn't notice that Idris teased him and so sputtered in passion. "No, to take my place in the world. If it's true that God made me, He didn't make me a goat herder or sheep—" He used a word that people in Barcelona saved for profanity.

"Miquel, your grandmother isn't deaf," Idris said, pointing to where she sat under the shade of an olive tree. However, Aurovita wasn't listening, having already kissed the boy goodbye and then settled in the shade to teach three granddaughters what she called *mathematica* (as if those girls would ever have to calculate food and fodder for one hundred men).

Miquel shuddered, as if shaking off a shiver. "*Àvi*, I'm sorry. My cousin Amir will be a much better steward for this village than I could ever manage. I've given him my house, so now he can marry. And I'm not made for that either."

"Yes, I think I see how you might be right." What Idris saw was that the too-handsome Miquel was like Jamal in other ways. Eager for adventure. Too much passion to stay home in a tiny village.

"And I'm a better fighter than most men." Even though Idris was agreeing with him, the boy repeated the argument he'd made all winter. "I learned crossbow, sword, and spear from men who fought with El Cid. I learned to ride and hunt from the best. That's you, my *àvi*."

"Also, you learned to gamble from the greatest Berber hunters who ever tossed bones." Idris had to say something because he was about to laugh at the boy's earnest pleas, which wouldn't be fair to that pure passion. "Of course you will go, *fadrin*. It's your turn to shape the world. To make the world serve your needs."

He walked with the lad down the trail to the east, both of them leading horses. Miquel held the reins of the finest Arab gelding that Idris had ever bred. At the place where that spring bubbled up from deep inside the earth, Idris made the boy stop while he showed him where the wealth of the sons of Musa was buried, giving the boy half the hoard. The sun caught in the boy's hair, and Idris was struck again by how much Miquel looked like his brother Jamal, passionately burning to be in the world.

"The rest is here if you decide to return, *fadrin*, since the Count of Barcelona will always see you as the don of Morella."

The boy slapped his knee, chortling. "The don of Morella! The count of copulating sheep!" Then he noticed that Idris wasn't laughing. "I'm sorry, *Àvi*. I'm honored to receive what the Cid gave you."

"You are the don of Morella. Others you meet will only be servants to a lord. You are a lord. What does that mean?"

Miquel dipped his head. "That I'm responsible for the men around me. That I care for their lives as much as my own."

Idris handed over the short sword and the silver dagger that never kept an edge. "Keep these, even when you earn better weapons. The Cid's own wife cast a spell on this blade. Though I never learned what the spell was. Perhaps it keeps you from cutting yourself when you shave."

"Your gifts from the Campeador?" At last Miquel saw the weight of the moment. He buckled the sword in place, then swung the gilded baldric over his shoulder, arranging the dagger to ride across that leather cuirass he'd spent the winter beating into shape. "Thank you, *Àvi*. I will keep these always."

Miquel held out his hand, to offer the kind of farewell that *cristiano* knights exchanged in these parts. Idris touched Miquel's hand, but instead of shaking it, he pulled the young man into the kind of embrace hunters shared in the ancient mountains.

"*Fadrin*, one of my old friends longs to see the waters of Babylon again. I think it's near Damascus. Or maybe Persepolis."

"I don't know where that is, *Àvi*."

"No matter. Please carry my friend to the Outremer."

"I need to travel light."

"It's no great burden, Miquel."

Out in the sunshine, the separation wasn't as dramatic as it had been in Silina's darkened mud-spackled house. Still, the qareen spread its wings, broader than an imperial eagle, and shrieked its full name for any spirits of this spring and its standing stones to hear. Again, the beating of wings was like thunder, the shriek like worlds grinding their edges together.

Miquel had his hands over his ears, and then over his face to protect from claws, but the qareen chose the boy's unruly black hair for its perch, then craned to murmur in his ear.

Idris pulled his grandson close again. "I have another name, my real name. Only your grandmother knows it. It will be lost when we are gone."

"Am I to carry that, too, *Àvi?*"

"Yes. My true name is Idren, the son of the milkmaid and Musa the hunter, who was lost here until I made a home for him and all the uncles."

Miquel rubbed at his ear, already quarreling with the qareen so he couldn't possibly hear what more his grandfather said.

"Farewell, *fadrin*. My heart tells me that you shall never return." He repeated what Viggo said so long ago. "Go with whatever gods will have you."

E N D • THE BLUE DOOR

Characters • *The Blue Door*

Aurovita: A Mozarab woman of the Rodriguez clan.

Badr al-Malik al-Makkzan: A Veiled Ones' captain from Tunis.

Benito: A goodman *compador* in Valencia.

Cristina: Aurovita's younger sister.

Diego: A Rodriguez steward.

Gonzalo Garcés: A self-styled count on the Castile/Aragón frontier.

Idren: A hunter from the Atlas Mountains; later, Idris ibn Musa; later still, Idris al-Makkzan.

Juba: Idris's middle brother; later, Jamal ibn Musa; later still, Jamal Abu Rashid al-Makkzan.

Meri: Idris's youngest brother; later, Amir ibn Musa.

Moshe: A Jewish *compador* in Valencia.

Ramon Berenguer: Count of Barcelona.

Rodrigo Díaz de Vivar: Campeador, "the commander"; later called El Cid, "the lord."

Silina/Susa: Idren's great-great-grandmother.

Viggo Torbjornsen: A northman from the Dane land.

Umar, Ali, and Tariq: Berber fighters from the village near Idris's.

Ximena: Rodrigo's wife; a Rodriguez clanswoman.

Yusuf ibn Tashfin: General of the Veiled Ones, serving the Abbasid caliph of Baghdad; later, Amir al-Muslimin ("Prince of Muslims").

Zirari: A qareen from Persia; Artasi Tasiri, "marvelous by truth."

Places in Idris's World, 1090

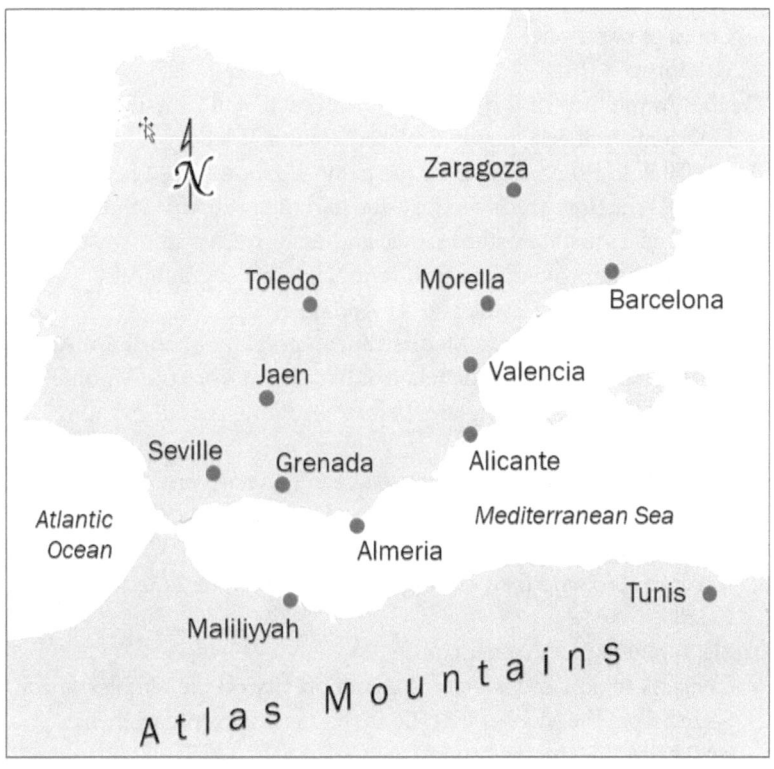

Al-Andalus (in country; Andalusia in Christendom): The land of the
    Moorish caliphates on the Iberian Peninsula.

Al-Broma: A fictional *castillo* on the Castile-Andalusian frontier.

Al-Mería: A port and fortress city on the southeastern coast of the
    Iberian Peninsula.

Aragón: At the time of Idris's story, a smaller territory than what
    became the Crown of Aragón, it was first established when the
    Kingdom of Navarre was divided into three parts. It grew in size
    through conquest of Andalusian territories and through dynastic
    marriage.

Atlas mountains: A range in north Africa, across Algeria, Morocco, and Tunisia. Idris calls the mountains *adras*, or home. Early Berbers appear to have inhabited the range since the Neolithic revolution.

Barcelona: At the time of Idris's story, territory in Iberia held by the Count of Barcelona; now approximately the political entity of Catalunya.

Castile: At the time of Idris's story, one of medieval Christian kingdoms in Iberia, newly centered around Toledo.

Iberia: The old Roman name for the peninsula now called Spain.

Ifriqiya: At the time of Idris's story, the part of north Africa that included Tunisia, western Libya, and eastern Algeria.

Jaén: A city and province in south-central Spain, geographically strategic between Castile and Al-Andalus.

Maliliyyah: Now Melilla, a Mediterranean port city in northern Africa.

Morella: A town on the Valencia frontier, taken from the Moors by Rodrigo Díaz, lost again later before becoming part of Aragón in the Reconquista.

Morocco: At the time of Idris's story, a region in northern Africa, including Marrakesh, that was part of the Abbasid caliphate.

Toledo: A city in central Iberia, taken from the Moors by Christian forces in 1085, and then serving as the capital of the Kingdom of Castile.

Tunis: A city in North Africa.

Valencia: A region and ancient Roman port city on the Mediterranean. Seized from the Moors by El Cid in the eleventh century, then retaken in 1102 by the Moors.

Zaragoza: A city in Aragón on the Ebro River. Originally founded by Caesar Augustus to settle veterans of the Cantabrian wars, it was subsequently conquered by Visigoths and Muslim invaders. It was taken by the Aragón king Alfonso I from the Muslims in 1118 and made the capital of the Kingdom of Aragón.

Glossary • *The Blue Door*

Abu: An honorific name as the parent of a child (Abu Rashid is the father of Rashid).

Almoravid dynasty: A fundamentalist Berber Muslim movement in the tenth and eleventh centuries that spread from the Sahara through Iberia. Chroniclers in that century called them the Veiled Ones, from the practice of wearing a veil below the eyes, marking them as separate from the decadent customs they fought against.

Almohad caliphate: A Moroccan Berber Muslim movement in the twelfth century that came to rule North Africa and Islamic Iberia.

àvi, àvia: Grandfather, grandmother.

Banu Hud: The Arab family that ruled the taifa of Zaragoza from 1039–1110. They led the resistance in the region to the Almoravid invaders.

Berbers: An ethnic group in North Africa. The invaders of Iberia in the eighth century were mainly Berbers. The Almoravid invaders who established a new dynasty in Al-Andalus in the eleventh century were also Berbers from Morocco.

booty: Treasure; throughout medieval times, the primary way warriors financed their armies or paid their mercenaries. That is, rather than "looting" as we now think of booty, these cultures thought of booty as legitimate plunder. ("To the victor goes the spoils.")

burnus: A loose, hooded cloak.

castellano: The romance language spoken in the Castile regions of Iberia.

castillo: A castle; most typically, a stone-and-timber hilltop fortress.

Catalan: In the Middle Ages, a language, not a political entity.

compador: A businessman, managing finances in a pre-banking age.

crucesignati, cruzados: Crusaders.

cuirass: A rigid armor covering the torso. At this period, it was still made of leather.

Dar al-Islam: "The House of Peace."

dhimmi: Non-Muslims in Al-Andalus under the protection of the caliphate.

djinni: A supernatural creature in Arabian mythology.

don: A courtesy title for a gentleman from the landed classes.

emir: At the time of Idris's story, any leader of the various *taifa* principalities in Al-Andalus, roughly equivalent to a prince or a king.

fadrin: A lad, a term of endearment.

ghul: In Arabic mythology, an evil spirit that eats human flesh and is commonly associated with graveyards.

goodmen, goodwomen: A reference to the people whom the Catholic Church called heretics; now commonly called Cathars.

hola: Hello.

ibn: A patronymic name ("son of...").

ifrit: An infernal djinni who lives underground.

isfiriya: A fluffy, egg-rich pancake with spices.

Madre de Dios: Mother of God.

migdiada: Midday rest.

mirkas: A spicy lamb sausage, with cultural roots in Tunisia and Algeria.

Moors: A reference used colloquially in medieval times by Europeans to describe Berbers, Arabs, Muslims in general, or any dark-complexion *mestitz* person.

Mozarab: Iberian Christians living under Moorish rule in Al-Andalus. This is a modern term. In medieval times, they would have been designated *dhimmi* and required to pay a tax.

naqala: A count-and-capture game or mancala-type game, where the objective is to capture more game pieces than the opponent.

nisse: A household spirit in Nordic folklore, who is responsible for the prosperity of the farm.

Outremer: The lands across the Great Sea, where the Crusader States were founded and other territory seized by Christian invaders.

parias: Tributes demanded by an Iberian king of neighboring Muslim kingdoms; a major way that African gold entered Europe.

qareen: A personal companion who is a lower-order djinni.

qutun: Cotton

rafraf: A long tail on a turban.

sarawil: Trousers.

surcoat: A long coat worn over other clothes or armor.

tagelmust veil: A ten-meter length of indigo cloth used as veil and turban by certain ethnic Berber men.

taifa: Any of several independent principalities in Al-Andalus.

Veiled Ones: How people at the time referred to the Almoravid dynasty.

Visigoth: Germanic nomads who held a kingdom in parts of Iberia from the fifth to the eighth centuries.

Visigoth rite: Also called the Mozarabic rite; the Christian liturgy followed by people of Hispania who lived under Muslim rule. The old rite was gradually replaced in Iberia from about the time of Idris's story.

Timeline ▪ The Dons of Morella

Morella is a real place in Spain, but the dons in Accidental Heretics tales are fictional.

1040: Rodrigo Díaz de Vivar, now known as El Cid, born. Almoravid (the Veiled Ones) fervor begins in southern Morocco.

1053: Almoravids spread ways to Berber areas of Sahara via desert trade routes.

1057: Rodrigo fights for Castile against Moorish control in Zaragoza.

1059: Almoravids conquer Berbers holding "heretical" form of Islam.

1062: Almoravids conquer most of Morocco, Western Sahara, and Mauritania.

1066: William the Conqueror of Normandy crowned king of England.

1072: Sancho of Castile murdered; Alfonso VI becomes king; Rodrigo loses rank, treated with suspicion.

1075: Idren born in the Atlas Mountains.

1079: Yusuf ibn Tashfin captures Tangiers.

1081: Banished from Castile, Rodrigo takes work fighting for Muslim taifa rulers in Zaragoza against Aragón and Barcelona.

1084: Battle of Morella, where Rodrigo worked for taifa rulers of Zaragoza versus Aragón.

1085: Castile captures Toledo. Many Andalusian emirs begin paying tribute to Castile.

1086: Taifa princes invite Almoravids to defend against Castile. Rodrigo is made general *miolitar* by Alfonso of Castile.

1087: Rodrigo sets sights on Valencia, independent of Alfonso, while supporting the Banu Hud against the Almoravids.

1090: Yusuf ibn Tashfin returns to Iberia to drive Islamic law. Rodrigo's daughter marries Ramon Berenguer II, Count of Barcelona.

1092: Muslim ruler of Valencia becomes Rodrigo's tributary.

1094: Rodrigo captures Valencia with an army of Moors and Christians.

1095: Idren comes to Iberia, age 20.
 Pope Urban II preaches the First Crusade to the Holy Land.

1097: Almoravid siege of Valencia; Rodrigo's only son dies.

1099: Rodrigo dies. Rodrigo's wife Ximena rules Valencia.
The Kingdom of Jerusalem is founded by European crusaders.
1102: Second siege of Valencia. After seven months, Ximena sets fire to Valencia's great mosque and flees to Burgos with Rodrigo's body.
1105: Miquel's father born in Morella.
1120: Almohads engulf southern Iberia, displacing the Almoravids.
1131: Miquel born in Morella. Pèire Leteric born in Catalunya Pyrenees.
1147: Miquel serves as mercenary in the Outremer; meets Pèire Leteric.
Franks abandon alliance with Damascus; Second Crusade collapses.

Pèire and Miquel Go to Sea

Pèire and Miquel Go to Sea
AN ACCIDENTAL HERETICS TALE

A Scribe's Note
These tales represent a faithful accounting as dictated by
Pèire Leteric, baron of Castel-de-Valerós, liege subject to
Pedro d'Aragón, presenting his account of deeds and acts
performed while he served as a faithful Christian in the
Outremer in decades past as a comrade of Don Miquel of
Morella.

Pèire Leteric swears by his father's hand, and upon the
paratge of his domus and his countrymen, that these
accounts are true, as much as men can perceive truth in this
world.

— *Tomás de Morella y Cyprus*
Feast of St-Mark
Anno Domini 1210

I, PÈIRE LETERIC SWEAR EVERY WORD of this is true, as true as the
milk from your mother's teat. I swear it on the bones of a saint,
even a real one.

First, you best understand, we were on crusade and even in
Jerusalem long before that hairy-assed Ricart Coeur-de-Lyon or
snot-nosed Philippe of France persuaded ten thousand men to lay
down their lives to expiate their sins. Let me tell you about real
crusading, not sheep stealing, the way the Angevines and Franks
thought to do it the last time the pope called on men to sew a cross
on their tabards and rot their sorry asses in the desert.

We are both sixteen, old enough to do most of what a man gets
to do, but neither of us has ever been farther than where the shepherds camp in the high hills at summer.

I come to the docks at Narbonne as trusting of men as a lamb
is of his shepherd. I believe in my heart I'm going to be earning
good gold, and getting my sins forgiven all the way to the golden
heavens guarded by all the singing angels. First man I meet on the
docks is this tall Norman (they all get to be towering size, from
what I know), dressed in velvet, a pile of fancy armor at his feet.
We get to talking, and it turns out that he's going to the Outremer
for the fourth time, he'd just come back to bury his dear old
mother, and I figure this is a good one to know, someone who's
been to the other side of the world and can give me a hint about
how it will be when I come there. We're waiting for the tide to turn
so the ship's captain will let us all onboard that wicker basket he
calls a boat. I'm not going to ask this old soldier what I'm
thinking—*Do I have the correct armor for the Saracen desert? Is this the
best helmet for fighting in the land where Jesus walked? Are there really
camels?* Instead, I say to him, "What's it like after fighting and all
your sins are forgiven for all eternity?"

Not too personal a question, not letting him know I'm as
ignorant as a lamb lost in a thicket.

He says (as much as a Norman can say a word that somebody
can understand), "It's not just fighting that relieves a soul. In the
Holy Land, when I first arrived, an ancient priest near Jerusalem
shared with me—"

He stops, stares out at the Great Sea, where swells roll and clouds float overhead. Just over that horizon is the Holy Land. "What? What did he share?"

That old velvet-coated knight shakes himself. "I know I'm safe forever in Abraham's bosom. But I'm thinking about you coming to that new land like I did. Unseasoned. Unprotected. Perhaps it's time I shared what kept me safe. Perhaps the Holy Spirit led you to me."

He produces from inside his fine, embroidered vest a sliver of wood, as long as your little finger. It had been dipped in molten silver and a red stone like a garnet had been craftily wired to it, so it looked like a drop of blood on the silver. He leans his head close to mine and says, "It's a piece of the True Cross. Where our Savior hung when he died for our sins."

I stretch my hand for it, wanting to look closely. It seems as old as a stone crypt.

He pulls it back, out of my reach. "I can't let you touch it until you're fresh from having a priest absolve your sins. The holiness of the True Cross will strip the skin from the bone of a man who's sinned. Get a priest to bless you, and I'll let you take this with you, so it can guide and protect you like it has done for me."

My heart is all afire. I'm looking about, wondering where there's a church, because I hadn't thought that getting free of my sins was part of packing up to sail the Great Sea. The old Norman fellow says, "There's a priest who writes letters for sailors, he's always by the chandler's store, where you buy a sailcloth to wrap your armor. He does intercessions for crusaders. You give him three silver morabatins, he forgives your sins, and I shall let your carry the True Cross back to the land where Jesus walked."

I'm a graceless idiot from the hills, so I'm half way up the dockside, and standing in line for the black-robed priest who's writing good-bye-mama letters for a bunch of lickspittle, would-be crusaders like me. Another smaller group of knights lingers nearby, tossing dice while waiting for the tide to turn, which I'd been doing till that knight got me all fired up about salvation. I'm nervous, looking back at the quay where the Norman knight was waiting. I hoped to heaven he was waiting. And I'm ready, silver from inside my belt now in my hand, getting sweaty while I wait.

"What do you wish me to write, seigneur?" the priest says. Like I'm the seigneur, and not the little brother sent off to make money in the Outremer.

"I only seek forgiveness of my sin."

The priest looks past me, where the old gentleman waits. They don't see each other, but I'm jiggling around, eager to part with both my sins and my silver.

"Do you renounce the devil and all your sins?"

"I do."

"Then go and sin no more. That's four silver morabatins."

"Four?" I stood there like a puppy wondering how the dog ate his dinner. I count out more silver and hand it over.

"*Renrén.*" Behind me, this golden voice calls me a fool in pure backcountry Catalan dialect.

I scowl, turning to face one of the dice-boys, and past him I see the Norman fellow is gone from the docks. So, turning back to the priest, I see just his black skirt swishing around a corner into an alley.

"There's no magic," the gambler says. "You're the fourth one they picked out today for a fool."

■

Not an auspicious beginning, having this boy from the hills call me a fool, especially since I'd just been one. But I learn that Miquel had seen what tricks men play and always expected them. By that time, Miquel, had already studied enough so that he was the man who got his tricks in before the cheating shills could see his game.

"Come on, *baquelar*." He grabs my arm, and we were running up the alley together, and he got a sword out, and the black-robed fellow is lying in the muck, Miquel's boot on his privates, and Miquel's slender sword poking his arm, demanding the silver back.

Which is about when I see that the "priest" fellow has boots, and woolen knickers, and leather strapping on his calves like a Narbonnese foot-soldier.

"Only the coins you took from my friend," Miquel says when the false-priest tries to hand over his entire purse. "Unlike you, we aren't thieves. Count them. Four. All silver. No brass."

My silver is in my hand once more, and after I tuck it back into my belt, I look up to see that Miquel's gone, and the priest is trying to crawl out of the puddle of horsepucky, mud, and who knows what wet stuff.

I head back for the dock and find Miquel's gambling friends guarding my armor and pack, while Miquel's off arguing with the captain of the wattle-and-daub boat about what we'll all agree to pay to sail out of Narbonne. It reminds me that, for every war I rode off to fight, the men that moved the fighters and sold them horses and armor made more than any mercenary I ever met, here in Christendom or off in the Outremer.

It's half a day again before Miquel looks my way or speaks to me. After we sort out how we are all to huddle together on this trip, Miquel manages to clear enough room among us to restart his dice game, and they're tossing the bones again even before most of us are tossing our breakfast over the sides of the rocking boat that's scooting its way slowly onto the swelling Great Sea.

Me, I can't stop watching the fellow who watched me humiliate myself. Miquel, like me, is outfitted for war. But the way I see it, he probably made that cuirass himself, sewed it better than a girl does her veil, and pounded those brass tacks so carefully to armor it, that he must have made his grandma ashamed of her embroidery. Yet it was there to see, if you know to look. He likely had a personal acquaintance with the bull he took that hide from, and he likely stuck his sticker in the bull's neck just a heartbeat before the bull woke up knowing he was dead. Every single body on that basket we sailed to sea in began to strip their shirts as the day wore on, basking in the sun, but Miquel keeps his cuirass on as if it's part of his body, that oiled leather the same color as his skin gleaming in the sun. (Don't forget to put that part in: that he's half Moor, though little did I know then it was Miquel's granddaddy who slipped some color into a fancy Mozarab clan.)

And of course he's got that sword tied to him like a third arm. Miquel had an old sticker-picker he got from his father or uncle, stuck in this homemade scabbard that he must have carved and painted all the last winter. Can't help but wonder if his people sat around the fire at night while he's carving away, not knowing he's about to break out of that goat-pen.

He invites me to join his gambling partners.

"I can't be throwing my silver away gambling," I say to him. "Everything I earn goes back to my *domus*." I was thinking, of course, that he's like me, a son sent by the household to fight for pay, for how else is your *domus* to get on? Fifty households can't pay their taxes if they're just growing olives and spelt, and minding their own business.

But no. Miquel says, "The home folk get not one brass barcelonese from me. Let them suck goats." And that, plus squat, was what he had to say about what he left behind in Morella.

There we were, about the same size, Miquel and me, though one of his grandpas gave him the shoulders of a roustabout. He could run faster than me, but whenever we were riding or fighting on horseback, I had him beat every time. "Like, maybe they only rode goats where you come from," I said to him once. He said he didn't spend his time talking to pure animals like they were people. He said it like he thought talking to your animal was a bad thing.

He and I have the same reach with a quarterstaff or a sword. I didn't want to learn that kind of close work with a dagger that he knew. I suppose Miquel had to learn that, coming from the part of the country he did, where spitting in the street or noticing a woman or wiggling your nose is like to get you into a knife fight every day and twice on Friday. We are the same age, and when camp's sitting still, no one with any immediate work, then some man or another begins chomping on his cud and picks a fight. There's nothing like those pirate Normans getting an itch in their pants and they have to start something. Many times one of those Norman bastards started picking on us for not being as tall as our horses. From that, I got to be the master of the quarterstaff, taking that stick to bruise a man who's an elbow's length taller than me. Miquel wouldn't fight just because of what some Norman said. He'd lash out with his tongue in a way that a drunk northman wouldn't understand, but who'd then charge after Miquel, only to get himself cut where it hurt, and then getting sticky with his own blood.

.

Later, the next time we talked about what we got paid was one of those rare times when an Outremer lord paid up all of what we were owed. Those lords in the Crusader States and other territories across the Great Sea still were always bad about paying their bills. I don't mean to say those Franks who settled the Holy Land were cheats and liars. I'm just remembering how many paydays there were when all we got paid was horse feed.

You know that lesson we all get to hear every year during the Twelfth Night season, when the priest tells the part about Our Lord's family? I think it goes, "Abraham begat Isaac, and Isaac begat Jacob, and Jacob begat Judah" and then they all go on begetting sons until we get to Our Lord and Savior? Well I'm here to tell you that in the Frankish kingdoms of the Outremer, the lesson that would be written about them, if anyone was telling the truth, would be: "And one Baldwin cheated with Joscelin's wife, so Joscelin took Conrad's wife, even though he already had three wives and a half dozen Saracen slaves in his bed, and then they all got together for a half a moon and cheated all hell out of another lord because he was a leper and his wife was a raving bitch." Yeah, the story would be more like that, and so on to the ninth degree of cousins cheating each other over a wife, a field, or whoever got the most slaves out of the last raid. Maybe, I'm only saying maybe, that's something that Ricart and Philippe put to rest for a while when they were crusading, even if was just getting Guy de Lusignan out of Jerusalem so he couldn't have shat on yet another attempt to get Outremer lords to pull together.

When we were working, hired out to this one Outremer lord, the order of the day wasn't to practice battle formations (those lords only had but one form). Instead, it was about who had now cheated their way to being in charge.

.

Two kinds of soldiers took up the Cross then or stayed on after they saw what it was to live in the Outremer. There were the rough boys, like me and my new friend Miquel. We needed to be paid because it was our job and lots like me had to send silver home to our domus. We were there to protect vineyards and goats for one Outremer lord or another who couldn't make an alliance with his neighbors.

And then there were those who went to battle for God's sake alone, going on a spiritual quest, longing to see Jerusalem. These fellows started out as the kind likely to tear up his own shirt to sew a cross on his surcoat, or to get his wife or mama to do it. And as things went on, those kinds of boys often ended up following a batch of black-coated Templars. Those kind did love their pretty surcoats and their secrets and having people whisper the name of their order with awe, all the while hoping the crosses their horses wore didn't collect too much dust.

Awe, spit. I love God as much as He cares to love me. But when your job is to carry the sword in the Outremer, I don't see what good comes of having secrets and special shirts to wear. Though I know pretty well there's lots who've been there that disagree with me. Or maybe you think I'm bitter or jealous of the spirit-moved boys? Maybe so—when I was sixteen and green as a June peach. But you know me, brother. I'm just practical. You can't plan and fight a war just from how the spirit of God moves you. Of course, the Templars—the real ones, not their swanning followers—knew this. They were smart boys. Still are. If they'd just give up wearing their pride on their fancy sleeves, it'd be better for them in the long run.

Though looking back as far as from here, sixty years later, I don't know how long the long run is. It's already two hundred years since Jesus was supposed to come back and take us to heaven and end this world of hurt and travail. Not that I'm complaining. I have my family and my villages that God gave me to care for. A woman loves me and keeps me warm at night. So I'm not complaining to Jesus about him and his Father in heaven leaving things the way they are for a while.

But let me finish this part of the story.

Miquel and I were sent out to the wide world in the Year of Our Lord one thousand one hundred forty-seven on a crusade that most in Christendom called failed. But we went there to do our jobs and stayed on to be paid. Though, our captains said, we were there because the local Saracens had been trampling saints' relics under their bare infidel feet. I never saw a Saracen do any stomping. But neither Miquel nor I were the kind that could afford to carry a sword just for the remission of our damned sins.

Enemies of the Cross were what they said we were being paid to fight. Boredom, the bloody runs, and camp thieves were more what we spent our time fighting.

When we got there, we found we lived in a new-world Babel. No, we didn't get a tower, because nobody there had enough free time to play in the mud and build one. I mean, every other row of bivouacked tents spoke another tongue.

I thought I was plum fancy myself, because I could make myself understood to men who come from around the Great Sea, Barcelona to Genoa. A Gascony man would jump when I called the captain's words down the line, as ready as any Toulousain donzel who got dressed up to fight Saracens. Miquel could add the tongues from Toledo to Valencia, though not so many boys from Iberia were there.

But then there were those that God flung farther from the tower of Babel, so far up north that they could talk their gibberish only with each other, leaving the rest of us alone. I mean, if you took the time, you could hope to understand a Frankish man or a Norman, and maybe some from Venice. And hope it was worth the time it took to figure out what they had to say. But then you get to the one who comes from the north end of the Rhone, and you start to think that maybe those boys should have stayed home and fought their own infidels.

Sometimes you'd see a Norman lording it over their foot-soldiers who all seemed to speak a weird tongue that was more like what those Germans spoke. To tell the truth, I thought whatever those northern fighters had to say likely needed to be filtered through their fancy helmets with the wings and birds on top.

Whatever. I should probably do like I heard about in those stories from the fancy crusaders, who keep having their scribes write a line now and again that says, "It was the will of God that" and so on. Then I could tell the part where it's the will of God that a sandstorm almost made me choke because it turned my snot to mud and also almost blinded my horse.

Or the part where God willed the entire camp to get the bloody runs, so that six in every ten men died, and their captains, if they lived, got to send letters home full of lies about fighting and dying for the glory of our Savior.

But dead is dead. And more men than not ended up dead who went on that crusade, glory or not.

We were lucky to be in a camp with a mad captain who cared more about new latrines every day, placed far from the wells, with more time spent laying down lime than practicing at bashing each other with wooden swords. He swore that's why we fared better than other camps, and I decided to believe him and follow his practice all the years I was marching men through anybody's countryside.

Miquel and the rest of us baby-crusaders were late to the whole party. Me, I was late because my uncle Sanç wouldn't let me go till I was sixteen, claiming he was too old to go riding across the world to watch out for me. But now, looking back, you and I know forty-two isn't too old to go riding anywhere. He probably let me go just so I'd shut my yapping flytrap about fighting Saracens for honor.

As if any Saracen anywhere was traipsing on anyone's honor in the Pyrenees hills for the last five hundred years.

Miquel never said what took him so long to join up, but I suspect he left Morella walking in his own goatskin boots and gambled his way to Narbonne, raking together enough winnings for armor and a horse and the silver it took to pay for transport to where the crusader army was trying to mount a war.

What we found ourselves doing was fighting the little pocket wars of the Outremer lords, who were more likely to be spitting fire at each other than at Saracens, keeping busy stealing each other's

wives, land, and slaves. It kept off the boredom of hot summers in
a dusty place. I guess.

.

Ai, Tomás, I talked myself dry and you said not one word while I
was running my mouth like a race pony. I'm too old to work a
whole damn day. And that quill's likely rubbing the wrong way
on your sword callous. Maybe, perhaps Katelina has a jug of wine
and some *brioix* and sausages for supper. Let's write more another
time. I've a mind to tell you about the time Miquel and Hugues de
Beaurain got into their first tussle over an Outremer princess.

E N D • PÈIRE AND MIQUEL GO TO SEA

. . .

BONE-MEND and SALT

Bone-mend and Salt: A Preview

In Book 1 of the Accidental Heretics adventure series:

> Tomás, the son of Miquel of Morella—mutilated and left to die, harangued by his father's ghost—seeks justice with a sharp dose of revenge.

> Jean-Luc, a French knight banned as a Cain, seeks respite—with a sword to battle his betrayers.

> Isabella of Valerós, a Catalan widow, holds her own fate, until a gold-sniffing priest accuses her of heresy.

> Pèire Leteric, a famous crusader, teaches paratge, the honor that pumps life's blood in the world of the troubadours, but finds treachery and murder instead of the honor he earned in the Outremer and at home in his castle at Valerós.

These ruined crusaders battle conspiracy and disaster while trapped in a new war that has run amok: Simon de Montfort has invaded the south in pursuit of Cathar heretics.

.

TOMÁS DE MORELLA Y CYPRUS skulked through the alleys of the
Valerós castle-village, the linsey-woolsey scribe's robe he'd stolen
in Toulouse scratching through his linen undershirt. He'd gone
looking for Clémence but found only the man's doss-kit. And no
letters. More than itchy wool was getting under his skin.

He'd been in the mood for a good street fight ever since he and
Chrétien left Toulouse, wanting more chances to test whether he'd
recovered his speed and agility. Up here in the back of nowhere,
people attack you for no reason, and you can't fight back. Your
mortal enemy appears at dinner, and—

"You have to sit and swallow watered-down wine and tall
tales." Miquel joined him, chuckling, looking sprightly and joyous.
Young. Dressed in the studded black-leather cuirass of an old-
fashioned Aragón mercenary, a warrior with more honor than
coin.

"It was a mistake to come here." Tomás didn't turn his head to
look. It was no surprise. His dead father appeared often in the past
year, telling him how to think, how to move, how to plot and plan.
As if he were twelve again, a young *fadrin* in need of guidance.

"This is the most interesting place for your hunt." Miquel
stretched and yawned. "And there's dicing in the armory."

"I know. I heard at dinner."

"You'll let Chrétien get there first? And then you spend tonight playing foolish gambler, like I taught you?"

"Go away. You have nothing more to teach me. You're dead."

"Not so dead that I don't enjoy watching people deceive themselves. It brings back such good times. *Ai*, I know.

"Go away!"

It wasn't healthy that he let his mind toy with him, even
believed sometimes that his father was there. But in truth, they'd
hit his head too hard when he took that beating on Cyprus.

Tomás bolted ahead through the alleys and then backtracked
toward the armory. Before going in, he stopped at the midden
heap behind the stable to relieve himself, looking around to see if
Miquel had left him alone, startled when the Marquis de Beaurain

came up, as silent as Miquel in his approach, stopping at the manure pile for the same purpose.

"Pèire is as crazy as ever, isn't he?" Hugues said.

Tomás was at a loss for an answer, but then saw that Hugues addressed Father Anselm, the chaplain of Valerós. Lamplight from the armory shone on their faces, while Tomás stood in the shadows.

The chaplain said, "Crazy as a fox. It's reassuring, don't you think, that certain people never change?"

"But you, Anselm? You in a cassock?" Hugues said. "How did that happen?"

"You know I took up the Cross for more than the joy of battling Saracens. I left the Outremer believing I had a vocation."

"There's no man better to help the dying and the battle-sore than you, Anselm."

"Thank you for saying it, though all my gifts come from God."

"But what of Yasmin?"

"I lost her in childbed," the chaplain said.

"*Ai*, my friend, I am sorry. Words won't do. I know what she meant to you."

"She's with God, where I try to be every day."

"Is it enough for you up here, playing confessor to sheep-herders? If you came to me, I'd find you a good place, perhaps in one of the knights' orders."

"I don't require your simony, Hugues. There's enough work for me here. I don't need a gift so grand."

When the men walked to the armory, Father Anselm said, "Is that priest Clémence in your entourage, Hugues?"

Tomás listened more keenly. Clémence carried the letter Tomás needed to save his inheritance from Renard.

"No," Hugues said. "Why do you ask?"

"Don't you remember him in the old days?" Anselm said. "Pèire never trusted him as far as we could fling him with a mangonel. I pray God has indeed saved his soul."

"You can't know what's in another man's heart, Anselm. But I shouldn't be the one preaching forgiveness. The pope's prelate, Arnau Amalric, is using Clémence as a gold douser."

"That old mountebank? Powers to sniff for gold? Is he using a witch-hazel fork or that great snout of his?" The chaplain spat in disgust. "In the Holy Land, when Clémence tried that gold-dousing swindle, Richard threatened to have him whipped in the streets and stripped from his order."

"I'm staying out of Arnau's way," Hugues said. "They are doing everything to find the wealth that seigneurs and heretics in the south have been withholding from the Church. The pope's people haven't asked my advice, and I don't offer."

"And what of your companion, Senhór Renoud of Montcava? Pèire doesn't trust him," Anselm said.

"He made that obvious at dinner."

"Pèire's granddaughter Isabella lived an unhappy life in the Montcava household."

"But she must like what Renoud has done for her son," Hugues said. "He's made the Fontcours estate wealthier than his brother ever managed."

"I didn't know that," Anselm said. Tomás did know, from his searches in Toulouse, and it made him hate Renoud more and long to snatch Clémence's letter, then to run to the bishops' court. "And I shouldn't judge, since tonight is the first time I've seen the man."

"In mixed company, Renoud plays the overbred city-lord," Hugues said. "But in action, he's a fierce business man. He did well after his brother was killed, when he took command of the brigade in Constantinople. I'm betting on Renoud this summer."

"You always knew how to temper your bets," Anselm said. "It is to be hoped that you've retained that skill."

When Father Anselm entered the armory, voices greeted him casually. But when Hugues entered, everyone stood, disrupting the game underway. He motioned the men back to their dice; he wanted to join. The players shuffled positions, because only the knights presumed to play with the marquis. Backed into a corner, Chrétien glanced around and then stayed in the game. Tomás admired his brother's boldness.

Father Anselm seemed to play only for the camaraderie, gambling casually, like a man who makes love for relaxation. Hugues, however, cherished the game. He smiled when he lost, but you could see him recalculating the odds. When he won, the marquis threw everything right back into the game.

Tomás leaned forward, eager to be in a game with this man, but he was supposed to be a lowly scribe. He stayed in the shadows, pulled up the cowl of his robe, and tugged the leather wrapping around his wrist.

■

Tomás felt that tooth, loose ever since the beating on Cyprus; in the last fortnight it had begun to ache. Tired and affected by wine, he listened to the series of stories told while they gambled. Pèire Leteric wandered in to watch. While tossing the gamers' bones, Hugues de Beaurain described the new war machines Simon de Montfort had brought south with him. Tomás let his attention drift, trying to judge how well-trained the bordoniers and house-knights here might be.

"Thinking about French mangonels reminds me of a time with Don Miquel," Pèire said. "That mestitz rascal."

Tomás jerked, knocking into the man next to him. Chrétien dropped his dice, as if clumsy.

Pèire settled back to recite a story. "It was when we were young lads baking in a stinking wasteland outside of Edessa. Miquel and our captain sneaked into a Greek camp to spy on their siege engines. After that, Miquel made a little one to show our engineers how to build it. That baby mangonel had a kick to it, though it was only about so big." Pèire flexed his arm in a gesture, the ropey knots of muscle more like the arm of a fifty-year-old soldier than a man of eighty. "Miquel brought it out at supper to fire beans and hard biscuits at squires in the next camp over. He'd send cobbles flying as far as where the Knights Templar bivouacked just east of us."

Hugues looked up with a smile and murmured to Pèire. Tomás barely caught the phrase, "Hadn't thought of that in years."

"Those Templars' black surcoats and red crosses caused a lust for glory to seize some fellows in our camp. Of course, those boys lacked a few Templar essentials. Like discipline and virtue."

The old man chortled at his own joke; Hugues de Beaurain was the only other person laughing. Pèire said, "One evening a couple of those lads were in their tent with a few Joans and Marias from the baggage train. You could hear them clear over to where we sat. All of a sudden, ol' Miquel bet me he'd win a horse-race."

"To my memory," Hugues said, "you always sat a horse better than Miquel."

"I won't deny it," Pèire said. "I took his bet, but I lost sight of Miquel in just two shakes after the race started. Sweet dancing angels, I had the finest pony then. But when I came to the finish line, everyone was with Miquel at the other end of camp."

Pèire quivered, trying to keep back his own laughter.

"What happened?" another knight called out.

"When Miquel rode by where the baggage girls were visiting, he had an accident that pulled the tent down. Which drew a crowd."

"Did your Templar neighbors see?" someone called.

"By my saintly balls, they surely did," Pèire said. "And that was the end of Templar dreams for those boys with their breeches around their knees."

Hugues, still laughing, said. "My brothers were in that tent, you know. They were mad as the devil. But I thank God Miquel saved them from the Templars."

"*Bon Dèu!*" Pèire exclaimed. "Those Templars think they're holier than a whole race of priests."

A man called out to Pèire, "Did you ride with Miquel or Hugues after that, senhór?"

Pèire said, "Those two stuck together for years, and I rode with them many a time. If you needed a well-trained general," he tipped a finger to point to his visitor, "Hugues was your man. But if you wanted pure guts, you went with Miquel, because he'd save your sorry hind end. Miquel was the best fighter God ever made."

While the story was being told, Chrétien wiggled his way to stand beside Tomás so he could whisper, "These old *peccadors* aren't the same as the others we hunted."

Pèire Leteric offered a toast to riding with Don Miquel de Morella, passing a stone jar among the men. A dozen knights and bordoniers in the room raised their botas and cups. None raised a cup higher than Hugues de Beaurain.

"*Qui s'ho creu?*" Chrétien whispered. *Who'd believe it?*

Tomás still didn't. He treasured the small comfort that no one here knew them, so this scene hadn't been played to seduce him into thinking these people might be friends.

■

The marquis left, which removed the interest for Tomás, since it wasn't his night to gamble. He departed when Chrétien proposed to teach the gullible gamblers a card game he'd learned in Cairo. In the dark, Tomás couldn't find a decent passage through the maze of alleys. Outside what must be the kitchens from the smell of banked-down fires, roasted meats, and garlic, he heard a man's loud whisper echo against the stone walls.

"Hey you! Bastard boy! I'll whip you till your arse bleeds."

Then Tomás heard a stick cracking on flesh. He stepped toward the bully and stuck out his right foot to sweep him down. The man fell but rose up again in a flash. Tomás heard the whisk and clang of a sword being drawn.

"Run, boy!" Tomás called. "Go home now!"

He pulled his dagger from his boot and freed the cord of the cursed scribe's robe, swinging it like a lasso. He whipped at the bully's sword hand, deflecting the thrust of the blade. Then he leaped to attack the brute. When they both fell to the cobbles, Tomás pressed his knife at the man's throat.

Renoud of Montcava cursed him.

Surprised at who he had at knifepoint, Tomás made sure Renoud felt the prick of his blade. Fear—Tomás hoped it was fear—twitched across Renoud's face, puckering a scar in his cheek. Tomás fought a desire to sheathe his dagger in Renoud's throat. Too much yet to be learned from the man.

"Here now. What's this?" a man growled.

Tomás faced Pèire Leteric and his marshal, leaving Renoud on the cobbles, denying himself the pleasure of killing the man who stole his legacy. Before Tomás could answer, Renoud rose, swearing. He kicked Tomás's hand. The knife clattered across the alley.

"This bastard Moor jumped me," Renoud shouted. "Why do you allow mestitz trash in your house, senhór? He needs whipping."

"I didn't know you in the dark either," the marshal said.

"He's just a vagrant bastard."

"No, this man is my scribe," Pèire said. Tomás stepped away from Renoud, astonished. "He's a member of my house."

"You allow your men to attack their betters in the dark?"

"I allow my men to exercise their good judgment. In the dark as well as the full light of day."

Strangely, the old man had declared Tomás his ally. Because he too distrusted Renoud?

"My sword will be the judge if that mestitz *baquelar* ever crosses me again," Renoud said.

Ai, just you wait until your time comes, senhór. Tomás stood, head bent, as the humble scribe he was supposed to be—and to make sure Renoud never had a good view of his face.

"Marshal, help Senhór Renoud find his quarters. I'll go with Tomás the scribe to remind him of the way."

Ten steps beyond, when Marshal Guillem and Renoud were gone, Pèire said, "Never did like that *punxor*. How did you end up with a knife at his gullet?"

"He was beating a child."

"Maybe it was his child to beat."

"I didn't think to ask," Tomás said. "And I lost my best knife."

"Isabella always said Renoud is the devil's own. Yet I can never catch him at it. Hunt for your knife in the morning. Then come talk with me. I'd like to hire your services, Master Scribe."

"Whatever for?"

But Pèire disappeared into the darkness without answering, whistling through his teeth. Worried that the old baron toyed with him, Tomás walked through the twisting alleys, seeking the bachelor-knights' barracks where he'd been given a cot for the night.

"*Qui s'ho creu?*" Tomás muttered. *Who'd believe it?*

"I told you, didn't I?" Miquel hung his arm around Tomás's shoulders, leaning on him as they traversed the cobbled alleyway. "But you boys never listen."

"Make yourself useful. Find the knife that bastard lost for me."

E N D • BONE-MEND AND SALT: A PREVIEW

∎ ∎ ∎

The Mad Woman of La Catalane

The Mad Woman of La Catalane
A Novella

The Accidental Heretics Come Home…

For some, peace is never possible.

ISABELLA, THE STEWARD OF Castell-de-Valerós in the eastern
Pyrenees, has twice been falsely condemned as a heretic. In 1210,
Isabella and Tomás, the mercenary she married, identified their
archenemy: a secret society called Crux Lunata. At the siege of
Minerve, Isabella narrowly escaped being burned with the town's
heretics.

To avoid the crusade against Cathars in the Languedoc,
Tomás, Isabella, and her son Sebastián traveled to Cairo, where
Tomás claimed his son Yusuf.

In late summer 1211, Isabella, Tomás, Yusuf, and Isabella's son
Sebastián set out for Barcelona to join the Valerós knights, who are
training soldiers for Pedro d'Aragón's long-planned invasion of
Andalusia.

1
The Market Town

The Narbonne-Girona road
September 29, Michaelmas, 1211

"AI, DONZEL. IF YOU DRESSED better, you'd get more respect."

A southern seigneur pushed his way inside the market booth to purchase a painted leather baldric, shoving past Isabella, who held the modest cuirass she intended to buy, forcing her to stumble and knock over the vendor's stand of freshly tanned belts and baldrics, the smell of hot leather filling her nose, cows-foot oil smearing her hands. The seigneur's dog, more wolf than Great Pyr and big as a vintner's pony, buried its nose in her breeches. After regaining her balance, she scratched that place near its ears. The beautiful beast looked up at her as if in love, slobbering over her hand and sleeve.

"Leave my dog alone, boy. If you don't want to lose your hand and half your *punxor*."

Being mistaken for a man was good. The disguise had kept her safe while travelling with Tomás and Sebastián in Cairo and on Cyprus. Now they were traveling from the Languedoc to Barcelona, but even on this peaceful road between Narbonne and Girona, she preferred having all the benefit of unadorned squire's leathers and light chainmail.

Being shoved aside: not so good. Isabella glanced back at Tomás, who was dickering for woolen stockings at the stall next door. She waved off Tomás's concern about the man who brushed against her. It was her duty to assert the honor of the inheritors of Castell-de-Valerós. In this part of the Pyrenees, even these lower hills, household honor was a newborn's first breath.

"Girona, isn't it?" She guessed from the man's accent that he hailed from a Catalan city further south. "The town that's never under siege? High walls? That's why your fathers don't have to teach their sons honor?" She called it paratge: the honor as practiced everywhere between the Rhone and Dordogne and Tyr rivers. People in this southern part of Christendom held paratge as an ancient tradition, the honor one owed to forefathers and to every person in one's household. She addressed the big dark dog in an elegant Narbonne accent, while scratching its head: "Who's a good dog? Who's so pretty? Yes, God made you good and pretty, didn't He?"

The dog loved her.

Behind Isabella, Tomás sighed, likely thinking he'd have to rescue her, though he surely knew better. She'd married him, yes, but when dressed as Vidal of Valerós, she invited only problems she could solve without his help.

"I'm the seigneur of Xirgú." The arrogant knight dropped silver in the shopkeeper's hand, not bothering to look her way. "My father died carrying the Cross to Jerusalem. I know paratge."

"Your father knew honor, but died before he could teach it." She didn't remember Xirgú in any crusader stories told by her grandfather, Pèire Leteric. "I am Vidal of Valerós. The seigneur who raised me saw Jerusalem. And Jaffa. And Damascus. And carried home more honor than you've pissed into the gutters of Girona."

Grabbing his fancy baldric from the shopkeeper's hands, the man confronted her, a sneer distorting his too-handsome face.

A leonine mane, like the yellow-haired crusader Simon de Montfort, only in the ruddy shade you find in the south. A bold chin, never challenged when jutted into others' business. Dark, southern eyes under heavy brows. A familiar stare, like in a forgotten dream. Growling, while his dog panted amiably.

"Did your honorable seigneur warn you that undersized donzels must defer to their betters?"

"My seigneur was Pèire Leteric of Valerós. He didn't have betters. Anywhere in the south."

Tomás again stirred behind her, likely ready for a brawl.

The man's brows twitched, his eyes flashed, as if trying to remember a forgotten message. He shoved her aside again and strode past Tomás, intending to bump him in the same way as he did Vidal of Valerós. Tomás stepped back, so the seigneur missed and stumbled. The tall seigneur righted himself and stared down at Tomás. Then he sneered.

"How our blood has weakened. Paratge is sunk in heresy. Our race of men dirtied by blackamoors and Saracen filth."

"It's Kurd and Berber and a landed Castilian grandmother." Tomás quietly repeated his heritage after the rude man had passed out of hearing.

Isabella entered the narrow stall, which smelled of sun-warmed leather tanned just enough for road- and battle-wear. The leatherworker glanced up, more intent on the lunch he'd spread on his workbench than the altercations between seigneurs. He quoted an unjust price, and Isabella considered how badly she wanted this particular cuirass.

"Seven silver morabatins? How about four?" She agreed to five, since the tattered cuirass she'd worn for the past year's travel wouldn't hold up to any more repair. When she pulled off her old vest, that wolf-dog prodded at the gap of her breeches again, wanting another scratch.

"*Hola, gos!*" the rude seigneur called, then whistled for his dog, scowling when he found his pet, its big, beautiful head being scratched by the irascible donzel of Valerós. The dog followed its master, one last look back at Isabella.

"You are a mad woman." Tomás's burned-honey voice in Isabella's ear. "Was that really necessary?"

"It was amusing." She tugged on her new cuirass and left the old one to the leatherworker, to do with it what he might. "Your brother Chrétien would have—"

"Been able to protect himself if his challenge came to blows."

"And what would you have done if he insulted your honor and your family?"

"Punched him in the *punxor.*"

• • •

Yusuf's and Sebastián's perpetual banter pulled Isabella back into the world, to the scents and sounds of the market.

"This is the best market town since Toulouse." Yusuf insisted on his claim, likely so that Sebastián might argue against it.

"I can't agree, Yusuf. Narbonne has a better market than Toulouse. Anywhere is better."

"You're prejudiced. You hate Toulouse. Admit it."

"It's no secret. The gutters of Toulouse are full of false crusaders wanting to burn heretics. Even if you call them heretics, it's a point of honor for people in this land to protect their own. We don't need French invaders telling us what's moral and right to do."

"Perhaps you can buy a charm here, to scare away the French." Yusuf pointed at the red bag of salt tied to Sebastián's belt. "Like you paid to ward off toothache. *Renrén.*"

At being called a fool, Sebastián punched Yusuf's arm. Yusuf rubbed where it hurt, but still hadn't learned to punch back. "Come on. There's more to see."

Sebastian and Yusuf twisted their way through crowd and the aisles of vendors, two paces ahead of Isabella and Tomás. When they'd gone to Cairo the year before to fetch Yusuf (Tomás's son; now hers), Sebastián (her son; now Tomás's) had bonded immediately as a brother with Yusuf. Though they couldn't be more different in appearance or temperament. Sebastián promised to be tall, and at thirteen already had broad shoulders as magnificent as any Valerós knight. Yusuf's beautiful face was just like his father's—or like Tomás's had been before enemies slashed it to ribbons—but he was lighter skinned, slim as a Persian greyhound, and walked like a scholar from the universities of Cairo. Which he was. An exotic creature compared to the Catalan backwoods heritage that Isabella and Sebastián carried into the world.

Yusuf and Sebastián stopped dead still, each chewing on a stick of sugar cane (alleged to have come straight from Cairo), to watch a prize-fight that was beginning in the market square. Men crowded against each other, closing the circle around the fighters, until the four travelers were close enough to be doused by flecks of the fighters' sweat.

One, dressed as a crusader knight, wore a much-mended Templars tunic, stealing glory from Jerusalem's heroes. The other man, bare chested, wore a stained turban and loose cotton trousers like Arab mercenaries. He was darker than Tomás, and many in the crowd were shouting, "Kill the Moor!"

A shill wriggled through the crowd, taking bets. Tomás, the perpetual gambler, waved him off.

"I thought you liked betting!" she shouted in his ear, most words lost in the noise of the crowd.

"Not when the winner is chosen before the fight."

Sebastián called to Yusuf. "Our uncle Chrétien is better than that crusader. Too bad you didn't get to see him fight when we were in Toulouse."

"And yet, our father is better than both of them." Yusuf glanced at Isabella, seeking confirmation.

"You don't know that." Sebastián punched Yusuf's arm. "You haven't seen Chrétien—"

Tomás grasped both boys by the elbow, steering them free of the crowd. "Our Vidal is better than the fellow in the kerchief."

Isabella barely heard his words, busy instead staring across the ring of shouting men at the rude seigneur, who held his dog by its studded collar, either spurring the dog to bark at the fight or holding it back. The intention was hard to interpret, since the seigneur seemed to attend only to Vidal of Valerós, tossing daggers of hatred with his eyes while jutting that proud, too-handsome jaw.

■ ■ ■

When Isabella caught up again, the boys were still arguing about that fight.

"No one fights better than our father. I saw him in Cairo." Yusuf defended Tomás as best in the known world.

"He was being kind to that old man who used to be his teacher. If you saw Chrétien in a dagger fight, like that one in the market between a Saracen and a crusader—"

"The Saracen loses." Tomás interrupted them. "Every time."

"Why?" Yusuf asked, always eager to learn from Tomás.

"He's too dark."

"He's not as dark as you."

Tomás waved away Yusuf's claim before Isabella could say it:
But just as dark as you, dolç Yusuf.

"This isn't for scholars to debate. The purpose of that fight—
and every mummers' show in the south—is to make everyone
believe that Christians will beat the Saracens when Pedro goes
crusading in Andalusia."

Sebastián continued to argue. "The Saracen was a decent
enough fighter. As good as the other fellow."

"The dark one with no shirt? He's no more Saracen than I am.
But if he wins, the crowd will rip him to pieces. His job in every
marketplace is to beg the fake-crusader for mercy."

"His job?" Sebastián remained puzzled.

"They split the winnings. Then ride to the next town and play
at daggers-and-infidels again."

"And riding to the next town is what we should be doing,"
Isabella said, since it was her job to be the most practical.

• • •

After they reclaimed their horses and joined the small train of merchants they traveled with, Isabella recounted the hostile stares
from the rude seigneur.

"What were you doing staring at a man?" Tomás said. "Don't
look at men. You're supposed to be a grown boy. At your age, you
should be watching skirts."

"Is that what you teach our sons?"

"Never in this life."

This good life, where they were all four together, on the road
to Barcelona, to prepare for battle and to ride with Pedro, the king
of Aragón, to recapture Andalusia.

Sebastián rode jittery with anticipation, eager to join a real
army and fight a real war.

Yusuf, curious, wanted to see the king's court and his scholars,
and longed to see whether Andalusia was truly the fabled place
he'd learned about in school.

Tomás admitted he longed to be in action again, after a year
away from the mercenary work he'd been trained to do since leaving his cradle.

Only Isabella rode relaxed, content with the moment, a good horse to ride, a peaceful journey, and to have all she loved with her. In just weeks, they'd join the Valerós knights who'd been hired by Pedro d'Aragón to teach battle tactics. Drowsing on the sunny trail, she couldn't imagine what a better life might be. The sound of the boys' mild squabbles drifted on the breeze. Tomás half rose and turned in his saddle to share that lovely twisted, ruined grin: he, too, couldn't be happier.

Sebastián was tutoring Yusuf on kings and counts in Christendom. "Count Raymond of Toulouse is supposed to be a vassal of Philippe Augustus, but that doesn't amount to much. Raymond's entire strategy was to just wait until the French knights got too hot and went home."

"That didn't turn out to be true," Yusuf said. "There are French knights everywhere we've been."

"That's because Philippe lets his Pays de France knights go crusading in the south. He's not worried anymore about disruptions from John, the king of the Angevines, or from the count of Burgundy or his other counts."

"He *lets* them go on crusade?" Yusuf murmured.

"Keeps them from fighting at home." Tomás interrupted Sebastián's lesson. "The best place for an army of trained knights is in someone else's countryside. Cheaper that way."

Ignoring the interruption, Sebastián resumed teaching. "Alfonso, the king of Castile, took Gascony from the Angevine king John because his wife is a daughter of Eleanor of Aquitaine. John's brother was Ricart Còr de Leon, whom we despise."

"He's dead now," Isabella said. "And whether that king is in heaven or hell—"

"Hell," Tomás said. "Definitely. If there is such as place."

Sebastián again disregarded his parents' intrusion on the lesson. "That leaves Pedro, the king of Aragon, who also holds Barcelona, Catalunya, and Provence. He's a Catholic, so he has to do what the pope says to put down heresy, but he respects paratge and doesn't want to fight his own people. Our Valerós knights are his mercenaries, and our father is his friend. He's the only king to whom we pay tribute."

"Happily." Tomás interrupted again.

"How can you be happy to pay tribute?" Yusuf asked. "Men in Cairo shout in grief when they have to send tribute to the Ayyubid sultan."

"It's what you pay so you have an army great enough to do good in the world. My *àvi* Pèire said that merchants and seigneurs who don't pay their taxes don't understand how big the world is. They think their little personal armies can defend against a king's army. Of course, nobody wants to pay a shaved brass bareelones if they owe tribute to a fool like King John in the Angleterre."

Isabella felt the thunder of horses vibrating in her breastbone, before she could trace the direction of the sound or warn the others. Mounted bandits galloped into the midst of gentle, armor-free merchants. Out of the thunder of riders, someone hurled a javelin, striking Tomás, who toppled from his horse.

Yusuf lost control of his horse and fell near Tomás. The merchants were screaming for mercy, but the attackers slashed at neck and shoulder, butchering them.

The last that Isabella saw, Sebastián stood alone, unhorsed, in the middle of the massacre, his dagger in one hand, sword in the other, screaming a Valerós battle-cry: "*Desperta, ferro!*"

Awake, steel!

2
The Song

SCRATCHING TO GET A HOLD.

Rock and moss. Lichens. The pungent odor of Stone pine. The ferric tang of blood trickling down her throat. Choking, she tipped her head—tried to...

Enough movement to startle a crow that wandered close by, alone, away from its friends who cawed and gargled at each other, arguing over a feast for—

She scrabbled again for a handhold. If she lived, perhaps the others lay as she did.

Open mouth. Call to whoever might—

Gag on blood.

She hated blood.

Scratch for a hold.

The murder of crows rose, as if all of one mind, cawing, their abrupt flight releasing wind in their wake, their communal cry one long note of mournful regret.

A dog snuffled nearby, then sniffed and licked her face, panting over her. It tipped its head, as if studying her, deep brown eyes like a concerned child. It nuzzled against her hand, wanting to be petted.

"*Hola, gos.* Come, dog!" A voice shouted. The dog pricked its ears. It was the pretty beast from the market-town. "Nothing more for us here. Come!"

The dog pattered away, and then one horse pounded up the trail, the beat of hooves fading in the distance. Only Isabella left to hear the echo.

Alone.

And near the sea. She smelled it on the darkening fog, the waves echoing up the hillside, matching her heart beat.

It still beat.

Yet she was alone, lying here with crow food and—

More pattering paws. Growls. Signals to each other, like those mercenaries had when they checked the bodies. They'd missed her, not seeing where she'd fallen, broken, in a cleft amid granite boulders.

A howl—a wolf calling to friends—and more pattering. What was it Master Guillem taught her to do when the wolf comes? Make yourself big? Swing a stick? Shout?

Wait until they come for you?

Three. She counted that many rumbling voices as the animals claimed the crows' dinner. More than they could consume in a night or carry back to their den. So they had no reason to come for her. Though better if they came now. If she joined her family right now, instead of slowly bleeding in the night fog, waiting for the sleep from which one never awakes. Until final judgment.

If this wasn't the final judgment.

The paws, padding near. Slavering breath.

The judges decided: all is for naught.

Fire flashed. Then flashed again.

"*Hai-ee!* Off with you!"

A fire brand, swinging nearby, struck one of the wolves, which yowled and scampered away.

"Go! I shall take what's left!"

Fire flashed again.

Now a human scrambled among the fallen bodies, searching like the bandits had, scavenging, kicking at rocks, complaining. Finding less than the crows did.

Fire. Too close to her face. Isabella closed her eyes, the only thing she could move.

"*Ai!* This one lives." A caw.

Just one of the crows.

• • •

Isabella burned, afire in fever and pain because the Arab doctor took the infant from inside her. Blood. So much blood. Drenching her hand when they let her let loose. Head pounding with bright-red pain, the same red as her bloody hands and thighs and—

The bleating cry of an infant.

"He's calling for you, you lazy wench. Get up and care for your child."

Her mother-in-law. Scolding in that round Toulousain accent, always scolding. So Isabella tried to move, but hands held her down, murmuring voices bid her be still. A woman spoke, a voice too warm, too deep to be her mother-in-law, who must have abandoned Isabella to the servants.

"This head wound is bad. Help me, *cor dolç.*" Sweetheart. The woman spoke in the Catalan accents of these hills, not Toulouse. "We need to clip this man's hair close so I can tend the wound."

When the infant cried again, Isabella cradled it close to her breast, pain radiating, throbbing everywhere, as if pain ran in her veins instead of blood and rubbed against her bones to set them on fire. *It's a boy. You must feel true joy. And red-headed, like his father. The very image of Nicolau as an infant.*

"No, his grandfather!" she cried.

"*Shh.* Let go. Let God do His work. You are only dreaming."

Her hands empty, Isabella stood alone, dressed in another woman's azure-blue robes, her linen shift whiter than it ever came from the washer-women. Her head ached. And no wonder: a metal circle wrapped around her brow, pressing down.

"He opened his eyes, *Àvia.*" A soft voice, like a child or a rock-spirit, speaking to her grandmother.

"*Hola, mon amic.* Are you with us?"

"He's sleeping again."

"If only that were so. Well, let's get busy. You and I shall do the best we can with herbs and prayers."

"I wish a doctor could help us. That Moorish man, Ibn Jafar."

"He's gone back to Toledo, dear. At least, I hope he's safe. If we can stitch this one gash, it's the worst. All the blood on his cuirass is from his scalp."

Warm water bathed Isabella's skull. She tried to speak, but instead dreamed more of fire. A child chanted prayers.

"*Àvia,* I keep saying the prayer from Our Lord. But look, his breath scarcely moves this feather. Let's console him before he dies. That's what Rixenda says we must do for bonhommes."

Bonhommes. Goodmen. Goodwomen. Heretics. That's who cared for Isabella.

"*Ai*, dear heart. We don't know what kind of man he is. Perhaps he's one of the murderers. So many dead in that swale."

"No, *Àvia*, we must help even murderers to come to God."

"*Òc*. There's no time to find Rixenda to come say prayers. Fetch more water. I sat in the candlelight enough times when an old man or old woman was being consoled. I know the words."

Isabella felt drops of water, like rain trying to fall on a hot summer day, sizzling against her hot skin. She'd heard those prayers chanted before, but not from a priest.

"You will come soon before the Father, the Son, and the Holy Spirit. You are the temple of the Living God, who says, 'I dwell in you and walk with you; I will not leave you without comfort.'"

The child's voice: "I like that part best."

"With my breath," a wisp of warm air, scented with clove, passed over Isabella's fire-hot face, "receive the Holy Spirit. Whatever sins you give unto God, they are forgiven. May God bless you and bring you to your good end. For this world will soon pass away, but if you do the will of God, you shall abide forever."

"Shall I say the next words for him, *Àvia*?"

"If you know them."

"I do. Rixenda taught me to say, 'I long to do the will of God.' And then I pray for this stranger to receive the power of God."

Again, drops of water fell over Isabella's face. The fire burned inside, leaving her so parched, she couldn't move her tongue or open her lips to speak.

"Very nice, child. Now we say the last consoling words. '*Parcite nobis*. We pray God that you accept this blessing, which God has given you.'"

"What is *parcite nobis*?"

"It's in Church tongue. It means *spare us*. Will you say the answer for him?"

"*Parcite nobis*. For all this stranger's sins in thought and deed, I ask pardon of God and of all Christians."

"Well done, child. Now, pray to the Holy Mother while you help me remove his shirt. We'll look for more wounds, and then tie the red thread around—"

The light voice, the angel voice, said, "*Àvia*, it's a woman."

"*Ai*, and all that lovely hair gone."

...

Isabella opened her eyes, hoping to see the sweet face of the woman who'd cradled her when she last fell asleep.

Instead, a very white girl gazed down, solemn, so close her breath tickled Isabella's face. White hair, white brows, rose-pink at the edges of her eyes, a pink tongue darting at soft lips.

"Are you dead, ma dòmna?"

"No." Only a ghostly whisper came out. Isabella, therefore, wasn't sure if she spoke the truth.

"May the Holy Mother of our Lord make you well or deliver you to heaven." The white child stroked Isabella's face, but instead of warm, human touch, the strokes scratched, as cold as metal, as if Isabella were indeed dead and in her grave.

"Blanca!" A woman's deep voice called. "You mustn't. Our saint's hand is only for a priest to use, to ask God's blessing."

"Rixenda says we don't need priests, *Àvia*." She called the other woman grandmother.

The white girl stepped back, tracing a cross in the air above Isabella with a jewel-encrusted object. The child grasped a finger bone, as old and weathered as anything a dog might unearth, but wrapped in a filigreed net of silver that trapped rubies and sapphires, gleaming in the rushlight.

"Give it to me, dear. That's a good girl." The warm voice of the grandmother. A rustling. "Here's a new, clean cloth. Can you wipe her face for me?"

The white child leaned close again, her nearly transparent fingers stroking Isabella's cheek. In the same delicate way that baby Sebastián stroked Isabella's earlobe while nursing, seeking and giving comfort. The girl laid a cool cloth on Isabella's forehead. "We pray that the Good God has not turned His face from us."

"No, Blanca, we only pray for comfort." A gentle correction, in a deep earthly rumble, as deep as any woman might speak. "God never turns away."

"Rixenda said that this morning when she lit the fire for us. When I told her about the dead men in the swale." The white child merely explained, not arguing.

"Mmm?" The earthy hum of a woman who listened and considered. "That isn't what Rixenda meant. She knows, like you and I do, that Jesus and his Holy Mother and our dear Father in heaven, they care for us."

"Rixenda says it's a wonder the sun still rises."

"Will you please fetch more cool water, Blanca? And another clean cloth? Let's do the chores God gave us, and let God worry about the rest. Then you can do your work for today."

All dead in the swale.

Isabella opened her mouth to speak, but her swollen tongue filled her mouth, no room for words to come out. Drops of cool water dribbled onto her lips.

"Just a little water, my girl. Don't try to swallow too much. You'll make yourself sick again."

Isabella drifted again, as if she lay in those comforting arms, rocked by a holy, sweet mother who murmured honeyed nothings, the way one sooths a nursing infant.

. . .

"Ai, los lobos!"

"It wasn't wolves, dear. Only feral dogs. Everything's gone feral in this part of the world." A husky voice, but a woman's. No crows. The woman who'd chanted the heretics' consoling prayers. With the clove-scented breath.

Isabella strained to open her eyes, which seemed swollen. Stone above her. A stone wall beside her. The woman who spoke hovered just out of where Isabella could see. Isabella strained to turn her head, but pain shot through her like lightning after thunder.

"We cut your hair so we could stitch up your scalp." The woman's voice rumbled near Isabella's ear as she again cooled the heat of Isabella's face with water. "We didn't know you were a woman then. Else we'd have tried harder to save your hair."

"So much blood." That too-white child appeared again, staring down at Isabella.

"*Òc*, Blanca. But let's not worry her about that."

"We couldn't see to work, there was so much blood."

"It's all washed away now, *cor dolç*. You helped save her."

"Like how we are washed in Jesus's blood." The child sounded thoughtful. "So much blood."

"Don't think on it, Blanca. Just draw the Holy Mother, the way you do. The shedding of blood is done. It's long ago. We are all clean now."

"But those bloody gashes, *Àvia*."

"Look how fast God heals when He puts His hand out to save us. Go do your work now, Blanca."

"It must be sad for her to be all alone. All those bloody bodies. Everyone dead except her. As if God—"

"Shh, Blanca. Our new friend has you and me with her. You shouldn't have seen that swale. Please go to work now. Think how the Holy Mother consoles her children. How she keeps us safe here in our cave."

All alone.

All dead in the swale.

Isabella couldn't speak, only ache beyond belief, and burn. Wolves-aren't-wolves. The crows. All the bodies in the swale.

She wasn't alive. Tomás and their sons dead. This was hell.

All alone.

■ ■ ■

Isabella lay on a pallet in a cave. Rush lamps illuminated enough that it was possible to make out pale stone walls and, amid the shadows, folded blankets, foodstuffs wrapped in hemp-cloth and stacked on ledges out of the way of vermin.

Distracted by a scratching sound, Isabella watched through swollen eyes (it hurt too much to weep any more). The girl called Blanca drew on the wall, creating a larger-than-life image of the Holy Mother, a crown on her brow, a halo sketched behind her, fingers raised in blessing, like the blessing Jesus offers in the frescoes painted in every church in these southern hills.

The drawing was the woman Isabella dreamed herself to be. This fresco had taken weeks of work, so it must be what Isabella saw in her fever-dreams. The girl was working on details of Our Lady's face, making her even more kind and beautiful.

"How is her robe so white?" Isabella's voice sounded even rougher and hoarser than before.

Before she lost everything.

She squeezed her eyes closed. Each time she wept, she fell into a crevasse, deeper and darker than this cave where she searched for and never found Sebastián and Tomás and Yusuf.

Blanca went on working, not looking around. "It's called lead white. My uncle gave it to me. The blue is made from ground stones, real stones. My uncle bought these in Narbonne, too. I need more. Do you think I can find blue stones to grind? If I look very carefully in the hills. That's how I found this."

The girl nudged a scabbard that clattered to the floor. She kept painting, while she talked. "Is that why you cry in your sleep? Did you kill someone?"

Tomás's sword.

The clanking sound brought the other woman in, who retrieved the sword and placed it back a stone ledge. Isabella squeezed her eyes tight again, feeling the pull across her scalp, a slight tearing of the cuts at her hairline.

"*Ai*, you're bleeding again. Let me help you."

"Who are you, ma dòmna? Where am I?" Isabella spoke more words than she had since she first woke here.

"I'm Rubea of Castel-St-Jean. We found you in the forest and brought you home with us. Such as home is."

"Above Portvendres?" Isabella tried to remember the last village they passed. "We're safe? Here at St-Jean?"

"Far uphill from Portvendres. We aren't at St-Jean. This is the safe shelter God has provided for us."

"I visited St-Jean once with my grandfather, when I was a girl. He bought horses from the seigneur." Refusing to weep, Isabella remembered that village. "There's a Roman church in the village, with beautiful frescoes."

"All dedicated to the Holy Mother, from time before our grandfathers can remember." Rubea seemed busy, abstract, while washing and tending Isabella's head yet again.

"We rode over the ridge one day," Isabella said, "and men were out with the swing-ploughs and oxen. The yellow of the terraced fields between the rock ridges shone like gold in the sun. Such a beautiful day."

"I hope those fields are being harvested," Rubea said. She straightened her brown linen robe, then brushed at her eyes. "Though I wonder who's there now to do the work."

"And we sat in your courtyard while two jongleurs sang songs about love and dying. One was from the north and sang about linden trees and birds and lonely streams, sad enough to break the heart of..."

Tears welled up again. Isabella hovered on the edge of that crevasse of grief.

Rubea said, "Here in the south, our troubadours write the best poetry. Our jongleurs sing the best songs."

Blanca whispered from where she was working. "Like cypress in the wind. Songs that smell of lavender and thyme." She began to sing a troubadour's song about an old warrior remembering with his last breath when he first made love.

This time, Rubea wept. A choking sound. She threw her apron over her face at the same moment that Blanca turned around.

"*Àvia*, are you well?"

"It's the toothache, dear heart."

"The cloves are almost gone, *Àvia*. Rixenda doesn't know when she can get more."

"Not to worry, Blanca. I asked Rixenda to find a blacksmith who might come here. I'll have that tooth out. No worries." Rubea tended to Isabella again. "It's time we learned your name and how you came here. What grandfather brought you to my house?"

"Pèire Leteric. I'm Isabella of Valerós. We—"

"May the Good God preserve us!" Rubea dropped the cloth she held, fumbled to hold on to the bowl of water. "Valerós is condemned, too? And then the crusaders hunted you too, like animals? Are we all lost now?"

"No, it was only bandits." Isabella, startled by Rubea's loss of composure, asked, "What happened at Castel-St-Jean?"

"It's my fault," Blanca said. "Their hearts could not open to the Queen of Heaven." She pointed to the figure she painted. "You can see Her, but only if you believe that heaven is here with us, right now. Then you will know Her."

"It wasn't your fault, dear heart." Rubea tied a clean cloth around Isabella's head. "Those men mistake the Dark God for the Good God."

"They called me a Magdalen and burned our chapel." Blanca turned her own calm attention to her painting again. "I don't know what a Magdalen is, but it must be very bad."

"You aren't a Magdalen, and you are very good." Rubea set her bowl aside. "I'm going to bathe our friend, dear heart. It's time you went to find Rixenda, to help her bring up food and firewood."

"Of course, Àvia." Blanca laid her brush carefully on a tile, beside two finger-sized pieces of charcoal. She covered her cup of paint with another piece of tile, and then slipped a shawl over her shoulder and left them, once again singing the dying crusader's sad song.

3
The Corona

WHEN BLANCA WAS GONE TO find Rixenda, Isabella asked,
"You're a Good Christian, ma dòmna? One of the bonhommes?"
That was the word she'd heard others use to describe themselves.
"Is that why the priests and crusaders chased you from Castel-de-
St-Jean?"

"I was a good Roman Christian. A woman of paratge. Until I
found myself living in this cave, accepting the help of bonhommes
to keep my girl's soul stitched in her body a few more years."

Rubea turned back the quilted covers and tugged open the ties
of the linen shirt Isabella wore—not a shirt Isabella recognized.
Rubea talked as she washed her patient, who weakly tried to help,
usually failing.

"The only heresy I ever whispered before now was the same
as every woman in the south thinks: Why pay a priest to ask God
to forgive my sins? God's right there in my garden, amid the birds
nesting in my orchards, in the heart of my poor dear girl. He's so
close by, I can ask whatever I need."

"Then it's Blanca they condemned as a heretic."

Rubea tut-tutted that notion. "The poor girl isn't a heretic. She
just sees the world in ... simple terms. But a passel of priests
traveling through visited our chapel, and then reported her to the
bishop. You see, I can't make her stop drawing the way she does."

"It's beautiful." While enduring the bath, Isabella studied the
white-robed figure that gleamed in the rushlight.

"Except she always paints Sancta Maria as larger than our
Risen Lord. When the priests questioned her and asked her to say
her creed, I couldn't help her." Rubea wetted her cloth again.
Isabella stared into the warm eyes of the woman in the fresco.
"Blanca believes all prayers she hears, dear girl that she is. You
can't discuss a creed with her. She just knows what she knows, and

paints as she does, because a force inside moves her to make these pictures. The priests became quite unhappy when they asked why she painted St-Maria."

Parched, Isabella asked for a drink, interrupting Rubea's story. It took a moment to finish swallowing before she could speak. "What did she tell them?"

"The worst possible answer." Rubea wiped a balm on Isabella's parched lips. "I still hear her soft voice, excited and happy to talk about her paintings. Blanca said, 'We call her Sancta Maria, but she's really the glory of the world the Good God created. I paint Her so that men will know bliss, like I do, and the Dark God will leave their hearts.'"

"*Bon Dèu!*"

"Since she's innocent as a lamb, Blanca repeated what she'd heard the bonhomme teacher Rixenda say: 'This church holds the treasure of the Perfects.' The priests began shouting, calling her an evil Magdalen and a heretic. Called me a mad woman for sheltering her and allowing her perfidy."

"How did she get away from them?"

"While they shouted for the knights they travelled with, I grabbed Blanca and we ran. We scarcely took time to pick up our shawls while running for the forest as fast as we could."

"But the knights who travelled with the priests?"

"You know these hills if you come from Valerós. There are footpaths only people of our domus know, trails horses can't follow. When night fell, many bonhommes from the village joined us. Then we walked through the forest for three days, until we came to this place. Many travelled on to join cousins who could shelter them. We depend on the bonhommes here in the forest for food."

"Your own knights wouldn't fight for you?"

"My knights are off serving Pedro d'Aragón. We've lived in peace for generations, so who knew we'd need them in our own domus? Likely they haven't heard what happened. How Castel-St-Jean has lost all honor."

"The Church and its knights destroyed your domus." Isabella fought memories of burning and destruction in Minerve, of disfigured knights in Bram. She shivered, then blamed it on the chill of Rubea's wet cloth against her hot skin.

Rubea said, "Their knights burned our chapel and castle, if you call our little tower a castle. Then they burned every house in the village where people didn't stand in the doorway and shout their creed. Now my village is under interdict, and the Church sent new priests, who teach everyone left behind how to say their prayers properly, and who follow my people into the woods to discover whether they succor heretics. Their food is rationed, so the Churchmen can tell if any is being smuggled out to the forest."

"What do they still want with you?" Isabella asked. "They have your property. Is it just to judge your soul? Or to call you back to pray to God in the proper way?"

"They awarded my land to Frankish crusaders, who took my people's food stores to feed their horses. I don't know what more they want. They've taken everything."

Already tired of lying helpless on that pallet, Isabella pondered that burned village and all that was lost. "When I'm well, when I can travel, come with me to Valerós. We'll be safe there. Not all our knights are gone with Pedro. And Valerós is rendered to Pedro. The crusaders will never touch it."

Rubea helped her to sit up, then tugged this way and that to replace Isabella's linen shift with a clean one, worn soft from many washings. "We shall see. Blanca won't want to leave her painting."

"Winter is coming. You can't live here. You'll freeze."

"We shall see. God still provides for us."

"Perhaps it's at Valerós that God means to provide for you."

■ ■ ■

Isabella ate now: broth, a bit of bread and mashed beans. She struggled less in her sleep, though Blanca whispered that Isabella cried.

When awake, she watched Blanca paint the Queen of Heaven. And prayed the prayers she knew for souls of the dead. *Grant them eternal rest, and may light always shine upon them.*

At one time—with the darkness lit only by rush lamps, Isabella wasn't certain about morning, evening, or night—she woke to the sound of pounding on the stone walls.

Blanca stood close to the wall, seeming perplexed, hammering her picture of St-Maria with a rock.

"What are you doing?"

The girl held out a sheet of gold leaf. "I want Her corona to be shiny. Everything gold belongs to the Holy Mother."

"That's not how you do it. You need *guix*."

"*Guix?* Like horse-glue?"

"No, nicer than that."

The girl listened closely while Isabella explained how to create a sticky substance that would keep the gilt stuck to the stone wall. Blanca recited what she needed, counting off the items on her thin, white fingers.

"Honey. Two eggs. Chalk."

"Can you find those? Then we'll use some of your white lead."

"People from the villages want to give us eggs, but only my *àvia* eats them, which is bad. Rixenda says if you eat food from the congress of animals, you cause souls to be caught in the world of the Dark God."

"Yes, I know. But you aren't going to eat the egg."

When Blanca returned, Isabella guided her through the mixing. Blanca had enormous patience for the tedium: whipping the white of the egg and then keeping only the residual liquid; grinding the chalk with a mortar and pestle until it was smooth, mixing in the honey and egg and lead; more grinding, grinding, grinding.

"How do you know this, ma dòmna?" The sole curiosity that Blanca showed over the entire time that Isabella instructed her.

"I used to make—" how to describe what she'd most loved doing in the old days, when Valerós was peaceful "—copies of the gospel. Like priests read to us."

"Did you have lots of gold?"

"No, none. I used yellow paint. But a friend showed me how gilding is done. When I lived in Toulouse."

"There is no such place."

"Of course, there is, Blanca. I lived there for five years."

"But it's gone now. I heard the knights say, before they chased us into the woods, 'We lost Toulouse.'"

"The city isn't gone. I was there this summer. They meant that Simon de Montfort's siege failed, not—"

"But they did take all the gold from Toulouse. That's how I found the Queen of Heaven's crown. Is this smooth enough? Is it *guix* now?"

"Yes. Now brush it over the wall where you want the corona."

Blanca was busy immediately, the white lead in the *guix* doing its job to show where the *guix* had been painted.

"Blanca, what do you mean, you found the crown?"

"Her gold. The priests carried it with them, all the way from Toulouse. But all gold belongs to the Queen of Heaven. So when we ran, when they were shouting at me, I put it in the basket with my paint pots, wrapped in my shawl. I spilled a little white lead when we ran—only as much as always trickles into my fingertips when I paint. But I saved all of Her gold. Can I pound on the corona?"

"No, the *guix* has to dry. You'll know it's ready when you touch it. It will make a scratchy sound as you lift your finger."

Blanca was already busy again, cleaning up. "Do you want to see it? The Queen of Heaven's gold?"

"If you want to show me."

The girl, with great effort, pushed aside the block of stone she stood on while painting, and reached into a crevasse in the cave's wall. She dragged out a leather bag and then opened it to show a pile of gold coin. Isabella couldn't make out the figures on the various coins, but among them was a red bag. Some priest had carried a charm for toothache.

"My *àvia* knows I have the gold leaf. But I'm saving this for a surprise. I shall gild this cave to show the Queen of Heaven in all Her glory. Do you want to help pound this gold into leaf?"

"I think you'd better tell your grandmother about the gold."

Blanca tilted her head, considering. "No. I want her to be surprised when she sees the Queen of Heaven in all her glory. For my *àvia*, her heart will be filled with joy. I'll wait till then."

...

Isabella woke from a bad dream. Rubea sat nearby, knitting in the dim rushlight. Blanca wasn't with her.

"Ma dòmna." Isabella was still surprised by her hoarse voice. "May I have that sword you found?"

With a curt nod, Rubea fetched the sword, still in its carved scabbard, from the ledge and laid it on the pallet near Isabella.

"Your killers plundered everything useful. The bodies were stripped. No other weapons left behind."

"Then you came."

"To steal from the dead, you mean?" Rubea took up her knitting, wooden needles instantly clacking. "You'd steal too, if all you owned and everyone you loved were stolen from you by Frankish wolves."

"Indeed, they were."

"Sorry, my dear. I was lost in my own sorrows. I've a toothache that makes me selfish at times." Rubea held her work a bit closer to the rush lamp. "Now tell me your story. It's many days since that attack. You should talk about it, and not just weep in your sleep."

"First, ma dòmna, I have to tell you a secret, though it isn't mine to share. Blanca carried away a bag of the priests' gold. She hid it here."

The wooden needles stopped clacking.

Isabella continued. "She plans to gild the cave. I wouldn't betray her secret except it means—"

"They shall never stop looking for us."

"Indeed. I need to travel soon. You must come with me, home to Valerós."

"Is Valerós far enough to be safe?"

"If you don't tell anyone where we've gone."

"Then I, too, shall share a secret. I don't believe bandits killed your friends. It was the same Frankish knights did it as burned my home." Rubea resumed knitting. "Tell me your story, cor dolç. Who did you lose in that swale? Whose sword do you hold?"

"It's my husband's. He died there. With our two sons. One from my body, the other my husband's. The others we travelled

with were strangers. Just a small merchant train we rode with for
safety. We were about to turn off that road to go to Valerós."

"From Narbonne? Toulouse?"

"From everywhere in the world. We'd been traveling. I
wanted to be gone from this part of the world. I was—I was inside
Minerve when the French laid siege. And my husband needed to
fetch his son from Cairo and his mother from Cyprus. We were
coming home from the Outremer."

"You've lived a more exotic life than mine, ma dòmna. To sail
across the Great Sea!"

"Yet here you and I both are. Will you help me up? I have to
learn to move again."

• • •

It hurt to walk. It hurt to sit. Weak from too many days on the
pallet. What hurt most still: her head.

In spite of the pain, Isabella walked, leaning on Rubea, who
was as old as Isabella's mother would have been. They walked to
the far side of the hill, where Blanca had painted another St-Maria
on a rock near where a spring bubbled from the group. They slowly,
so slowly, followed a narrow trail around the hill, where a rock
ledge just above the cave gave them a bench to rest on and gaze
out over the forest and hills below.

"There's a monastery on the other side of that mountain,
above the Great Sea." Rubea pointed, but clouds had caught on the
mountain top, so Isabella couldn't discern mist in the trees from
smoke rising out of monastic fires. "Some of their servants help us,
bringing bread from their ovens and beans from the abbot's store."

Beyond that mountain was a thin line of no color, since the sun
wasn't shining. The Great Sea.

"From up here, one can't see good or evil in the world,"
Isabella said. "It's only magnificent." Her head pounded, but she'd
decided that she couldn't nurse illness any longer.

Rubea said, "I've listened to the bonhomme teachers, who say
that life isn't good versus evil in the ways the Roman priests
taught us. It's not about angels and demons. The whole of life is

merely to be aware of itself. Beyond that, we only hope to do good and be comforted."

Isabella closed her eyes against the beauty of hills and sea, and considered Rubea's words. But then she once more saw Tomas and Yusuf fall, and Sebastián holding his sword high over his head, shouting. "Good and evil seem as real as these trees and rocks."

"Òc. I still feel it. I'm not likely to be perfected in this life." Rubea sighed again. "I lost my husband early in life. But I believe that I did everything God asked, since He placed me over others in my domus, making me responsible for their well-being. Keeping them safe. I made good children, then lost them young. I can say that I helped make our gardens grow, to provide food and medicines that helped others keep their children alive."

"When it's all taken away by men who seem to incarnate evil, are the bonhommes' teachings any more comfort?" Isabella folded her hands, as if praying. Then caught that, and sat on her hands.

"The Church has stolen my land, sent men to chase me through the hills. Calls me heretic and mad woman. I'd been loyal to the Roman church, though paying a priest to pray hasn't brought God closer. But you can't ask God for anything more than peace within your own heart. That's what the bonhommes mean when they wish you a good end."

"You prayed their final prayers over me. I remember it like a dream. I couldn't stop you." Isabella tucked her hands into her sleeves, feeling chilled and tired.

"Yet I omitted saying their creed. I'm not sure I understand all that yet. But after the fire at St-Jean, I believe what the black-robed teachers say, that there's a Good God and a Dark God."

"Two Gods cannot rule life."

"Yet you and I believe that the Father, Son, and Holy Spirit live in the one true God. Still, our own priests call me heretic and mad woman. So here I am, sweeping out a cave every day. Baking thin, hard bread in an old kettle, mashing lentils, and peeling onions." Rubea's voice cracked for a moment, as if she choked on a sob. "I am a woman without honor, no longer able to take proper care of the people of my domus. All I can do is pray that the people from my domus found safety. Only God can help them."

"How many were lost?" Isabella wanted Rubea to keep talking. The trickle and splash from the stream where they sat wasn't enough to drown out thoughts about her own lost ones.

"My steward died when they burned the tower. The kitchen girls ran for the woods. I hate to think how the crusaders treated those poor women if any were found. The laundry women—I know they're resourceful. Perhaps one of the armies moving through here needed laundry women. The little boys who kept the geese and ducks, and fed the puppies in the kennels? I hope they ran off with their mamas or their fathers. Or found an uncle to shelter them in the woods, the way we found our Good Christian friends here."

Rubea stood up from where they rested by the spring.

"Let's get you home, ma dòmna. Rixenda will be back with Blanca, and they'll worry about us."

Shakily, Isabella stepped down the nearly hidden trail, one hand on Rubea's strong shoulder, the other persistently making a sign to ward off evil.

• • •

"It's tacky." Blanca held up her finger, the one that had tested the *guix*. She sat patiently on her stone block, brushes and charcoal spread out beside her, a packet of gold leaf in her hand.

Rubea said, "Where did you find gold, my dear?"

A guilty person might have glanced to Isabella, perhaps condemning her for betraying secrets. But Blanca didn't feel any guilt. "When you called me to run, I picked up my paints and the gold that had come to our chapel for Our Lady. She needs me to paint her, to help people see Her."

"The gold, my dear?"

"It belongs to Our Lady. All gold belongs to the Queen of Heaven."

Exhausted from that walk, Isabella stretched on her pallet again, pulling a blanket over her, finding that she shivered in exhaustion. But Blanca was determined to start her work. So,

Isabella gave her instructions, one idea at a time, the way her friend in Toulouse had taught her.

> Find the flattest tile.
> Wash your hands.
> Lay a gold leaf on the tile.
> Wrap your hand in that cloth.
> Blow on the *guix*. Lightly.
> Lift the leaf with just your little finger.
> Wave it over the *guix*. Let it fall in place.
> Repeat for the next leaf.

"Very nice, Blanca. It's perfect."

"Oh, ma dòmna. It's like in my dream."

"Now press down on it with the cloth. You can burnish the leaf until it sticks to the stone. Don't press too hard."

"It's just what Our Lady wanted."

"Wash your hands before you do it again," Isabella said. "Grease on the *guix* keeps the leaf from sticking."

"It isn't very shiny, ma dòmna."

"In the morning, when it's dry, you can burnish it again to make it shiny. You're doing a wonderful job, Blanca."

"It's because when I breathe on the *guix*, a little bit of God inside me leaks out."

"Maybe so."

"Oh, it is, ma dòmna. That's why we aren't afraid to die. It's just God inside of us whooshing out, to help Our Lady do the work that must be done, to comfort the world."

■ ■ ■

Later, alone, Isabella found she wasn't convinced. In the dark, after Rubea extinguished the rushlight and the three of them lay under blankets on thin straw pallets, Isabella again whispered prayers for the dead, not convinced that the brush of breath on her hand was anything Divine leaking out.

■ ■ ■

That night (if it was night), Isabella dreamed of Valerós. She stood on the castle parapets, gazing out over mountains, as far as the Great Sea. A hawk soared overhead.

A wind rose. Not the freezing mistral of early spring, but the kind that warmed your bones in May, carrying scents of lavender and pine. Bordoniers—farmer-soldiers home from fighting—plowed the lower fields with oxen, while young boys tended freshly-sheared sheep that browsed in a vetch field left to lie fallow. The boys alternated a game of tag with fetching lambs that wandered into the buckthorn hedge. In the peach orchard, several pairs of women propped up boughs that had been overburdened with fruit the past season. They worked carefully, since the blossoms awaited in a pink-tinged fuzz, ready to pop into bloom on the next warm day.

Closer by, the kitchen girls chatted while they culled beans that had soaked in spring water over night. The tall brown one declared she was in love, but couldn't tell if the man knew she breathed and walked the earth. She had no brother or mother to speak to him. What to do? Each had a favorite charm:

> *If you can get a hair from his head, I have a red thread to bind him.*

> *It's wormwood you need, to put in his wine.*

> *I know a chant that calls down rays of the sun so that he sees only you.*

> *My brother sleeps in the dormer with that man. He'll put a binding talisman in the straw where he sleeps. If you saved a baby tooth, that's the best charm.*

The old mistress of the cooks and maids, Ermessen, came out of the inner kitchen, to ask why they dallied. She listened to the excuses, and then promised a real charm, guaranteed to work.

> *Take this bread to where he works in the field, and say an Our Father when you give it to him. Don't argue, girl. I know it works on account of he already had a charm off me to bind you.*

On the track far below that ran between the spelt and vetch fields, two horses raced, one carrying Sebastián and therefore sure to win, and the other with Tomás, almost keeping up in spite of that lurching way he rode. Yusuf waved a banner at the end of the road to signify the winner.

No, not a banner. That painted scabbard that held Tomás's sword, both the gilding and the red paint gleamed in the spring sunshine.

• • •

Blanca stood over her again, shimmering white in the rushlight. She once more traced a cross over Isabella's face with the saint's finger, its touch dry as dust, feeling if it left a mark where she drew it across Isabella's forehead, nose, and chin.

"Don't leave us," Blanca whispered. "We'll die if you leave us. I dreamed that you were the last soul to see Our Lady's glory."

"You won't die. But I do have to go home. Come with me."

Rubea joined them, carrying an armload of firewood. "Blanca, let our guest sleep. She needs her strength. Don't bother her."

"She isn't a bother, ma dòmna. I was saying that I need to leave. To go home to Valerós. Today. Now. Please come with me. I can offer you much better shelter at Castell-de-Valerós."

"Òc," Rubea said, agreeing readily. "We have little to carry. Just enough to keep warm on the road, and some food."

"Thank God you agree." Isabella felt relief, both for the promise of bringing them to safety and for the promise of their company on the way to Valerós.

"But I can't leave Our Lady again," Blanca said. She stayed busy with her work on the wall, painting another patch of *guix*, preparing to gild rays of gold from the corona. "People can't see all Her glory."

Gentle talk and persuasion carried on for a long while, until Blanca stopped responding to their pleas.

After bringing warm porridge from the fire, Rubea sat beside Isabella.

"You should come with me now," Isabella said, still unwilling to leave them living in the cave. When Blanca went to the fire to fetch hot water, Isabella whispered a desperate idea. "Perhaps we can carry her away when she sleeps."

"You know that would be wrong," Rubea said. "It'd break her heart. We'll follow as soon as she's ready."

"Can you travel alone?"

"We came here."

"I'm not happy with the idea of you on the road alone," Isabella said. "It's All Saints in two days. You can't trust this weather. I'll send people from my village to fetch you."

"I'm staying with Our Lady," Blanca said, rejoining them. "Look at Her. How can you bear to leave Her?"

"She'll always be in my heart," Isabella said. "I promise you can make new frescoes in our chapel. More people will see Her glory."

"The Queen of Heaven prefers to light this cave."

A glance from Rubea, a shake of her head: no use arguing.

Isabella struggled with disappointment and remorse as she packed. She wanted to keep arguing, but the remaining argument was which of the three of them was most touched by the moon:

Blanca, who served St-María compulsively.

Rubea, whose worry for the people of her village gnawed at her soul, while care for Blanca and life in this cave were wearying her body.

Isabella, who would wail at the moon and plead with God, as soon as she was alone in the forest.

With little to carry away—Tomás's sword, the small packet of beans, nuts, and turnips from Rubea, a borrowed knife and flint, a wool blanket that Rubea had stitched to be a cloak—Isabella dressed as best she could in her remaining serviceable clothes (washed and mended by Rubea) and a borrowed shirt and linsey-woolsey coat. She could walk to Valerós in these boots, but only just, and she needed to pray for modest rain and no snow.

Her modest pack tied with a hempen string, Isabella heaved it over her shoulder, and then embraced Rubea.

"I owe you my life, ma dòmna."

"We only do what pleases God."

When Isabella tried to embrace Blanca, the girl held her at arm's length and stroked Isabella's cheek, her pale fingers as cold as the cave.

"Carry this with you, so you are always consoled."

Blanca slipped a cold stone into Isabella's hand: a broken roof tile that had been chipped to form a rough circle, its edges not fully smoothed. Isabella tipped it so that rushlight caught the white glow of the painted image: another sketch of the Queen of Heaven.

"*Mercé*, Blanca. Please come when you can. All my domus— my household and villages—they need to see Our Lady, too."

Blanca tilted her head, as if listening. "I'll ask. *Bon día.* You are consoled wherever you are."

4

The Church

ISABELLA DIDN'T TRAVEL CONSOLED, her body and mind too busy ignoring pain, remembering the trails that led to Castell-de-Valerós, worrying about Rubea and Blanca left behind. She whispered admonitions and calculations for the journey, keeping company with her own voice. If she didn't talk to herself, she heard Tomás's voice: *Are you sure this is right?*

By midday, she'd only just reached the road that led to the nearest village. Not even a league from the cave, Isabella rested on a boulder, reconsidering what she might be able to achieve. It became harder with each step to ignore the pain. She'd stumbled too often. Valerós was much farther than four days' walk if it took this long to go such a short distance, hurting this badly. She lingered under a holm oak, considering alternatives.

Rixenda slipped from the woods onto the deer-path that served as a trail. They'd been introduced at the cave, but Isabella had seen the bonhomme teacher only enough to recognize her: a tall, bone-thin woman with dark hair escaping its scarf to cascade down her back. Eyes as dark as that cave, but always probing, watching.

"*Dèu els beneeixi.*" Rixenda began the bonhommes' blessing. For a woman so thin, she had a smooth, honeyed voice, every word spoken as if it were part of a mother's lullaby. "We ask God to make you a good Christian and lead you to a rightful end."

Isabella, too tired, couldn't remember the response, and couldn't rouse herself to receive the kiss of peace.

"Rubea's prayers didn't make me into a different kind of Christian. I don't think you can convert me."

"We don't seek converts." Rixenda sat, folding her long, thin frame beside Isabella on the boulder. She rested her hands on her

knees as if in prayer. "Your own soul will lead you to what best consoles you and brings you closer to God. I will only try to persuade
you in one case: if you tell me that what you believe now keeps
your soul from God."

Isabella had spent too much time on the pallet considering that
question. "A vestige of God lives in all things. People wish their
souls could be the image of God. But I think it's better just to
recognize that God is in all things. We can't truly know the divine
in this life, except to believe God is within us."

"Then you do believe as we do." Rixenda passed Isabella her
bota of water

"No, I don't. You bonhommes reject prayers for the dead."

"Because the dead are gone from us. If perfected, they're with
God. If not, we don't know. But they aren't lingering somewhere
that we can beseech God to protect or forgive them, not if they
themselves never asked for forgiveness."

"I can't endure that thought."

"You want to join those you lost?" Rixenda declined to take
the bota back, indicating that Isabella should keep it. "And yet you
must go on living. This world—the material world that holds
evil—it still holds you, doesn't it?"

"Òc. I have to go on. To help the people in Valerós, if nothing
else." Isabella remembered that dream of Valerós again. Once she
began describing it, she couldn't stop. "In my village, some
women are swingling hemp, getting ready to comb it through the
winter days. Other women are spinning wool and flax. The
woodcutters are up in the hills, bringing down firewood to sell in
the lowlands. Farmers are gathering in cabbages and leeks, and their
wives are laying this summer's bounty down in the cellars, nestling
provisions in straw. Their children are in the woods, gathering nuts
and mushrooms. All that comes from God—and I need to do what I
can to protect them, because that's what God gave me to do in this
life. I must do it, for the sake of my family's honor. Else, I shall truly
go mad."

"Yet you aren't well enough to go now. Do you want me to
help you back to Rubea's cave? Or shall I find people in the village
who can care for you until you're well enough to travel?"

"I must go on."

"Then wait here while I find friends."

. . .

Waiting: what Isabella had learned best in Rubea's cave. Waiting to wake from nightmares. Waiting to sleep and escape all thought and pain. Waiting to watch Blanca busy at her work, the only release from monotony and grief. Waiting for Rubea to bring water to ease her burning thirst. Waiting to return to Valerós, to safety and the balm of everyday life.

She dozed, waiting for Rixenda, and so was startled when the teacher slipped in beside her again.

"You must return to shelter with Rubea."

Isabella roused and shook free of Valerós dreams, not knowing she'd been asleep. "I want—"

"A new priest came to this village yesterday with a passel of knights. It's Sunday. He's preaching against heresy at three masses. Let me help you up. You can lean on me. We'll reach Rubea's cave before nightfall."

"I must go forward. I'm a Catholic. My castle is rendered to Pedro *El Católico*. The priest isn't my enemy. I can ask for his help."

Rixenda leaned back, away from her. "Ma dòmna, are you mad?"

"No."

"You're feverish again. This is madness."

"No." Isabella now saw the logical way through this pain and misery, as if a veil had been lifted and her vision cleared. "Pedro was a friend of my husband's. My knights are working for him, training soldiers to fight in Andalusia. Madness would be *not* asking for help due me as a steward of Castel-de-Valerós. Or to think I can travel alone in this forest. I need to be home with my people."

"If that's what you want, I'll help you."

. . .

At the edge of the village, Rixenda disappeared back into the forest, whispering, "*Dèu els beneeixi.*"

Isabella missed her immediately. Not for the sake of a shoulder to lean on and an arm that caught her whenever Isabella stumbled, the bony fingers that grasped Isabella's elbow to guide her. She missed the lull of the woman's comforting voice. Her calm sureness in the world. She missed the way Rixenda smelled: of herbs and the forest, the odors of her mountain home. Rosemary. Lavender. Rowan oil.

Entering the village, one might think it deserted. But it was Sunday and there was a new priest. Following the track to the center of the village and finding the church? A child could do that.

The church was a simple one, in the old style, not even a tower to distinguish it. Only a large arched door broke its stone walls at the level of the road. High up, square windows allowed light inside, the openings sealed with waxed goatskin. She's already seen that this village would never be able to purchase glass or make their own. Not on the main merchant road, they'd never manage more each year than what they could live on.

Inside, Isabella stepped into the back, joining the tallest of the villagers, remembering to stand on the men's side. The dim interior felt like Rubea's cave, with its barrel-vaulted ceiling, and only enough candle branches to illuminate the priest at the altar, and perhaps the first few rows of ranking lords who sat on backless benches. Along the sides, on the walls under the vaulting arches, someone had painted the twelve disciples, each standing formless in white draping robes, the faces nearly identical. Each could be identified only by a symbol in their crudely painted hands, like the keys that St-Peter held.

The priest was repeating the familiar words of the mass, not yet preaching. He had a heavy French accent, which made it difficult to recognize where in the mass he was. Rather than listen, Isabella studied the fresco showing the Holy Mother holding her infant, attended by angels. Unlike Blanca's white-robed lady, this figure was dressed in black, as if already mourning the death of her son. No one in the village had a rich uncle who'd give the painter white lead or gilding. Only a circle of brown-and-ochre paint denoted Our Lady's corona.

Isabella repeated prayers with the men around her while staring into the figure's eyes. But the fresco painter had provided only dark wells, a dark void, with no talent to explain comfort and love as Blanca did with her brushes and homemade paint.

After looking over the villagers—in their best linen and wool, faces washed, and eagerly anticipating their visitor—Isabella studied the five knights who stood in front, to the left of the altar. The kind of knights Tomás detested: much better dressed than the people around them. Clinking about in chainmail at the wrong occasion. *"The cow that gave her hide for those boots was a nobler creature."* Isabella tended to be more forgiving of mere vanity than Tomás ever was. From the colors on one man's surcoat, they were from Narbonne. Not Frankish knights out riding after crusading season had ended. One Narbonnese knight (barely past the age of donzels) turned in profile to gaze on his friend, revealing such a beautiful face that he could challenge the angels for shedding light from heaven. Isabella judged quickly (he was in love with the friend upon whom he gazed), and then noticed that another man kept glancing at those two men, his brows furrowed and mouth drawn up in jealousy.

The priest bowed to kiss the altar and then faced the crowded church. Around her, people shifted to get a better view, and Isabella gave way. In the rustlings, a huge shepherd next to her, a rich band of lanolin across his tunic as if he often sheltered lambs in his massive arms, purposefully stepped aside so she could see the priest's face: a round-faced, round-bellied man no older than she was, wearing a Cistercian's white robe. He was many French-inflected words into his lesson before Isabella stopped looking around and listened. The priest preached in the local dialect, but his French accent made it hard to understand the words.

"Heretics consider our beloved Jesus Christ to be an imitation of flesh, not true flesh. They reject alms and tithing in a way that also rejects the Holy Cross."

Ai, Dèu!

"Heaven is forbidden to heretics."

The Frankish priest used many of the same old, grievous words that Isabella had heard for years from white-robed preachers on the streets of Toulouse.

"The communion of saints is forbidden to all members of a family if any one of them shelters even a single heretic, until all persons in the family shall throw themselves upon the mercy of the Church for judgment."

So familiar, the words lulled Isabella, so exhausted she could sleep on her feet. Then the priest woke her from muzzy thinking.

"Of all villages of the hereticated and the damned, Castell-de-Valerós is the worst among spawn from hell. For Valerós lords plot with the heretics, inviting Saracens to invade Christendom."

Valerós!

Isabella, sheltered among the tallest of the town's people, glanced around, afraid that anyone might recognize her. She wanted to move toward the heavy arched door, but the way was blocked by shuffling field workers.

"You are called upon to spit on these fools' shadows or any print in the dust where their feet have tread."

A chill froze her spine as the priest read names of villages and seigneurs and their families. As hideous as it was to hear the church's condemnation of one's friends, living and dead, he hadn't finished.

"Worst among the heretics and witches is Isabella of Valerós, condemned as a heretic in Toulouse and Minerve, who claimed herself redeemed by our Lord and Savior. But we know this woman to be sunk in heresy. She's believed to have died, but if any should find her or shelter her, her sins shall become yours, and you shall be judged and condemned."

The ice in her blood, the air stuck inside her, the voices inside screamed for her to run. But she remained trapped in the crowd.

Then that shepherd next to her sneezed. And sneezed again. After his third mighty blast, the men around them murmured, "*Dèu els beneeixi.*"

The priest paused. After a torturous silence, he barked in anger. "Who calls blessings in the common tongue? It is an abomination and heresy. Who is it?"

As if they were five heads on one body, the knights at the front swiveled to see. The knight in the middle, beloved by the angel-knight and spawning jealousy in another of them, was Matheus of Xirgú, the rude knight from the leather stall, that hand-painted baldric draped across his broad torso. As crowded as Isabella was among the villagers at the back of the church, his gaze caught hers. It took him a heartbeat longer to recognize her and begin to bellow.

"Vidal of Valerós!"

Isabella, weaving through the woodcutters and shepherd-boys, made it through the heavy wooden door before hearing chainmail clinking at the front of the church.

Outside, she ran.

5
The Mountain

LIKE MOST EVERY VILLAGE in these steep hills, one riding trail led through town. The stone-and-plaster houses crowded the trail and the terraced hillsides, each against the other. Beyond the village walls, just high enough to keep children and goats and milch cows in, lay an expanse of unfenced pasture.

Isabella darted across the square and past the village well, seeking any alley leading off the road. Down the first narrow walkway, she sprinted toward what she assumed was the village wall, only to be stopped by the muck heap waiting to be tossed over the wall. No space left to scale the wall here. A cow mooed from inside the byre in the understory of the nearby house, pleading that it was past milking time. A wooden cart lay in front of the byre, the kind built to be pulled by men, not donkeys. Its bed filled with threshed grain stalks, the cart wasn't large enough to hide in. Hiding in the byre wasn't possible—the knights could search such a small town before the villagers made it home from church.

She ran on, wiggling through the space between wall and house, listening for pursuers. Another muck pile, this one well-rotted and ready to be hauled to the fields.

With no other passage, she ran into the kitchen of a house, its door held closed only by a wooden latch. Hearing the knights shouting at the other end of the town, she peeked through the front door cautiously, then darted across to another narrow alley where the town wall was visible at the end. She leaped over the wall.

And slid down a ten-foot granite cliff, scrambling over rock-rose and hawthorn, scratching her hands when she grabbed to slow her fall.

With no time to catch her breath, Isabella bolted through the open grass land and ran into the woods, as deep as she could go, forgetting about pain, busy orienting herself under dark clouds and seeking the footpath. Praying that she could disappear faster than armored knights could pursue. When she heard horses, she found a footpath that led in the other direction. Three times she waded across narrow streams that flowed down the mountain to the Great Sea.

She had to rest. In spite of the jabs of pain, Isabella scaled a holm oak and lodged herself in upper branches. The evergreen leaves blocked sight of the rocks below. The clouds thickened, making the afternoon so dark she couldn't judge how long until night. She couldn't do more than feel the throbbing in her head and bones while she quieted her breathing enough to think.

A wolf howled, far up the mountain, perhaps another mountain over. Another answered.

She shivered. So cold, though it was only All Saints, the last of the harvest season. Was the Feast today or the next?

She'd left the warmth of Rubea's cave only because she wanted to be home, sheltered at Valerós. But the Church was on a mad quest for Cathars, looking under straw beds in every cottage and under every rock in the countryside. So she couldn't go home, even if she were strong enough. Not if it was under interdict. Not when the heretic-hunting Matheus-of-no-honor was seeking her as the lone survivor of the massacre that had killed Sebastián and Tomás and Yusuf.

Winter was coming—her bones felt the threat of the first storm, soon to blow into the mountains. It was too far to go to Toulouse to join Chrétien, Tomás's foster-brother. And she'd drag danger to his door. Her sister was safe, far away, married to the newly declared marquis de Beaurain. But Isabella couldn't walk a hundred leagues to reach safety with her sister, unless borne on the wings of angels.

And not one angel seemed to take interest in Isabella's fate.

■ ■ ■

"You are a mad woman."

Tomás whispered in her ear, the way he did when Isabella woke him in the morning, but he only pretended to complain.

"*Eu vos amor,*" she whispered, declaring love. She reached for his hand.

Grasping lichens and twigs.

She'd slept in her tree-bough cradle. The clouds might be thicker or it might be nearer to sunset. She needed to find a familiar path before it was dark, to go back up the mountain. Because the only possible action was to return to shelter with Rubea, get stronger, and then—

The choices shrank as she pondered them. Get a letter to Pedro d'Aragón or Chrétien and beg them to help Valerós? How, exactly, to do that from a cave in the Pyrenees? She considered what she'd often said she'd do if nothing were left in her world: retreat to a women's convent, find solace in studying scripture and doing each day's work. Where was the closest women's cloister? Up the Aude valley; again, a hundred leagues from here.

Her teeth chattered and her bones rattled. She couldn't continue to sleep out in the open. The first winds of that promised storm crackled through the autumn leaves of her tree. Time to travel.

Her sense of direction—and the many years riding horses in this kind of country—proved worthy. She'd run much farther than seemed possible, carrying all that pain. The first comfortable sighting, just as night closed around her: Rixenda kneeling near that trickling spring where Blanca had painted Our Lady on a boulder. The teacher was filling three botas with water. Rixenda glanced up as if expecting her when Isabella collapsed by the spring, exhausted.

"*Dèu els beneeixi.*"

"May God console you," Isabella answered. Though she longed for more consolation than the world had.

"Our friends have agreed to flee. Can you go further tonight?"

"In the dark?" Isabella didn't know if she could move from where she'd sunk to sit. Rixenda had lit Blanca's rush lamp. In its iron cage, the burning reed cast both light and shadow on the rock above where the spring trickled from the rocks.

"I know the way. It's best to go now. Can you walk more tonight? It's only a league to another place that will offer safe shelter."

Only a league. Isabella had walked three that day, at least.

"Òc. I'm glad you convinced Rubea."

"I didn't. Blanca believes that her saint is calling her to go out into the world." Rixenda shook her head, her shadow doleful in the rushlight. "Rest here a bit. Then join us. They should have finished preparing to travel. Are your clothes warm enough for the storm that's coming?"

"I have a cloak Rubea made for me. Why are you coming?"

Rixenda stood, slinging the botas over her shoulder. "I learned in the village today that they took my family. All I had left was my daughter and her two sons. The crusaders took them. Burned their house. I have—" she hesitated "—nothing but God to console me. I can at least help my friends."

She touched Isabella's head, like a priest does. But instead of a blessing, she said, "You have a fever again. I'll fetch another blanket for you."

Rixenda slipped silently away. Isabella rested a few moments, changing her prayers from desperate pleas to gratitude for having friends to travel with her. And a safe destination, wherever it might be in these woods.

She picked up the lantern, which flashed one last time on St-María's white robe. She made her way over rough ground, pausing at that ledge above the cave, the place where Rubea showed her the surrounding mountains. She untied her small travel pack, found that extra linen shirt, and wiggled into it. She set the cloak aside along with Tomás's sword, deciding to wear the sword instead of carrying it in her pack. After she tucked that tile icon from Blanca and the packet of food inside her shirt, she tugged her jerkin back on and wrapped up in the cloak. Her hands were already icy. She'd ask Rubea for rags to wrap her hands, since the night was turning colder by the moment.

She straightened, ready to join her friends when five knights entered the clearing below the cave. She hastily pulled the lantern's shutter closed. She hadn't heard horses, but then, no horses could come within a quarter league on these rocky footpaths.

The knights arrived on foot, carrying hastily-made torches: pine branches ripped from trees, the rough ends hacked enough to keep a smoky pitch-fire burning. They milled about the trampled earth surrounding Rubea's cooking ring. Their leader, Matheus of Xirgú, stood with his hands on his hips before the cave and shouted.

"In the name of our Savior, I command you to come forth and face judgment."

While his voice still echoed in the night, bouncing on trees and boulders, his dog appeared beside Isabella. As if they were back in that sunny market-town, the huge dog cozied up to her, nuzzling her hand, begging to be petted. She scratched its ears to keep the dog from whining. The dog settled closer, warming her where she'd been freezing just heartbeats earlier.

Matheus shouted again.

Rubea emerged from the cave. The mistress of St-Jean was dressed to travel, a blanket around her shoulders as a cloak and a small bundle held in front of her, like a soft shield.

"Indeed, senhór, I am prepared for judgment. I ask forgiveness of my sins, and I say my creed as any true Roman Christian would. Who sent you to judge me? Shouldn't a priest stand in court and judge whether I say my creed with conviction?"

Matheus didn't answer her challenge. "You are loyal to the Roman Church? Not a heretic? What are you doing out here in the wilderness?"

"I'm a poor widow. This is the shelter that the Lord our God has given me. The Church does not yet condemn a woman for being poor. Is that still true?"

The other knights were grousing about coming such a long, rough, and dirty way on foot, in the freezing cold. In another moment, this mutiny would take them back down the trail.

Except Blanca appeared.

She carried a candle, a good beeswax candle that illuminated her too-white face so that she glowed like an angel. Or a ghost in a child's tale. She too was dressed for travel, in Isabella's ragged left-behind boy's clothes. Rubea had spoken in her usual warm, commanding voice, but Blanca's rang out shrill, child-like.

"*Parcite nobis*. We are here to sing the glory of the Queen of Heaven."

"*Ssh, ssh!*" Rubea hushed her. "Not now, child."

Matheus roared. "Vidal of Valerós!"

"*Òc*," Blanca said. "We are going to Valerós now."

"Rushing to join your hereticated kinfolk?" Matheus misidentified her, angry beyond reason. "Out to rebel against the Church with filth?"

"I only praise the Good God. And serve the Queen of Heaven."

It was over in one interminably long moment.

Better if they'd taken Rubea first. because Our Lady would console Blanca. After Matheus pierced Blanca's heart with his sword, Rubea endured twenty heartbeats until his friend slashed Rubea's throat.

The dog nuzzled and prodded again when Isabella's hand froze and she stopped breathing. She'd led those knights here. To invade her friends' safe place and murder them.

Like she'd caused Tomás and Sebastián and Yusuf to die, foolishly arguing honor with the master of Xirgú.

Matheus wiped his sword on Blanca's tunic—Isabella's—and commanded the knights to search the cave.

Very little was found. While the knights complained about wasting their time, he ordered that the worthless goods they found be dropped on the bodies in the clearing. One of the knights—the one who looked at Matheus with love and longing—fumbled with the flint-and-tinder box Matheus handed him, striking several times before a spark caught and ignited the ticking on the top of the piled good.

Isabella's straw pallet.

Flames rushed quickly. The knights called Matheus and his would-be lover back into the cave, exclaiming over the gilded image.

"There's more gold hidden here." Matheus's voice echoed from inside the cave. "There has to be. Look harder."

A second ransacking began.

Matheus appeared at the cave's entrance with his faithfully trailing knight. "We need to search these woods."

"At night?"

"*Hola, gos!*" Matheus shouted for his dog. "We have torches. We found three travel packs inside. So, there's one more filth-loving heretic to find. Help those bastards get the gold from the cave so we can search further. *Hola, gos!*"

The dog rose, but then settled again to let Isabella scratch its ear.

Matheus, now alone by the fire, called his dog again.

Rixenda appeared near him in the smoky haze.

"*Dèu els beneeixi,*" she said, her voice still as calm as a lullaby. "May the Good God console you."

Before Matheus could strike Rixenda, Isabella leapt from the ledge. Before she regained her balance, Matheus slashed at Rixenda with his sword, then turned to face Isabella. She swung Tomás's sword, wanting to send Matheus to the devil before she died. The scabbard smashed against his skull.

"*Desperta, ferro!*"

Isabella meant to shout, but only a rasp escaped her throat.

She struck so hard that she lost Tomás's sword, hearing it clatter in the underbrush. Matheus fell at her feet, across Rixenda, whose soul had already gone in search of its next incarnation.

The dog pattered down from the ledge, carefully choosing its way on the dark path. Coming to rest beside Matheus, the dog looked up at Isabella, as if questioning. Then it bent its huge head and licked its master.

Again, Isabella ran, leaping this time into the thicket. Across the clearing from where Tomás's sword had fallen.

■ ■ ■

As she crouched, breathless, the other knights discovered their fallen leader.

"*Jhezu del tron! Is he dead?*"

"*I don't think so.*"

"At least he got the bloody heretic before she managed to kill him."

"I thought these dung-eating heretics didn't raise arms. Afraid of killing babies' souls before they're born as rats or pigs."

"Lies. All lies."

"What do we do?"

"Carry him out of here. Find a healer."

"Hope we find the horses before we have to tell him the only gold is what we scraped off the wall."

"Look what I found. Booty stolen by heretic grave-robbers."

"Call his wolf-dog back from the bushes. Matheus will butcher us with a dull knife if we leave his dog behind."

"Hola gos!"

. . .

The dog didn't follow, still snuffling near where Isabella cowered, until the knights disappeared back into the woods, bearing Matheus in a hand-sling between two of them.

"Carried him home drunk this way once. In Narbonne."

"Òc. I about pissed myself when he woke up, grabbed his sword, and started shouting about lost honor."

Their noise echoed up through the trees, the knights having no need for stealth. Finally, the dog ran off after the knights.

When their shouts died, Isabella edged into the cave, her cloak pulled up close over her face. She wished it would stop the stench of the fire, but had no luck.

Our Father in heaven, forgive us…

She chanted prayers for lost souls, whispering, each breath begging God to console the dead. Inside the cave, lit by the flicker of the pyre, most of what remained was litter: broken paint pots trickling color and lead white across the dirt floor, paint rags set aside to be washed in spring water, dried beans spilling from slashed hempen bags.

Our Lady's corona had been peeled from the wall. Tiny slivers of leaf gleamed in the light of Isabella's rush lamp. The saint's face had been hacked with a rock, so only one eye now gazed, seeking to offer a last measure of comfort. The white hem of her dress was scarred brown, by dirt kicked up from the floor.

Smoke from the fire was filling the cave. Isabella pushed aside the stone used as a step whenever Blanca painted. Reaching into the dark crevasse, she felt pebbles and larger stones, finally touching the corner of that leather bag. Seizing it, she left the cave, pausing on the upwind side of the clearing to retie her now-miniscule pack and secure Our Lady's gold inside her jerkin.

Our Father, forgive us…

Isabella scrambled back up to the ledge. The rush lamp still smoldered. With the shade pushed up, she followed a footpath that led away from the ledge, with no idea of where to go. The knights had come up and then followed down the footpath that led to the village. Isabella had no idea where this other path might lead. But if there was a path, then people lived along it. She'd find shelter somewhere.

...

She had to stop too many times. The lamp served her well, though it wouldn't last through the night. The wind had picked up for a while, but blew at her back. She could see her way along the un-familiar path, though no sign appeared of even a woodcutter's shed.

She paused frequently to stop shaking. Clutching the lantern, grasping the cloak close around her head and shoulders, still she trembled.

It was the cold. Her nose burned with it, so she pulled the cloak up over her face, leaving her knees to the cold.

It was the uncertainty. She peered through the dark, seeking any possible shelter from the wind, finding nothing to do but to continue down the trail.

It was the fever, come back again. She'd lain on that pallet under Rubea's care, saying prayers for the dead, since a fortnight after the Feast of the Assumption until now, nearly All-Saints. Two cycles of the moon. Past time for fevers and chills. She was only tired, and could push on past that, to sleep when she found shelter.

It was the smell of the fire, which clung to the cloak.

She'd turned it over, so the other side was wrapped close to her face. That didn't help. She needed the cloak. Her jerkin wasn't enough to keep warm this night.

She breathed through her mouth, hoping not to smell anything. *Our Father, forgive us...* The warmth of her breath through the cloak sent a cloud in front of her, the departing spirit lit by the dull glow of the lantern.

Which flickered.

Isabella paused again, consigning herself to the loss of the lantern's diminishing light, peering deep into the woods for any kind of shelter.

Hearing the soft nickering of horses.

Following the sound, she walked out of the trees into a grassy swale where five horses were hobbled. She knew this swale. The last of her lamplight flickered on the pile of boulders where she'd lain undiscovered, until Rubea rescued her.

By that tree was where she'd seen Tomás and Yusuf fall.

The very center was where Sebastián had stood and shouted the Valerós battle cry.

No sign of that now, just a peaceful swale with horses.

Murmuring sweet things, starting in Catalan, she walked slowly among the animals. Shields and blankets tied to saddles. These belonged to soldiers prepared to bivouac, and the number left no doubt whose horses these were. She touched the flank of the horse that seemed most gentle, felt the mark burned there.

A mark she remembered from horses her grandfather once purchased. He wanted them for their Arab blood, and one stud had lived for years in the herd at Valerós. The mark of Castel-St-Jean.

Horses now ridden by the knights who destroyed Rubea's domus and made her a fugitive. Who had just slaughtered that kind woman and the gentle, moon-touched Blanca.

One horse had a different brand. She chose that one to make friends with, to carry her away. Isabella felt in her packet of provisions for the three wizened apples Rubea had given her. She whispered in the horse's nose, making friends, and slipped the horse a reward as it allowed her closer. She unbuckled the shield and let it drop beside them. The horse shook its head, happy enough to be done with that burden.

"*Ai, kalila.* Tired of standing out here in the night with your friends? Wouldn't you rather ride like the wind?" It didn't matter what she said. She simply repeated gentle words. And offered a wizened apple.

The snow began then, the first powdered flakes, stinging her face in the wind. She untethered the horse, slipping the last apple as a reward when she mounted.

"Go!" she said, leaning close, speaking in Catalan, guessing that might be the horse's training language.

The horse started down the road—the direction where Isabella had been traveling weeks before, not the direction she'd come from. Exhausted, she let the horse have its head, believing it had a better idea of where to find shelter from the storm.

. . .

The snow fell more heavily, laden with water from the Great Sea, but cold and sodden. She shook her shoulders every few moments to lighten the snow mantle from her cloak.

Which was now wet through.

The sound of the Great Sea was near, in a tumult of storm, which meant she must be near the merchants' coast road. However, the horse chose to go up the mountain, not pausing at the branch in the road. "*Horses see better in the dark than we do.*" Was she no more than five when Pèire Leteric taught her that? The snow more than dusted the road, but the horse continued. It knew where it wanted to go. Ahead, a faint glow up the mountainside indicated that they would indeed find people.

So long without sleep, so many leagues traveled that day, that night. She hadn't eaten since saying goodbye to Rubea and Blanca, almost a day ago. She couldn't trust her inclination to sooth her thirst by catching and eating snow. Each time she nodded in the saddle, she jerked herself awake, though that movement startled the horse. But they were going somewhere, together. With rest and this horse, and perhaps a tiny bit of Our Lady's gold, she could ride to Valerós. Pretend to be someone else. Be safe.

Then a wolf howled. Or a feral dog.

Another animal answered, so close by that the horse spooked. Another howl, and then the horse bucked.

...

Off the steep side of the trail, Isabella tried to breathe, her belly in spasm. No air came.

All of the spirit of God had leaked out. She had no more inside her. Wings fluttered overhead. A raven settled near, its head tipped, studying her.

When you no longer breathe, when God has leaked out of you, then you are dead. All consoling is done.

"*Aahhh!*"

She cawed. The raven croaked back.

Her belly jerked, and sucked in a rasp of air.

"*Dèu!*"

The raven raised its wings and rose up, leaving her alone.

Who knew it hurt so badly when God rushes back inside you?

She lay still, slowly breathing again. She'd fallen on a rock that jammed the purse of gold into her belly and ribs. When she could breathe, she got to her knees, nearly buried in snow in just the time it took to regain her breath.

May the Good God console us all. I commend to you Sebastián and Tomás. And Yusuf, who learned to be good without a teacher. Receive Rubea and Blanca and Rixenda, who consoled me and who were forgiven by their bonhomme friends.

The road was empty, but covered with enough snow that it was easy to follow in the dark, so she couldn't wander back into the woods. The horse must have continued up this way, but snow had already filled its track. She was alone on the wild road, her boots soaked now like her cloak. The sound of the Great Sea behind her, she walked toward the faint light she'd seen earlier.

Dawn appeared to be near. In her fever, her ears buzzed, as if filled with song, but not the song of angels.

Around a deep bend in the road, the forest gave way to farm sheds and a stone building crafted in the new style, with a tower and high walls. The buzz in her ears was the chant of monks in the chapel of that monastery Rubea had pointed out that day they talked on the ledge. Where the servants were kind to poor bonhommes.

Once again, she shook the layer of snow from her cloak, which was now heavy with snow-water. At the porter's gate, she knocked, her freezing fist stinging as she rapped on the lintel.

Still alive. Another day to pray for the dead.

After knocking a third time, she stepped away to leave room for the gate to open.

Parcite nobis. I pray for all of my beloved, for whom no priest will pray, for any amount of silver.

God alone knows there's no need to name Isabella of Valerós in prayers for the dead. Her soul had received consolation, and couldn't bear to be consoled any more. Vidal of Valerós also had been rendered unto judgment.

Who stood knocking at the gate? She might be anyone in the world, anyone who'd ever looked into the eyes of the Queen of Heaven. Whose face had been hacked from the wall. She might be Vidal, a donzel of Cyprus, where no one living here had ever been.

She threw back the sodden cloak, let snow fall on her bare head, and called out to the porter in Catalan. *Help me, grandfather.*

"*Àvi, m'ajuden!*"

I will give you all the Queen of Heaven's gold if you will let me sit by your fire and pray for the dead.

E N D • THE MAD WOMAN OF LA CATALANE

■ ■ ■

CRUX
LUNATA

Crux Lunata: A Preview

In Book 3 of the Accidental Heretics adventure series, French knights are helping Castile and Aragon invade Moorish Andalusia. So, the Troubadour world enjoys a brief respite from the crusade against the Cathar heretics. Yet for some, peace is never possible.

Tomas, the mercenary, is sent by Pedro d'Aragón to disrupt the Moorish defense. In Andalusia, some say that Tomas inherited El Cid's magical sword and demand he help his own clan. But destiny sends Tomas to meet his nemesis: a boy who is a djinni.

While the armies gather, an ink-stained monk uncovers a plot by Crux Lunata, a secret order of knights. A confraternity of Occitan and Catalan knights undertake a dangerous journey to warn Pedro: Crux Lunata plans total destruction of Pedro and his efforts to unify the south.

The men and women of the confraternity risk their lives and their dreams to save Pedro. But will they instead burn on a

heretics' pyre? Or be flayed for spying? How to both fight and
hide while Crux Lunata schemes to destroy all they love?

.

An Apparition in the Hills

Monasterio de St-Pere de Selva
Near the Great Sea
November 30, 1211, All Saints Day

PASCAL, THE PORTER AT ST-PERE de Selva, lingered outside the
chapel, his ancient bones as cold as the stone walls. Fat sodden
flakes of snow piled in the courtyard, making his chores a misery.
While the monks shivered in their boots during the dawn prayers,
that *chiflado* abbot repeated the three psalms.

Chiflado. That's what Pascal's old granny called a man touched
by the moon who carried more pride than kindness in his pockets.
The abbot chirped on, preaching about honor and apparitions of
saints and the coming hordes of Saracens.

Pascal expected neither saint nor Saracen to appear in this
frozen place. Just flocks of knights with crusader crosses stitched
on their surcoats, knocking on his gate to demand provender, as if
spelt fell from heaven like manna to feed horses and monks and
knights. It was just as Pascal's granny always said, "A man out
seeking glory is ducking his chores."

Chores, not apparitions, guided each day at St-Pere, all the
tasks that must be done to ensure the feeding of God's priests each
morning and night. Pascal left the noisy abbot to his preaching
and turned his attention to the animals under his care. The
chickens huddled in their thatched shanty, where neither rain nor
snow fell; they didn't care about odd weather. Pascal cleared the
snow scum from the water trough near where the horses stamped in
their shed, their misty breath the only ghostly sighting in these
quarters. In their byre, three milch cows chomped their cud. He
pitched an extra fork of hay for each of them. Cozier here, Pascal
thought, than in that cold stone breezeway they call a chapel.

Thirteen. Maybe fourteen. That's how old he was when it last
snowed this early, before the harvest was done. Winter provender

will be rotting if this mushy mess of snow lay in the fields too long. But nothing could be done about it now. In his own hut, Pascal fed more twigs into the fire and sat down to pull off his wet boots, soggier than they'd be if it merely rained on All Saints, down here where the Pyrenees tumbled into the Great Sea. Just as soon as he kicked one boot free, a knock sounded at the gate.

Wouldn't you know it?

Pascal tugged on his boot, the wet wool stocking all rucked up.

"Patience!"

He shouted in Catalan, then called again at the third knock, this time in the tongue of Narbonne, since that's what the abbot demanded. The priestly lord of this place didn't want his friends to think a huddle of shepherds kept house for his monks.

"*Àvi*, help me!"

The figure at the gate cried for help in backcountry Catalan. *A mal punt*, as his grandmother would say. A bad situation. No, worse than that. The old man couldn't refuse any soul in this weather. He kicked away the snow and dragged open the lesser gate, which creaked like the dead branches of a silver fir rubbing in the wind. The abbot would tan his hide with a stick if Pascal didn't get olive oil on those hinges.

In the storm-dark morning, Pascal heard the sea crash below. Snow blew into his face. Ten paces beyond the gate a slight figure hunched, either from age or from bearing the world's weight like a yoke. The visitor pushed back the hood of his cloak. White flakes fell on shorn white hair. More a ghost than a man. The pale face was both old and young, hollow and creased with pain, the life sucked out, the spirit within defeated.

In his lodge, Pascal hung the stranger's snow-soaked cloak near the fire. His visitor, hoarse from cold or illness, croaked out a few words in the accents of a young Narbonnese lord. The donzel had gold to purchase a place in the monastery and, though still shivering, asked to be taken to the abbot.

"All I love has been rendered unto God. Nothing holds me in this world. Best that I too render the rest of my life to God."

The porter disliked seeing young life squandered within these cold walls. This stranger—who walked more like a wound-sick girl than a pampered lad carrying a purse filled with gold—seemed so ill that "the rest of life" here couldn't be long.

"Òc, donzel." Pascal called him young lord. "But first, let's warm you up. Come sit by the fire."

• • •

Pascal had scarcely settled the stranger into the warmest corner, tucked him in with a sheepskin to stop the shivers, and forced a mug of hot wine into his hand, when he had to tend the gate again.

Five gaudy knights, friends of the abbot's, shouted for service as if St-Pere were a merchants' inn, their horses in more of a lather than a good man might allow. Just like they did on previous visits, most of them hurried off to the refectory, leaving Pascal to tend their horses. The only one with the decency to stay and wipe down his horse was the big broad-chested one with red haired, who always rode with his wolf-dog across his saddle. Perhaps his mother thought the fellow handsome, but contempt twisted his mouth and furled his brow too much, and those bad habits had spoiled his looks.

"Bon día, senhór. Cold as a weasel's tit today, isn't it?"

The knight was maybe deaf. Or perhaps Pascal was a ghost in his own stable and should best save his breath to comfort these overheated ponies. The big man heaved his saddle aside and got to his business, giving his dog more attention than Pascal got.

A few moments later, the abbot deigned to appear in the stable, eager to speak with his visitor. Pascal raised a hand and bent his head in a respectful greeting, but as usual, the abbot looked right through him, as if Pascal were invisible. Pascal returned to his task—ai, but his icy bones ached in this weather—taking care to properly clean the hot horses and tend their hooves.

"Did you find it?" The slender abbot, his hood pulled up against the snow, folded his arms like a raptor come to rest in his eyrie. "Those heretics stole a lord's ransom when they ran for the hills."

"Not a brass barcelonese." The visitor spit into the straw. He spoke with the tones of gentry but practiced worse manners than any cursing Catalan woodcutter.

"So, they fled deeper into their holes? Those blasted Cathars." The abbot muttered words in Church Latin. "That's what the bishop calls them now. Cathars. Says 'heretic' is too good a word for them."

"They're in their holes, but no longer breathing. We baptized our blades in heretics' blood last night." The big fellow drew his sword, twisting it to make it shine in the thin light of the stable.

"You wiped out the last of them? Any left to tell where their gold is hidden?"

"No, unless one crawled into the woods to die." Big man slammed his sword back into its fine, leather-wrapped scabbard. "All we found in their cave was moldy spelt and turnips."

"Crux Lunata counts on you to fetch gold for our work."

"Then we need to capture the castle-villages in the upper hills. When those cat-suckers run from the cities, they hide their gold deep in the sheep-shit towns that shelter them. Arracheuse, Quéribus, St-Féliu, Peyrepetuse. Especially Valerós."

"Why not take Valerós now?" The abbot buried his arms deeper in the sleeves of his robe, bracing himself in the cold.

"Your Church courts are slow. Especially since Valerós is under the king of Aragón's protection." He used one of Pascal's stable blankets to cover his horse.

The abbot cleared his throat. "That's your next job—to take care of the king of Aragón."

"Pedro isn't going anywhere until next summer. There's time enough to fix his monkey."

"Did you persuade your grandmother? We need Felip to take orders now. His fee can feed six knights for a year."

"I can't do everything at once. Lop! *Hola, gos!*" The knight called his dog, which was worrying one of the monastery's horses. "She insists that my brother wait till he's twenty-five. Damn my dead father for leaving money in the hands of a woman."

"Try again. Though if you can't pry gold out of her fist, at least Felip is valuable here."

"Valuable? That little squid takes space and eats your food."

"He's the best worker in our scriptorium."

"Writing gospels for the glory of God?" The man covered one nostril and blew his nose, wiping away the wet with his hand. "Is that worth an extra helping of beans on Sunday?"

"More. Since the last crusade, the lords and their troubadours clamor for illuminated gospels. St-Pere earns good gold from Felip's copies, especially at Pentecost and Twelfth Night."

"*Qui s'ho creu?*" The big man sneered. *Who'd believe it?* "The squid hasn't been worth jack-spittle since the day he was born."

"Unlike his modest older brother." The abbot reached out an open hand, waving a command. "Did you achieve anything last night besides sending ragged souls to hell?"

"*Ai*, just found the Cid's sword, tucked away in the heretics' lair. If it's a magical sword, the magic is that I found it again." The big man tugged a short-sword from a scabbard tied to his saddle.

"Praise be to God!" The abbot dropped to his knees when the knight handed him that short-sword.

"Praise be to me. This is a sign. I'm the man to carry this sword, to help fate do its job."

"No, I'm traveling with the bishops. I will carry it to Toledo."

The big man cursed, calling down leprous angels.

Calm as a barn cat, the abbot said, "You'll follow the discipline of Crux Lunata."

"That order chose me to use the sword."

"*Òc*, but I carry the sword and the Grail until the moment when we bring the king's end. You can wait and travel with me."

"I'd rather eat cat tripe than travel one league with a herd of scrofulous priests."

"Get some food. Warm up before you ride again." The abbot backed away from that wolf-dog, which was busy sniffing at his feet. "And for the love of God, leave that dog in the stable."

"Other men's horses don't like him. *Hola, gos!*" The fire-haired knight stomped off, the abbot and the dog trotting along behind.

Across the way, an apparition stood in Pascal's open doorway, letting in both the frigid weather and the icy humors of St-Pere.

Pascal hoisted a bundle of wood and toed his door further open with his boot, thinking how his grandmama believed in luck, but didn't hold with coincidence.

"By the graces of the Good God, there's pottage hot on the fire, donzel. More than enough for two."

His ghostly visitor stared out at the knights' horses until Pascal shut and barred the door.

"If my old granny was here, she'd insist you rest up. Get a bit stronger before you jump in with them ague-plagued monks." Pascal pulled that dented tin cup from its peg on the wall, the cup his granny gave him on his wedding day. He dipped into the pottage, making sure a goodly number of carrots made their way into the cup. "Stay here a bit. Keep warm and lend me your company."

"You are kind." The donzel reached out a thin, spectral hand to receive the cup. He stared into the hearth flames. "Perhaps for a day or two. Just until..."

Until, Pascal guessed, those heretic-hunting knights were gone, off in search of other souls to torture.

■ ■ ■

In the refectory, where the Silence was strictly enforced, Felip de Xirgú preferred to sit alone, hunkering down so no one noticed that he was the biggest man in the room, the only one not born a half century earlier. The only one starving for one more crust of bread.

Until he came to St-Pere, Felip hadn't considered food as an object of desire. Now, at every meal he yearned for more, spawning yet another sin of the flesh to confess. The ovens and kitchen fires had been built too close to the scriptorium, so he had to endure the scent of baking bread, braising fowl, and roasting onions while he worked. Each morning when he carried firewood into the kitchens, he stole from the pile of loaves the baker hauled from the ovens. Unquenchable hunger wasn't mentioned in the Ten Commandments, but stealing was, even if it didn't rank with killing or taking God's name in vain.

Worse, though, pure physical lust hounded him each night from the last evening hymn until he exhausted himself chopping wood in the dawn's light. During the harvest, a farmer's wife came along to unload grain into the abbot's big barns. Felip helped, just for a glimpse of the woman's breasts straining against her linsey-woolsey robe. Muscles bulged in her forearms when she wrangled sheep from a cart. Felip woke more than once, sure that she crushed him, burying his face in her huge breasts.

Felip had appeared at the gates of St-Pere, yearning to escape sin, but it pursued him through the monastery's maze of galleries and cells and chapels.

After breakfast, before the Silence began in the scriptorium, the bald, stooped script master shuffled over to give Felip a new task, an apparition testimony by a priest from Montpelhièr.

"Most stories come from ignorant villagers who drank too much and forgot to eat breakfast." The master laid a rough parchment for Felip to copy, an utterly unlovely piece that resembled a rapidly written letter to a farm steward. "This one is worth preserving. It's an inspiration to go and defeat the Saracens in their lair, before they invade Christendom."

Felip fetched the best piece of parchment and got busy ruling it while the master droned on.

"Illustrate the saint in the rubric. Do it the same as in the Legend we received from Genoa. With a rose inside the frame." As if Felip couldn't draw and color an original image of St-Jordí. "Our abbot is sending it to the pope. So, do your best work."

As if Felip didn't always do his best. However, if this piece was to be a gift for the pope, then when Felip finished, the master would sign his name. That's how it was done here.

The script master cleared his rheumy throat. "Ask for the key to the gilding cabinet when you begin the final decorations." Then he rang the bell for Silence.

AN APPARITION OF ST-JORDÍ
TESTIMONY OF ESAK OF AVIGNON
FEAST OF ALL SAINTS 1211

To meditate on our bond as the Church Militant here on earth with the purified apostles, saints, and martyrs of the Church Triumphant, the priest Esak prayed at the Church of St-Denis outside the walls of Montpelhièr. In the silence of the empty church, the priest felt warmth rising from behind his heart, as if the hottest sun shone on him. When he opened his eyes from prayer, the martyr St-Jordí appeared, the good soldier who died for his faith. As the priest Esak offered praise to God and His Son Our Savior, St-Jordí spoke to him in a voice like a gale in the pines, saying in these words:

"Saracen armies are crossing the Great Sea, called by their caliph Mirammolin to invade Christendom. Christian knights must rise up to stop their perfidy."

Just after Felip inked the details of the saint's plea—all the while daydreaming that he'd be one of the knights called to do Heaven's work—the master handed him a written request, waving it urgently but not breaking the Silence. *'Our abbot wishes to speak with you.'*

Indecently excited, Felip hurried through the portico to the abbot's room. At the last summons, the abbot entrusted Felip to recreate a beautiful but deteriorating St-Mark's Gospel. At the abbot's suite, a linen banner draped over the garish iron door-pull indicated that the abbot was welcoming all visitors. The door ajar, Felip knocked and then pushed the door open at a summons.

His brother lounged in the abbot's guest chair, that daunting wolf-dog at his feet, drowsing while Matheus scratched the beast's head. The abbot wasn't even present.

"*Hola*, you lucky *calamarson*." Matheus always called him a baby squid. "I bring good fortune. Heaven's promise is now yours."

Overwhelmed by Matheus's good cheer, Felip shrank into his woolen habit. His mother claimed they looked alike, but his grandmother's polished brass mirror didn't agree. Felip was just as tall, but Matheus was broader. Felip was dark, but Matheus's hair was on fire, like his unreliable temper.

"Heaven's promise is why I came to the abbey," Felip said. "To render my life to God."

"But this cold hell leaves you open to all manner of sins of the flesh. I bet a dozen old brutes already covet your sweet ass."

Felip stepped back in disgust. "No. It's not like that here."

Startled, that massive wolf-dog sprang to its feet, hackles up, growling at Felip until Matheus snapped his fingers and pointed to the floor. The dog sank back down, one eye glaring at Felip.

"Well oh well, *calamarson.* I've come bearing remission of all your sins, signed by the new archbishop of Narbonne." Matheus held out a parchment roll. When Felip didn't reach for it, his brother untied the ribbon and broke the wax seal. "I've been initiated into an order of knights. We're joining the crusade against the Moors, for which the bishop promises forgiveness of all sins in this lifetime."

"And I can c–come?" Felip's heart leaped into his throat.

Matheus jerked the parchment out of Felip's reach.

"No, you can't c–c–come. You know the abbot won't let you leave on any journey until you take orders. I'm offering you the chance to pay for a real knight to travel under your banner."

"B–but Grandmother doesn't want me to take orders yet." Felip bit back resentment. Their uncles declared Matheus of age when he was twelve, so he'd received most of what was left by their father. Felip had only limited control of his own small inheritance, though he was twenty-one. "She says I'm too young to decide the course of my entire life."

"You can deed that briar patch up the hillside in Girona to the order. Then we add your name to the order's rolls, and your sins disappear, like magic."

Felip finally snatched the parchment from Matheus and studied it. "I wish I c–could go on crusade. Like our father did."

"Then get your grandmamma to let you take orders now instead of waiting. But you're better off here. You won't end up dead like our dear old father."

"It was an honorable way to die." Felip read every word twice, studying the parchment. "Why can't I give my land to the order and also beg the abbot for leave to go with you?"

"What can a baby squid do in a war?"

"I can ride a horse."

"And battle the Moors with your wet quill and a parchment scraper? Yet thanks to you, the glory of God will advance under the Lunate Cross. Your banner will wave in victory over the Saracens."

Those words excited him, but Felip retained the caution he always needed around his brother. "The rents from my land go to our grandmother. Will your order of knights provide for her?"

"Don't be a squid just because I call you one." Matheus laughed. "I shall guarantee our grandmother's wellbeing, as I have since our father deserted us for glory as a crusader in the Outremer, hoping to regain Jerusalem."

"How is she? How is Serena?"

"If by 'she' you mean our grandmother, she's tottering on the muddy edge of her grave, as she has for the last ten years. Sign here." Matheus handed Felip a quill from the abbot's table. "Your little playmate Serena has sprouted a very plump set of titties."

"Don't t–talk about her like that."

"Why not, *calamarson*? You've been handling yourself at the mere mention of her name since she turned thirteen." Matheus waggled a finger, impatient for Felip to finish. Then Matheus sanded the ink and blew on it, sending dust speckles over Felip's dark robe.

"She's a respectable senhóreta."

"She's poor as a yellow-necked mouse. Since her father died, all she brings to market are those luscious and ample breasts. Else, she'll be seeking shelter with her dead father's goatherds."

"Matheus, you are such a bastard."

But his brother was already at the door, waving farewell with his usual rude gesture.

"Lop!" Matheus called. "*Hola, gos!*"

Matheus strolled down the gallery, whistling for his dog. That murderous wolf-beast cast one last red-eyed glare at Felip.

"Welcome to Crux Lunata," Matheus bellowed, his voice echoing in the gallery, "and the war against the evil blackamoors."

E N D • CRUX LUNATA: A PREVIEW

Characters – *The Mad Woman*

Houses of Valerós and Cyprus
Isabella of Arracheuse, Pèire's granddaughter
Chrétien, Tomás's foster-brother
Pèire Leteric, seigneur of Valerós (deceased)
Sebastián, Isabella's son; heir to Valerós and Montcava
Tomás, Isabella's husband
Vidal, Pèire's son
Yusuf, Tomás's son

People of the Road
Blanca, Rubea's granddaughter
Matheus of Xirgú, a Christian knight
Rixenda, a Good Christian teacher
Rubea, the senhóra of Castel-St-Jean

Historic Figures
Pedro II, King of Aragón and Count of Barcelona
Philippe II, King of France, called Philippe Augustus
Simon de Montfort, leader of French army; Viscount of Carcassonne

Glossary – *The Mad Woman*

The non-English phrases in *Accidental Heretics* stories are for fun and color, not linguistic purity. The characters in these stories speak or read several languages.

A–B

a mal punt: A bad state.

Ai Dèu: O God.

àvi, àvia: Grandfather, grandmother.

baquelar: Villainous rogue.

barcelonese: Coinage under the Count of Barcelona.

beneeixi: A blessing.

bon Dèu: Good God.

bon día: Good day.

bon nuoit, bona nuèch: Good night.

bonhommes: The community's term for itself; Good Christians. Also rendered in English as goodmen and good women.

booty: Treasure; during the crusades, the primary way crusaders financed their armies or to pay their mercenaries. That is, rather than "looting" as we now think of booty, these cultures considered booty as legitimate plunder. ("To the victor goes the spoils.")

bordonier: A freeholder who arms and fights, freely, for a baron.

C

Catalan: In the Middle Ages, a language and culture, not a political entity.

cor dolç: Sweetheart, an endearment.

crux lunata: Lunate cross, featuring lunar crescents at each terminus; a pagan symbol; war tokenism imported to Europe by returning crusaders, adding the Islamic crescent in heraldic and other symbols.

cuirass: A rigid armor covering the torso. At this period, it was still made of leather.

D–F

Desperta, Ferro!: Awake, steel!

domus: Household, meaning the larger economic household of a titled landholder.

don: A courtesy title for a gentleman from the landed classes.

donzel: A young gentleman, in training for knighthood.

eu vos amor: I love you.

fadrin: A lad, a term of endearment.

G–L

goodmen, goodwomen: A reference to the people whom the Church called heretics, and the community called themselves bonhommes; now commonly called Cathars.

gos: Dog.

hereticated: Having decided to adopt a heresy.

hola: Hello.

Jhezu del tron: Jesus in heaven.

jongleurs: Medieval minstrels who sang the songs of the troubadours.

kalila: Sweetheart, an endearment.

M–R

ma dòmna: My lady.

mercé: Thank you.

Moors: People from northern Africa who settled on the Iberian peninsula under Muslim leadership. Colloquially, a *mestitz* of dark complexion.

morabatin: Gold coins in Aragón. A horse cost about one hundred morabatins.

Normans: Descendants of the Viking Northmen who settled Normandy, and later invaded Britain and conquered the Muslims on Sicily in the eleventh century.

òc: Yes.

Outremer: The lands across the Great Sea, where the Crusader States were founded and other territory seized by Christian invaders.

Pare Abát: Father abbot.

Pare, m'ajuden: Father, help me.

paciència: Patience.

peccador: Sinner.

punxor: Prick.

Qui s'ho creu: Who'd believe it?

renrén: Fool.

S–Z

Sancta Maria: A woman's oath, calling on Saint Mary.

Santa Mare de Dèu: Saint Mother of God.

Saracen: Colloquial term used in Europe for Muslims.

seigneur: A man of rank who rules lands and a household.

senhór, senhóra, senhóreta: Titles of respect; equivalent to señor, señora, señorita.

squire: In the southern lands, a fighter of rank between knights and foot soldiers, for his lifetime. In the southern world, squires did not rise to become knights.

surcoat: A long coat worn over other clothes or armor.

viscount: A European noble rank, above a baron, below a marquis.

Place Names – *The Mad Woman*

Valerós, Fontcours, Montcava, St-Félíu, St-Joachim, and
Monasterio de St-Pere de Selva exist within the Accidental
Heretics' world, but nowhere else.

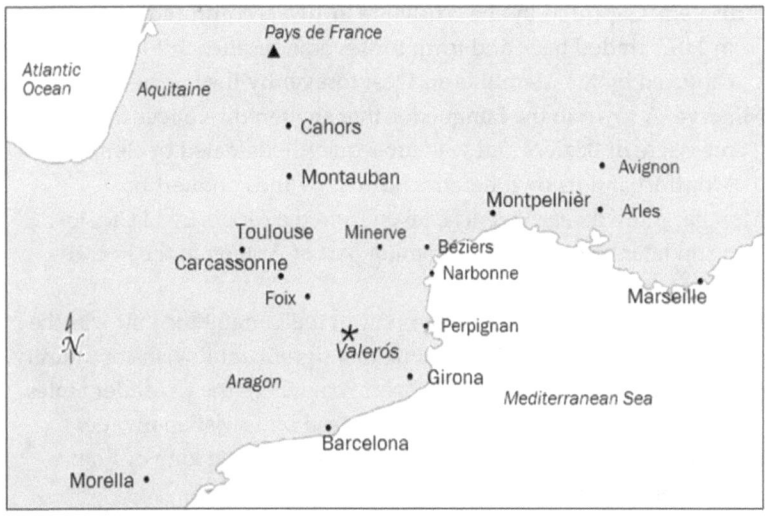

Al-Andalus (in country; Andalusia in Christendom): The land of the
    Moorish caliphates on the Iberian Peninsula.
Aquitaine: A duchy in what is now southwest France that was a key
    portion of the Angevine empire under Henry II and Eleanor of
    Aquitaine.
Aragón: In the mid-thirteenth century, a union of the Kingdom of
    Aragón and the County of Barcelona established the dynastic
    Crown of Aragón, with tributaries across the Languedoc at the time
    of this story.
Barcelona: A territory on the Mediterranean, now approximately the
    political entity of Catalonia, for which Pedro II held the title Count
    of Barcelona.
Cairo: The seat of the Ayyubid dynasty that Saladin founded, with the
    third oldest university in the world.

Cyprus: An island in the Mediterranean, south of Turkey and north of Cairo. During the Third Crusade, its Muslim rulers were conquered by Richard Lionheart who sold it to the Knights Templar, who in turn sold it to Guy de Lusignan.

Girona: An ancient city in the northeast corner of Catalunya; part of the countship of Barcelona at the time of this story.

Iberia: The old Roman name for the peninsula now called Spain.

Jerusalem: Captured by the crusaders in 1099, recaptured by Saladin in 1187, traded back and forth for several decades until finally captured by the Mamluks and lost forever by the crusaders.

Minerve: A town in the Languedoc that sheltered refugees from the massacre of Béziers and was subsequently defeated by Simon de Montfort and its own heretics burned by the conquerors.

Morella: A town near Valencia, taken from the Moors by El Cid, lost again later before finally becoming part of Aragón in the Reconquista.

Narbonne: A rich Mediterranean port in the Languedoc that was the seat of the archbishop and home to a significant Jewish community.

Outremer: The lands across the Great Sea, where the Crusader States were founded and other territory seized by Christian invaders.

Pays de France: The historic personal domain of the king of France; most of this area became the province Ile de France.

Provence: A county on the Mediterranean, ruled by the counts of Barcelona; governed by Pedro's brother Alfonso at this time.

Quéribus: A mountain stronghold near Aragón in the Corbières hills.

Toulouse: A county in the Languedoc, whose count owed allegiance to the king of France at the time of this story. The city, on a major trade route between the Mediterranean and central France, was a bishop's seat.

About the Accidental Heretics Series

Lost in the Languedoc Crusade

Find this series in your favorite online store
or ask your independent local bookseller.

ACCIDENTAL HERETICS SERIES
Book 1: *Bone-mend and Salt*
Book 2: *Trebuchets in the Garden*
Book 3: *Crux Lunata*
Book 4: *Song of Valerós*
The Mad Woman of La Catalane: A Novella
The Blue Door… and More Accidental Heretics Tales

LEGENDS OF VALERÓS SERIES
Wheel and Serpent: 1
Traitor: 2
Hero: 3

To learn more about these series, visit:
www.jugumpress.net

About the Author

E.A. STEWART, the author of the *Accidental Heretics* series, is the pen name of Annie Pearson, who lives and writes in Seattle.

www.anniepearson.com

From Jugum Press

HISTORICAL AND CONTEMPORARY FICTION

Nzinga, African Warrior Queen by Moses L. Howard

Nzinga is a brilliant leader during a time of violent upheaval. This fictional biography brings to life the 17th century flourishing African kingdom, now lost, where early explorers' maps of West Africa call out: "Here reigned the celebrated Queen Nzinga!"

Nine Volt Heart by Annie Pearson

He said, "I love you." She said, "You don't even know the real me." He said, "Great song lyrics. Key of G? Can we try close harmony?" Jason and Susi meet by accident in Seattle. Secrets, songs, and stalkers quickly entwine their lives in unpredictable ways.

This Charming Man by Ajax Bell

A chance encounter with an intriguing older man inspires Steven Frazier with visions of a more rewarding life. A vibrant snapshot of Seattle in the early 1990s, this story captures the drama of coming into one's own as an adult.

A Summer in Peach Creek by Michele Malo

Teenaged Faith travels to Peach Creek, West Virginia for a visit with relatives in 1932. When a scandalous murder occurs, Faith discovers the corrupt underbelly of Logan County. As summer progresses and peaches grow, Faith finds her own moral center.

PERSONAL VOICES IN HISTORY SERIES

Journey into Gold Country: Memories of a Forty-Niner

by Ralph Buckingham; foreword by Charles Barker

The California Gold Rush, remembered sixty years later by a New England younger son who went to seek his fortune.

We Were Walimu Once and Young, edited by Brooks E. Goddard

True stories from the Teachers for East Africa and Teacher Education for East Africa experience in the 1960s.

Find print and ebook editions:

www.jugumpress.net

Jugum Press